A Surreptitious Undertaking

An Arabella Stewart Historical Mystery-Book 6

D.S. Lang

D.S. Lang

Ebook ISBN: 979-8-9867318-1-0

Paperback: 979-8-9867318-3-4

Cover Designer: Karen Phillips

Editor: Alyssa B. Colton

This book is a work of fiction. All characters, places, incidents, and events are products of the author's imagination or are used fictitiously. Any resemblance to real places, events, incidents, or persons (living or dead) is purely coincidental.

Prologue

September 1921

Monday afternoon

As she walked to the mailbox at the end of the long driveway leading to Ballantyne Inn, Arabella Stewart wrapped her cloak tightly around her. Although the sun was shining, the brisk wind held a hint of the coming winter. A sigh escaped her. Bella loved spring, with its promise of renewal, and summer, with its shimmering brightness. Early fall, with the glorious colors, was pleasant—if only winter didn't follow. As October neared, her enthusiasm dipped. Business at the resort tapered off. Until Thanksgiving and Christmas, she wouldn't have guests to distract her. And she needed a distraction from worrying and wondering.

With a combination of hope and anxiety, she pulled the mail out and quickly flipped through it. Her heart accelerated when she saw a familiar scrawl. Although the envelope held no return address, Bella knew who sent it. She tore the packet open and pulled out the one-page missive.

Dear Bella,

I'm sorry not to write more regularly, but we've been busy night and day. Although we've made progress on the case, I may not make it home soon. I still hope to be in Moreley for Christmas, and I hope I still have an invitation to spend it at Ballantyne.

I miss you.

As ever,

Jax

Mixed emotions assailed her. He signed all of his notes *As ever*, but what did that mean? Jackson Hastings had been her brother Matt's best friend, her childhood buddy, her girlhood crush, and her sometimes college escort. Just when she'd thought their friendship would blossom into more, America had entered the Great War. All too soon, Jax and Matt had been called up with their National Guard unit. Shortly afterward, Bella had joined the Signal Corps and ended up in France ahead of them.

Ever since, time and circumstances had kept them apart. Although she'd worked with Jax on several homicide cases since her own return home in December 1919, he'd maintained his distance. At least he had until last April. Finally, he'd lowered his barriers, but they'd no chance to begin a courtship because he'd given up his job as town constable to become a Prohibition agent. Since then, he'd been hundreds of miles away trying to solve the murder of a buddy's wife. While she understood Jax's desire to help a man who'd saved his life in the trenches, Bella sometimes doubted they would ever unravel the case.

After another glance at the note, Bella resigned herself to more days, even weeks, of worrying and wondering.

Chapter One

Friday afternoon

Uncertainty plagued Agent Jax Hastings as he approached the unfamiliar office. His boss, Senior Agent Amos Derringer, must have a good reason for pulling Jax away from his current investigation to drive hours for a meeting. Why the man hadn't provided an explanation on the telephone was troubling. Because operators sometimes listened in? Perhaps. But what was going on? Bridgeling, Ohio was an hour southeast of Jax's hometown of Moreley. Not a typical venue for bootlegging or speakeasies. But Prohibition had led to increased crime in many places, even villages like this one.

When he stepped into the building, Jax immediately saw Derringer talking with a muscular man in his fifties. Clad in a sheriff's uniform, he had to be the local lawman.

"Jax, you made good time," Derringer said. "Sheriff Rufus Ayling, this is Agent Hastings."

The burly fellow extended his hand to Jax. "Glad to meet you, son."

Jax responded in kind before glancing back at Derringer.

"Let's sit down in Rufus's office," his boss said.

Jax followed the two older men into a room at the end of a narrow hall. He started with surprise when he saw a woman already seated at the big table in the middle of the room.

"Eleanor Corning, this is Jackson Hastings, the agent I mentioned," Derringer said.

The woman nodded, but said nothing. As Jax and the other two men took seats, he covertly studied her. Sturdy of build with her blonde hair swept into a bun, she looked to be in her early thirties. Her light blue eyes, ringed with mauve shadows, darted to him before settling on her clasped hands.

"Eleanor's younger brother is a patient at Poplar Pines," the senior agent said. "Since it's not too far from your old stomping grounds, I assume you've heard of the place."

"Yes, sir. It's a sanatorium catering to veterans who suffer from shell shock," Jax replied. Some of what he'd heard about the facility wasn't good, since treatment for mental conditions hadn't progressed much, but what would that have to do with Prohibition? He didn't have to wait long to find out.

"Miss Corning visited this week but wasn't allowed in, even during the regular guest hours on Sunday and Wednesday," the sheriff said. "That concerns her and me."

Jax turned to the woman. "Were you given a reason?"

She shrugged. "Sunday, I was told he wasn't well and couldn't have company, but no details were offered. I came from Pittsburgh, which is a long drive, so I asked about seeing him on Wednesday evening during the next scheduled visitation. The woman in charge said it all depended on how Aaron, that's my brother, was doing. I stayed because I've been worried about him and hadn't seen or heard anything for over a month." Her voice trembled, and she pulled a hanky out of her pocketbook. "I'm sorry," she said in a broken whisper.

"Let me tell Agent Hastings what else happened," Derringer put in.

Miss Corning nodded and wiped her eyes.

"When she went back, the woman in charge," Jax's boss glanced at the paper in front of him, "a Mrs. Lenning, reported Aaron wasn't any better, so Eleanor was turned away. On her way out to her automobile, she was followed by the receptionist, who overheard the conversation inside. Can you tell him about your brief exchange?"

She cleared her throat. "The woman, a Miss Bounder, said to come to the Bridgeling diner later that night. She indicated there were odd goings-on at Poplar Pines, including something about a Samuel James being of interest because he looked familiar to her. She couldn't quite place him. She was agitated, but we were interrupted by another employee, so she didn't say more."

Jax frowned at the revelation. "Is he a patient or a worker?"

Miss Corning shook her head. "I don't know. She said he reminded her of someone, and he might have *something helpful* to share, and that's when she stopped. When a young woman came out, Miss Bounder seemed very nervous. That's when she wanted to meet me later."

"What did she say at your meeting?" Jax asked.

"Unfortunately, Miss Bounder didn't make it." His boss made the reply. "Eleanor called me yesterday morning because she was even more worried. She's been staying at the hotel here and doesn't want to go home until she learns more about Aaron."

The woman contacting Derringer, and his use of first names indicated some personal connection. But what? The man was nothing if not formal and reserved. And why were they meeting in the sheriff's office? Was the case related to bootlegging or not? Jax looked at Miss Corning. "I understand your concern, but I'm not sure why I've been called here." He again focused on his boss. "Do you think there's a rumrunning ring at the sanatorium?"

"It's not likely," the man admitted, "but there are other problems which have made Rufus uneasy for a while."

Sheriff Ayling glanced from the woman to Jax. "In early March, one patient wandered outside at night and fell victim to hypothermia. Last month, another reportedly drowned in the river behind the place. He also supposedly got out and took off on his own."

The information troubled Jax. "Aren't the patients closely monitored?"

"Supposedly," the sheriff said.

The words *reportedly* and *supposedly* stood out to Jax. He held his peace while the conversation continued.

"It's what I was told." Miss Corning clasped and unclasped her hands. "Aaron's wife is the one who had him admitted, and she insisted it was a fine institution using modern methods with plenty of help to watch over the men. I didn't think he was bad enough to require hospitalization, but Constance said I wasn't the one dealing with his nightmares, hallucinations, and such. Since their home is near Columbus, I only saw them every few months. I was sick with pneumonia, and my physician forbid travel until this week."

"Does your sister-in-law have concerns about his care?" Jax asked.

"No, but she hasn't been to see him since he was admitted six weeks ago," the woman replied. "I called her after I wasn't allowed to visit, and she brushed me off. I would've come sooner if not for being ill. Now, I'm terribly anxious about Aaron."

Apprehension curled like a cobra in the pit of Jax's stomach. The situation was all too familiar. Although dealing with shell-shocked soldiers was arduous for relatives, some found a facility and left the men to sink or swim. He had two former comrades in those straits. "What were the modern methods mentioned to your sister-in-law?" A few mental institutions were trying new procedures, but, to his knowledge, many continued to employ age-old strategies.

"Proper diet, exercise, and such. She didn't give me much information." Miss Corning wrung her hands. "I honestly think she simply wanted to get rid of him, so she could have fun. When I telephoned her Wednesday night, the maid said Constance was out and wouldn't be home until late. The same was true last night. I believe my sister-in-law is out on the town every night. The last time I saw Constance, she certainly looked and acted like a flapper. She's young. Only twenty-two, and I understand not wanting to be tied down. I wish I'd been aware she was overwhelmed. I would've helped."

Jax mulled over her comments. Sympathy for both Miss Corning and her brother bloomed inside him. "How old is Aaron?"

Miss Corning was once again wiping away tears, so Amos answered. "He's twenty-five. He joined the army in 1917. Left college to do so. He and Constance married before he left. She was very young, maybe too young."

"You know her, as well?" Jax asked.

"I was at the wedding and met the girl then." Amos fingered his narrow mustache. "I probably should've said right off that the Cornings are old friends. Eleanor's older brother and I were best buddies growing up in Pennsylvania. He was a copper and died in the line of duty before Aaron left for France. I've stayed in touch with them, which is why she called me." He patted her hand. "I'm worried about Aaron, too. And about the overall situation at Poplar Pines. I didn't learn details until I spoke with Rufus early yesterday, which brought me here."

With puzzle pieces falling into place, Jax understood the concerns of both lawmen and Miss Corning. What he didn't see was his role. "Do you know much about the men who died?"

Ayling shook his head. "My deputies and I were out at Poplar Pines to investigate. We spoke with the Lennings, the mother and son who own the place, first. We all talked to the workers. Everyone gave the same information, which seemed very rehearsed. The first death didn't trouble me so much, but a second one put me on alert. Several people quit after the patient froze to death last March. The receptionist, Miss Bounder, was relatively new, but I spoke with her about the supposed drowning. She was nervous and troubled. I felt like she wanted to say more, but we were never alone. I suggested interviewing the employees in my office, which met with strong resistance from the Lennings. When we didn't find the body last month, I didn't push it like I should have."

"We can only do so much," Derringer put in.

"Have you been out to the sanatorium to ask about the receptionist?" Jax posed the question.

"After Amos and I talked early yesterday, we decided to wait to go there," Ayling replied. "However, I had my clerk, Edna, telephone and ask for Miss Bounder. Edna mentioned meeting for lunch on Saturday, as planned, as an excuse. The two of them have socialized a bit so that wouldn't put anyone on alert. Edna was told the woman left a note in her room saying she was resigning and going home, which is near Columbus. I haven't been able to get in touch with her. No one answered at her aunt's house, where she lived prior to working at the sanatorium. The operator down that way said the aunt and Miss Bounder used to visit other relatives near Portsmouth. She wasn't sure of the exact town, but told me them taking off unexpectedly wasn't worrisome. Even so, I had her connect me with the local constable. He wasn't concerned, either, but he'll send a deputy to the house tomorrow to look around and talk to neighbors."

"Probably a good idea, but folks in her hometown know Miss Bounder better than we do. Maybe she and the aunt truly are traveling," Amos said. "What about the employees who left a while back?"

The sheriff nodded. "I only located two who left since Captain Ward Falconer died in March. They weren't at Poplar Pines when Lieutenant Jeremiah Smith disappeared and probably drowned in August, and when Aaron disappeared more recently. However, they doubt any patient can slip out easily. In addition, both workers were bothered by the lack of effective treatment." He looked at Jax. "You must be aware of shell shock and the current remedies."

Jax ground his teeth. "Unfortunately, two fellow officers suffer from it. I visited them when I first got back from France. It was pretty awful."

Ayling looked grim, but nodded. "One of my interviewees had been a nurse, and the other was an orderly. Anyhow, the nurse said not much treatment takes place. Mainly isolation, sedation, and restraints."

Jax looked at Ayling. "Do you know much about the men who died?"

Ayling slumped back in his chair. "Smith, the one who supposedly drowned, hadn't had visitors for a few months. I'm guessing he really is dead, but we can't be sure. Anyhow, his wife was the main one who came, as his other relatives live at a distance. When his elderly aunt found out about his death, she called me to get the body. At that point, I wasn't even aware of the problem, so I went out and talked to Dr. Lenning. He said the body wasn't found, just evidence Smith jumped off the dock. Slim evidence, in my book. A pair of slippers turned up there the next morning and a robe, similar to those worn by patients, got hung up on the riverbank about one hundred yards south of the place. When I questioned Lenning about not reporting the incident, he hoped the patient was all right and would be found. Or so he said. My deputies and I tried to get more details but failed."

"Could a body completely disappear in the river?" Amos asked.

"It's deep in places, but I find the story hard to believe." Ayling released a long, low breath.

"You think Smith was killed and dumped?" Jax asked. "The Boxmore River is wide at some points, wide enough for a body to get washed a ways downstream. Is that true by the sanatorium?"

"It's about two hundred yards across there. It was running high and fast when Smith disappeared, but I'm not convinced he's in it," Ayling replied.

"What are the other possibilities?" Jax focused on the sheriff.

"He could've been killed and buried in the woods. There's an expanse of trees out that way. Who knows? I have possibilities, no certainties." The sheriff exhaled sharply. "We searched close to the sanatorium and found no sign of a grave, but there's a lot of empty land. We couldn't cover it all."

Thinking about the lieutenant being killed and dumped in an unmarked grave troubled Jax. "If we get to the bottom of Corning's disappearance, we may find out where Smith is, too. What about Falconer? I assume his body was recovered."

"It was. Our local physician did a brief survey and confirmed the cause of death for Falconer," Ayling replied. "After talking with the former nurse and orderly, I don't believe either man left the building voluntarily. Same with Corning."

"I wish I could've visited Aaron regularly," Miss Corning said in a broken whisper. "I'm so afraid something similar happened to him."

"He may just be doing poorly because of some treatments." Amos used a soft, consoling tone, but worry shone in his dark eyes. "I hate to think of him suffering, but he's young and can recover, if that's the case."

"I hope so," the woman whispered.

"We'll do everything we can to find him," Amos assured her.

Jax wondered how. His boss had already indicated the sanatorium wasn't a bootlegging location. What was his plan? Jax wanted to ask outright about being summoned, but Amos didn't seem eager to hurry things along, possibly because Miss Corning was so edgy and upset. Not that Jax blamed her. "You mentioned Mrs. Lenning. What does she do?"

"She manages the business end, we think," Rufus replied, "but they have a Major Billings who seems to be involved in various ways, but his exact role isn't clear."

"Constance mentioned him when she first took Aaron. She liked the man. He was with Mrs. Lenning when I was sent away without being able to see my brother." Miss Corning chewed on her lower lip. "I indicated I'd take Aaron with me now that I've recuperated from pneumonia. Although Billings seemed sympathetic, he said much the same as Constance: that I don't realize how hard it is to care for someone in Aaron's boots."

"How old is Major Billings?" Jax asked.

"Around fifty or thereabouts. He's still a very handsome man. Neatly dressed in his uniform and well-groomed. He looked every inch the army officer." Miss Corning glanced from Derringer to Ayling and back to Jax. "My parents left ample inheritances for us, enough for Aaron to spend two years or longer, in a sanatorium, especially if Constance is careful with her expenses. But I fear she isn't." She leaned forward and folded her hands on the table. "When I spoke with her about not being able to see Aaron, she said some patients had run off. Maybe he had, too. It was an odd thing to say. I think Constance realized because she ended our conversation right away."

Jax shifted to look at the sheriff. "The employees who left didn't think it'd be easy for a patient to get out. Right?"

"They didn't, and I don't, either," Ayling replied. "Not unless someone made it easy to do or took them out."

"Is it possible some patients are allowed to leave? Even encouraged to do so because their relatives no longer want to pay for their care?" Jax felt sick at the idea. Surely, no one would be that heartless. But if relatives dumped men off and didn't come back...

"I don't want to believe it's true," Derringer put in, "but it's a possibility. One we want to explore."

"Considering what we know already, I'm afraid it's likely." Ayling leaned back and folded his arms across his chest. "Both Falconer and Smith came from affluent families. Both had been there for over six months. Aaron hadn't been at the place as long, but whoever is behind these occurrences may get bolder. And greedier. We need to do a lot more digging. Hearing from Miss Bounder would help." Frustration underscored the last sentence.

"I'm sure it would." As Jax mulled over the bits and pieces provided, he saw a puzzle take shape. An ugly puzzle with too many missing fragments. "It sounds like there's one main issue, which has to do with people who'd prefer relatives die rather than live indefinitely in a treatment facility because of the cost. The same folks don't want to be burdened with caring for their loved ones at home."

"You're on track with our suppositions. Money may be the primary interest," Derringer said. "But we need to find Aaron. He might have disappeared prior to last weekend. We don't know exactly when. Miss Bounder told Eleanor not to despair, so he may still be alive. But we want to move quickly." His voice was taut with tension.

"And I want to find out for sure about Smith and Falconer. Was there nefarious intervention or not? Of course, locating Smith's body would be helpful and would give his aunt some peace. Letting patients wander away would be bad, but grabbing them and putting them out is much worse," Ayling added.

"That's a lot to investigate," Jax observed as he looked at his boss. "You said the Bureau isn't involved."

"There's no basis for our involvement." Derringer grimaced. "I'm here because Eleanor called me. I wanted to take leave and investigate myself, but the top brass wouldn't hear of it, which is why I called you. I figured you were familiar with Poplar Pines, and you're a veteran."

"Has the brass given me an okay to work this case?" Jax didn't see how that was possible. If they wouldn't allow Amos to take time off, why let him?

"No, they haven't because there's no bootlegging involved." Derringer drummed his fingers on the table. "Rufus could deputize someone."

"You want me to go on leave and work with the sheriff?" Jax asked for confirmation. Now, more puzzle pieces fell into place, but sizeable holes remained. From his time as a town constable, Jax knew Bridgeling had two deputies already. Why add him?

Derringer nodded. "You've never visited Poplar Pines?"

"No, I never have. It's a good hour's drive from Moreley. My job never took me that way," Jax replied. "There aren't many homes in the immediate area, are there?"

"You're right," Ayling said. "Poplar Pines is isolated. Not much else around, and you'd be going miles out of your way if you were leaving here for Moreley."

No one had mentioned him returning to his hometown at present. Jax still had little idea of why he had been called, but his mind swirled with possibilities. Most of Jax's work with the Prohibition Bureau had been investigating the murder of Jocelyn O'Donnelly, the wife of another agent. In fact, he'd only taken the job because he owed Mick O'Donnelly. Despite his focus on that case, Jax had sometimes gotten called to raid blind pigs and speakeasies. Legwork always occurred ahead of raids, and two cases had involved brief undercover stints. Did Derringer want Jax doing legwork or going undercover? Or would he be doing something else? "What role would I play?" Getting a direct answer would help at this point.

"Before we get to that, I want you to look at the patient list. It's not likely you're acquainted with any of them, but we need to be sure. Rufus got names when he was last out there. There are only twenty." Derringer shoved the sheet of paper across the table.

Jax scanned it. "I don't recognize any names."

"Good," his boss said before taking the paper back.

The situation seemed odd because his boss was obviously involved, but not necessarily in charge. "This investigation is being run out of your department, Sheriff?" Jax asked.

Ayling nodded. "I can't send one of my deputies, because they'd be recognized, and I don't want to involve any nearby department, since they might be known to folks at Poplar Pines, too. Getting a federal agency involved would be impossible, and we have nothing helpful at the state level. The best I can do is deputize people to help."

"Help in what way?" Jax asked.

"As for your task, since you're a former soldier, we want you to assume the role of a patient. That will involve pretending to have shell shock. I assume you saw men with it during the war. You already mentioned two buddies. Can you pretend well enough to convince the staff and other patients?" Derringer looked both hopeful and anxious.

The question required serious contemplation. Unfortunately, Jax had witnessed a few soldiers suffering from the awful malady. As he reflected on them, Jax recalled the wide range of symptoms. "Some mostly sat and stared in front of them. They spoke very little. I could manage that better than having fits of anger, which happened with others. That was true with my friends. They lost control at times and had to be restrained." The memory lashed him. Neither had deserved such poor treatment. Not after bravely leading their men into battle time and time again. Not after serving their country with valor.

"You need to be cautious about being too badly affected. Electric shock is used in some asylums, although I haven't heard about it at Poplar Pines," Ayling said.

The case deserved investigation, but Jax didn't want to become a shadow of himself due to going undercover and enduring harsh treatments. Instead of voicing his fears, he said, "I wouldn't be able to investigate much then. How am I supposed to investigate, anyhow? I assume patients aren't given the run of the place unless someone wants them to take off."

"They aren't," Miss Corning replied. "Not at all, from what I heard."

"But you can meet the patients and the staff. Someone, probably more than one employee, knows what's going on. We suspect a small group might be involved." Ayling drove his fingers through his hair. "I don't want more deaths or disappearances of veterans in my jurisdiction. I'd go undercover myself, if I could. As Amos said, locating young Corning is at the top of our list."

"I agree about involvement of employees," Derringer said.

Jax absorbed the information, but went back to a previous comment. "If the Lennings are in charge, aren't they the most likely suspects?"

"Maybe. Maybe not. They were both away when the supposed drowning happened," Ayling said.

"That doesn't mean they weren't involved," Jax said.

"It doesn't, but I'm not sure if they are. One might be and not the other. It's hard to say." Ayling's deep voice resonated with frustration. "I met Mrs. Lenning when they bought the place. She seemed sharp and articulate. The last few times, she was flighty and befuddled."

"How old is she?" Jax asked.

"Sixties," Ayling replied. "It's possible she's getting senile. At that age, my father-in-law was."

"If so, she can't handle the business end well, which means someone else takes care of that, and talks to relatives about costs and such." Jax returned his attention to his role. "You think I can find out from the inside?"

"We do," Amos told him.

"Are you sure I'll be admitted? There must be screening of some sort." Jax studied his boss as he spoke.

Derringer ran one forefinger inside his starched shirt collar. "You need someone to take you, so I spoke with retired Senior Constable Jenkins about him and his wife playing your uncle and aunt. They're agreeable. They'd drop you off, visit once or twice, and feign frustration about the cost of your care, while hinting they're well off."

"To induce whoever is involved to offer a way to get rid of me." Richard Jenkins was serving as Moreley town constable while Jax temporarily worked for the Prohibition Bureau. The older man and his wife were also living in the Hastings homestead, so they were close at hand.

"That's our hope," Ayling put in, "but it isn't apt to happen right off. In fact, we don't want that. You'll have time to make observations and report findings. Needed time."

Confusion shimmered around Jax. "If Richard and Jenny only come twice, how will I get the word out, if I find information?"

"We're working on that part. Our goal is to get you admitted this weekend." Amos studied Miss Corning, who was staring at her clasped hands. "Time is of the essence regarding Aaron, but we also want justice for the two others, and we need to protect all the patients. I wish I could stay, but I have to be back in Washington on Monday morning. I drove straight-through getting here, and I'll do the same heading home. Even though Rufus will be in charge of the operation, I'll check in when I can." Once again, Derringer acted as unflappable as ever. "It should work well."

Jax wished he felt the same way. Of course, his boss wasn't going undercover. "How am I supposed to get information? Look around at night? Talk to patients and workers, discreetly, I know. But what else?" The particulars of Jax's assignment needed clarification. A lot of clarification.

"Observe first. Some patients will chat more than others," Ayling said. "You'll also interact with the nurses and orderlies."

"How many employees are there?" Jax asked.

The sheriff flipped through a notepad. "Three nurses, two orderlies, a cook, a cook's aide, a gardener-handyman, and usually a receptionist. My deputies and I spoke with all of them more than once, and with the Lennings and Billings, of course. None of us know them well. Some come to town for a meal or shopping, but mostly they stay at Poplar Pines. A couple are local folks, but I haven't seen either one lately, except at the sanatorium. Could be people out there don't want them talking to me, so they aren't allowed to come to town anymore. Neither had a vehicle, so they need rides."

Jax put his hand to his head. The situation sounded worse and worse. He glanced at Miss Corning. "You'll be staying in town overnight?"

She ran one hand over her neat bun. "I will. Then, Amos thinks I should leave. I hate to do that, but I suppose he's right. Me staying might make folks at the sanatorium suspicious. I'll stop at a cousin's home on my way. We'll have a pleasant visit." The last sentence was more hopeful than certain.

"I'd like to tag along and see you get there. You must be worn out, what with not sleeping well. Right now, let me walk you to your vehicle. You can rest at the hotel, and I'll be along later this evening." Derringer stood up, helped Miss Corning out of her chair, and tucked her hand into the crook of his arm.

She offered a weak smile, bid the men goodbye, and let Amos escort her from the room.

"I'll get some coffee for us," the sheriff said. "I don't know about you, but I could use a cup."

"Sounds good." After Ayling left the office, Jax settled back in his chair but had little time alone because his boss was only gone for moments.

Once Ayling again took his seat, the senior Prohibition agent leaned forward and put his hands on the table. "You don't have to take this assignment, Jax. I asked you to come without telling you why because, as you often point out, operators might listen. This is a sensitive situation, and I wanted to avoid eavesdroppers."

"A wise idea," Jax replied, "I'm just not sure why you called me here, if you didn't think I'd take the job."

"You're an excellent lawman, and one of my best agents. You've been clear about wanting to leave the Bureau soon. I hate to lose you, but I understand." Derringer's expression was both solemn and sympathetic. "You can officially resign, and Rufus will deputize you before we leave today."

"And not go back to Philadelphia?" Jax wanted clarification. He was ready to quit. If accepting a deputy position hastened his departure, that was an incentive.

"I realize you didn't intend to stay with the Bureau this long. We all hoped to solve the murder of Mick O'Donnelly's wife sooner than we did." With one hand, Amos massaged his neck.

"We'll need you to testify, but the other agents can wrap up the case. You brought your things with you, like I suggested when we talked yesterday, right?"

Since Jax hadn't taken many personal items, he had put them all in his bag. "I did. I suppose you need my resignation in writing."

"Yep. My clerk can type it, so you only need to sign." Amos made the reply.

"All right." Jax hoped his stint as a deputy didn't last long, since he was eager to get home for good.

Jax turned to Ayling. "It looks like I'll be reporting to you for the immediate future."

The man's craggy features relaxed. "I appreciate you doing this, Jax. You come highly recommended, not only by Amos but also by Richard, who I've known and respected for years." Ayling leaned back in his chair. "I hope you don't feel like we've made all the arrangements without consulting you. Once Amos got here, we moved forward, since time is of the essence. I have a bad feeling, and unless we act quickly and decisively, I don't think Aaron Corning will be the last man to disappear."

"Do you think he's dead?" Jax hadn't wanted to ask in Miss Corning's presence, but it had been in the back of his mind.

Ayling ran one hand over his face. "I hope not, but I'm pessimistic."

"As much as I hate to admit it, I'm uncertain myself," Amos added. "Miss Bounder gave Eleanor reason to hope. Unfortunately, the basis of her optimism isn't clear."

"Then, I need to get there as soon as possible," Jax said. "What about a contact? I'll need someone to take information out for me. You mentioned a couple of locals working there."

The sheriff frowned. "I doubt if I can speak with either one ahead of you going, and I'm not sure they'd make solid partners. Too easily rattled, if the past is any indicator. If Miss Bounder hadn't quit or whatever..." His voice trailed off.

"Do you think she's another victim?" Jax asked with concern.

"It's possible, since she mentioned nothing about quitting to anyone. And I can't reach her." Ayling laced his fingers and let them rest on his broad chest. "We can't even be sure the note in her room was actually written by her."

"We want to put someone in that job, if we can." Amos rose and started pacing.

"Maybe there's a female agent who could take a temporary leave and apply to be the receptionist," Jax suggested. Some Prohibition agents went undercover, so that seemed like a strong suggestion, even though the Bureau employed only a few women.

Amos stopped mid-step. "I'm shorthanded. You know that. With you resigning, there's no way the big boss would approve such a scheme."

Jax slumped back in his chair and considered the situation while his boss went back to pacing. Periodically, he took a side-long glance at Jax. "Do the two of you have another strategy?" Jax asked. A sixth sense said they did.

The older men exchanged a long look. "When we discovered Miss Bounder had left, we discussed ideas with Richard. A new receptionist will be hired as soon as possible. They fill jobs quickly. Getting someone from our side in would be perfect. I'd suggest my clerk Edna, since she has the right skills and a sharp mind, but people at the sanatorium would recognize her." Ayling laid his forearms on the table.

The statements increased Jax's apprehension. "Did Richard have a plan?" He felt certain the senior constable did, and Jax had an inkling of what the idea was.

His boss turned toward Jax. "He does, and he'd like to present it himself. For that reason, we said we'd meet at your house around seven o'clock."

"What's his suggestion?" Jax asked.

Amos cleared his throat. "We have a general idea, but I want to respect Richard's request to let him reveal it."

"As do I," Ayling agreed.

"Of course," Jax replied, but the potential solution from Richard was cause for concern. Would the older man suggest involving Bella? While she was a fine amateur sleuth, she wasn't a law officer. Nor was she trained to be part of a potentially difficult, dangerous undercover investigation—one that wasn't simply a whodunit, but a whydunit, and howdunit, too. But who else was there? Jax released a pent-up breath. Even if Richard made such a suggestion, would Amos support it? His boss had balked at Bella's involvement in a previous case, so he wouldn't necessarily approve of her being a crucial player in this one and, if he didn't, what about Rufus? Women were few and far between in the police ranks, and civilians getting involved in cases didn't sit well with most lawmen. Did Richard know a policewoman to fill the role?

Jax couldn't shake a sense of foreboding as they wrapped up their meeting and made plans to be in Moreley later. As much as he yearned to see Bella, he didn't want her in danger. Not at all.

Chapter Two

Weariness dragged at Jax as he pulled to a stop in front of his house. On his way home, he had stopped at Ballantyne resort, but Bella was at a moving picture with Jenny Jenkins. That news eased his mind, since she had left for the theater while he was still in Bridgeling. Even if Richard, Amos, and Rufus had agreed about recruiting her, they wouldn't have had time to offer the invitation. Perhaps, he could quash the idea—if it was Richard's plan. But maybe the man had another strategy.

Buffeted by a host of emotions, Jax climbed out of the roadster and studied his family home. The two story Victorian sat close to the street. When his mother had been alive, she had grown beautiful roses in a profusion of colors. Unfortunately, with no one to tend them, some had died while he was in France. After coming home, his work had kept him busy—not that he knew much about flowers—but he was happy to see new growth along with the last blooms of summer. Clearly, Jenny Jenkins had been at work.

Light poured out of the front windows while a lamp burned on the porch. For the first time in years, Jax wasn't returning to an empty house. Warmth dispelled some of the chill encompassing him. Long strides carried him to the porch steps, which he took two at a time. At the door, Jax hesitated. He'd never knocked in the past, should he now? The decision proved moot when Richard appeared.

"Welcome home." The older man beamed as he ushered Jax inside. "Amos and Rufus are in the front parlor."

When Richard put out his hand, Jax did the same. The retired senior constable still had a lawman's bearing and appearance. Traces of white now shot through his gray hair and mustache. Otherwise, he looked much as he had when Jax first met him years ago.

After following Richard to the parlor, Jax exchanged greetings with the other men before taking a seat on the sofa facing the fireplace. A cheerful blaze flickered there, but his mood didn't improve. "I suppose the three of you have discussed Richard's idea about how to replace Miss Bounder." He had given them time to do so, since it was now a quarter after the hour.

"We have," Amos replied.

"We want to solve this case, and you've said you do, too. You've taken the oath as a deputy sheriff. I could order you to go to the sanatorium, but I won't," Ayling said.

"I'm not backing out. I'm just wondering what the plan is," Jax replied.

"We don't want you stuck there with no regular contact. It isn't safe," Richard said. "Or workable. We need you to get word out when you find clues."

All three of the older men sounded defensive and uneasy, which only increased Jax's suspicion. No policewoman was involved, or she would be here now. Not that many existed, but he'd been guardedly optimistic. "I'd like to hear your plan, although I probably figured it out already."

Richard nodded. "I'm guessing you have, so there's no need to dilly dally. With the receptionist's position open, I suggested Arabella apply. Then, she would be your contact. You already know all the reasons she'd be a good choice. I won't repeat them."

Jax knew all of Bella's positive points. In fact, he had spent the past hour weighing the pros and cons of having her involved. Bella's experience, skills, and insight weighed heavily on the plus side. "Have you told her about the case?" While he didn't think that was likely, he wanted to be sure.

The senior constable shook his head. "No. I wouldn't do that without talking to you."

"The girl has many beneficial aspects as an investigator," Derringer added quickly.

The support from Amos increased Jax's annoyance. He moved his attention to his boss. "You wanted to make sure she stayed out of the way in the case last June. And she was involved as a witness long before I got there."

"I did, but she won't be in the way at the sanitorium. Her primary job is to relay your messages to us," Derringer said. "That's all."

"Which puts her in the middle of a complicated, risky case. Involving a civilian is chancy." And not just any civilian. Bella would be the one in jeopardy, and he'd be hard pressed to protect her while in the role of a shell-shocked soldier.

Richard answered. "If I thought she'd be put in peril, I wouldn't suggest it."

The older man's assurance made Jax feel foolish. "I know you wouldn't. It's just that..." His voice trailed off.

"You want to protect her? Understandable." Richard's countenance held sympathy.

Jax didn't refute the assertion. How could he? "I do. Her well-being is my number one priority."

Richard grinned. "Progress."

Warmth rose in Jax's face, but he nodded. He had hidden his feelings for Bella much too long. He wasn't going back to keeping his distance. Or to concealing his emotions from others.

"If you're dead set against it, we might figure out something else. Having someone there every day is the best way to get needed information out in a timely manner," Ayling said. "Amos and I talked more on the way over here, but we don't have another quick solution."

Again, Jax couldn't argue the point, so he took another tack. "The resort season isn't over. Bella is probably busy out there."

"The season is winding down. You're aware of that." Richard made the observations in his usual calm tone.

Much of his boyhood had been spent at Ballantyne, the resort built by Bella's grandfather and his partner more than three decades earlier. The place featured golf, tennis, fishing, and boating during the season. After spending countless spring and summer days there, Jax knew fall was a lull before the holidays brought visitors for sledding, skating, and festivities. A long moment of silence passed while he considered how to respond. He was still thinking when his boss spoke.

"It's entirely up to you, Jax," Derringer said. "We want to get to the bottom of the situation, especially in regard to Aaron. It will be more difficult without someone else inside."

"It's more dangerous for you if you don't have a reliable contact at the place," Richard added. "And we need information in order to get justice for those men. We may even locate Aaron Corning, if we act fast."

Although the young officer might be dead, they didn't know for sure. Moving quickly could save him, so Jax knew they were both right. He also knew if Bella wasn't contacted and found out about this discussion later, she would be furious. Mostly with him. She deserved a voice in the decision, which led him to relent. "If Bella gets the receptionist's job, how will I talk with her? Patients aren't allowed much freedom, from what I learned last year during another case and from what we discussed earlier today."

"They aren't, but the receptionist takes on a lot of extra duties—escorting patients outside, feeding those who can't do it themselves, reading to them, and so forth. Miss Bounder told Edna as much, more than once," Ayling said.

"Which is a good thing for the case." The satisfaction in Richard's tone and expression were clear. "And Arabella would be perfect for the job."

"Are you willing to ask her?" Derringer looked directly at Jax.

After a moment's hesitation, Jax nodded. "We can talk with her about it, but she'll need to agree to only carry messages. Nothing more. I don't want her questioning other employees or snooping around the place."

"We'll make that clear," Ayling assured him.

"When do you want to meet with her?" Jax asked.

Richard pulled out his pocket watch. "She and Jenny went to a moving picture. They'll be back soon."

Jax felt ambivalent. Over the past few months, he had often thought about his homecoming. The current setting and circumstances hadn't been part of his imaginings. Not even close.

"You look uncertain," Richard said. "Why don't you take a few minutes alone with Bella before we go over the investigation?"

The older man's sympathetic countenance had Jax nodding. "If possible, I'd like to."

Richard spoke again. "I'll suggest refreshments and help Jenny with them."

"I'll say I need to wash my hands," Derringer said. "That will give you and Miss Stewart a few minutes to yourselves, but I'd rather you didn't discuss the current case until we're all together."

"I'll go outside for a smoke," Ayling put in.

Before Jax could form a reply, feminine laughter followed the sound of the front door opening. "All right," Jax agreed, mostly because they didn't have time for further discussion. As the voices grew closer, he felt a lump form in his throat and sweat break out on his forehead.

Jenny, a pretty blonde in her early fifties, led the way to the house and stopped inside the front door. "You must be wondering why Jax's vehicle is here."

That was undeniable. After seeing Jax's Chummy parked at the curb, Bella had been hard pressed to continue conversing.

His latest note had said he wouldn't be home for a while. What had happened? He must be well, or Jenny would have told her. Wouldn't she? Nothing in the older woman's countenance indicated something was wrong, but Bella had to ask. "Has he been hurt?"

"I haven't actually seen him, but he's not injured. I only know a little about why he, his boss, and the sheriff from Bridgeling are here. Richard wants to tell you himself, and I agreed. Come along." Jenny softened her words with a smile.

Uneasy and worried, Bella's legs felt wobbly as she approached the room. After Jenny stepped into the parlor, Bella paused beside her. Her gaze took in Richard, Senior Agent Derringer, and a stranger in a uniform—the man from Bridgeling, no doubt—before riveting on Jax. All of them had risen as soon as the women appeared in the archway. Bella only focused on Jax. "What a surprise to have you back in Moreley." *Shock* better described how she'd felt upon seeing his vehicle. Utterly and completely stunned, and she hadn't regained her composure yet.

"Hello, Bella." Jax's voice was a rough murmur.

She scanned his familiar face. His wavy blonde hair curled over his collar, and his green eyes were red-rimmed and ringed with shadows. "Hello." Her tone sounded as hoarse as his.

Jax shifted from one foot to the other while holding her gaze.

"Jenny, why don't we get tea and cookies?" Richard ushered his wife out of the room, while the other two men followed on their heels with some mumbled words about cleaning up and smoking. Bella paid them little heed.

When they were alone, Jax gestured to the sofa. "Sit down, please."

Emotion shone in his eyes. Exactly what emotion she couldn't tell. Since her legs still felt weak, Bella quickly perched on the edge of the cushions. "I got a note from you on Monday, but you didn't mention coming home. In fact, you suggested you wouldn't be back for weeks." Despite being glad to see him, Bella felt troubled. This reunion wasn't what she had imagined for months. He seemed stiff and formal. Why?

Jax sat down, but his gaze shifted away. "I'm as surprised as you are about being back here today. Amos called yesterday and asked me to come."

Her brow furrowed. "Come for what? Your note sounded like you were tied up with the O'Donnelly case."

He glanced at her again. "We found her killers and the guy who hired them, since I wrote that note. Everything happened really fast. I'll have to go back to testify, but not soon. There's wrap up to be done. I won't be involved in that."

As relief flooded her, Bella beamed at him. He didn't smile back, which tamped down her happiness. All the same, she strove for a bright note when she responded. "Wonderful. Mick O'Donnelly must be glad." The man had saved Jax's life in France. When a bootlegger's assassin had taken aim on Mick, a Prohibition agent, but shot his young wife, Jax had readily agreed to help bring those responsible to justice. Bella had been sad to see him leave their hometown, even temporarily, but he had made a solemn pledge to come home for good after the case was solved. Now, he was taking another job?

"He is. We all are."

"But you aren't back home to stay?"

Jax ran one hand over his face. "I'm afraid not yet, which is why I'm glad we can talk in private."

Bella's measured optimism gave way to deep dismay. "You came to tell me in person you're staying with the Bureau?"

"No. I'm not." Jax leaned back and folded his arms across his chest. "I came because Derringer has another case for me. This will be my last away from here, for sure."

For a long moment, she stared at him. "Jax, you made a promise to me. Now, you've taken another assignment." Resentment and regret warred within her, and both surfaced in her voice.

He bowed his head, and with one hand, massaged his neck. "This isn't a job with the Bureau, which is why we want to talk with you."

His tentative tone made Bella relent. "Talk about your case?"

Jax pressed two fingers to his forehead. "Yep. I only found out about the job late this afternoon. Remember when we heard about Poplar Pines last year? That sanatorium for shell-shocked soldiers."

"Sure. I remember. What does that have to do with you being home or another case?" Confusion filled Bella. Was he changing the subject or was there a connection?

Jenny and Richard, reappearing with a tray of refreshments, interrupted. Richard put it on the table near the fireplace, and Jenny poured cups of tea. By the time she'd given some to Bella and Jax, Derringer came back.

After they got settled, Bella glanced at each face before saying, "I still don't know what's going on."

Jax spoke first. "We were catching up, and I just mentioned Poplar Pines. Nothing more."

"Good," Amos said. When the other man entered the room, Derringer looked at Bella. "Miss Stewart, this is Sheriff Ayling from Bridgeling."

Ayling nodded before taking the chair he had used previously. The entire situation put Bella on edge. So had the revelation about Jax not coming home, as promised. They would discuss the whys and wherefores in more detail later because, despite his latest pledge, Bella wanted to be sure Jax wasn't going to take more assignments with the Bureau and use some other excuse. If other people came before her, she wanted to know. Breaking ties with him wouldn't be easy, but Bella didn't want to spend the rest of her life waiting for Jax. She had waited so long already. Didn't he feel the same way about delays and distance? If so, he needed to prove it. Not talk about it. She shifted her thoughts to the present. "The sanatorium is an hour's drive from here. Maybe a little more. Why do you want to talk with me? I've never been there." Bella looked from Derringer, to Richard, to Ayling, to Jax.

"Since you'll be the one directly involved, why don't you tell Arabella?" the senior agent asked Jax. "Richard, Rufus, and I will fill in, as necessary."

Bella glanced at Jax, who seemed even more uncomfortable. "Yes, why don't you tell me?"

After a long exhalation, Jax nodded. "As I already told you, I only found out about the case this afternoon." He cleared his throat before revealing the discussion in the Bridgeling constable's office. Once he wrapped up with the news of Miss Bounder's sudden departure, Jax let silence fall.

For a long moment, Bella absorbed the revelations. "Patients have died and disappeared. Now, the receptionist abruptly quit, missed a meeting with Miss Corning, and isn't at her old home even though she left for there."

"She supposedly left a note in her room at Poplar Pines saying she went back to the Columbus area to live with an aunt,"

Ayling said. "No one has reached her or seen her. We'll keep trying. There's not necessarily anything to worry about."

Despite the positive words, his tone and expression sent a message of concern, but Bella focused on the patients. "Do you think the latest missing man is still alive?"

"We hope so," Derringer replied, "but we're worried about him going forward, so we want to move fast."

Bella understood their concern, but not the genesis of the issue. "Jax just said the two men who died had relatives who complained about being burdened with their care, and the latest one's wife was upset about spending so much money on his hospitalization. Do you believe that's related to their fates?"

"We do. But we don't know for sure that the second one is dead. There's much more information in the file." He tapped the packet of papers sitting on the small table between him and Ayling. "If you agree to help, you'll see I've known Aaron Corning and his family since I was a boy. He's married, but it's his older sister who called me. His wife dumped him at the sanatorium and hasn't been back." Derringer continued with more details about the wife.

After hearing about young Mrs. Corning's social life, Bella saw an ugly possibility. "If the patients aren't free to come and go, someone might sneak them out, maybe to get rid of them."

"You've got a detective's mind," Richard put in. "That's exactly what we fear. It's what Miss Bounder hinted to Miss Corning. It's what two former employees mentioned to Sheriff Ayling. The problem is, none of them have solid evidence of who is involved. Or exactly what's going on."

With so much to consider, Bella asked a question related to *who*, not *how* or *why* although all three seemed critical. "More than one person, wouldn't you think?" Bella asked.

"Exactly." Richard set aside his teacup and leaned forward. "Miss Bounder planned to reveal her notions when she met with Eleanor Corning."

"It's strange that she quit so quickly. Is there any possibility someone planted the note, and she's still at Poplar Pines?" Bella asked.

Ayling looked grim. "I can't rule that out, but you and Jax might be able to clarify her status, if you're there. Miss Bounder only worked at the place for a couple of months. I haven't been able to locate the receptionist before her. My deputies and I spoke with a former nurse and a former orderly. And we've got dribs and drabs from various sources."

"Why did the nurse and orderly leave?" Bella asked.

"Both were uneasy about the death in March, and neither thought patients got real help," Derringer said. "The Lennings, who own the place, tout modern methods, but the pair I spoke with saw none being employed."

"Could the sanatorium primarily be a money-making scheme, not a real hospital?" The thought disturbed Bella.

"We all believe that's likely," Richard said.

She nodded. "Plenty to investigate. How do you plan to do it?" They had revealed the problems, but not Jax's actual assignment and not why they were telling her.

Derringer offered a tight smile. "Sheriff Ayling has deputized Jax, so he can help with the investigation. I wish I was able to be directly involved, but I'm headed back to Washington. Orders from my superior. I'll escort Eleanor on my way, and I'll stay in touch with Rufus and Richard, although not in an official capacity. As a family friend, I'm apprehensive. As a lawman, I want those involved brought to justice, and quickly."

The senior agent's deep concern took Bella aback. In previous dealings with Derringer, she had found him cold and aloof. But not now. "It's disturbing his wife spends so much time out-and-about, not to mention never visiting her husband." Bella couldn't imagine being so neglectful or selfish with a loved one. "I understand the need to investigate the place, but how do you plan to get more details?"

Seconds of silence preceded Derringer's response. "Jax has to uncover them."

"How?" Bella directed this query to Jax. So far, no specific answers had been provided. The men had outlined the reasons to investigate, but not their methods. "Are you planning to do interviews? Is that why I'm in on this discussion? To help question people? Employees, patients, relatives?"

Jax shook his head. "That wouldn't work in this case. If the owners are involved, they won't be forthcoming, if confronted. The same is true for employees and patients who might either be implicated or hesitant to tell the truth for fear of repercussions. As for relatives, those who might pay to eliminate a problem aren't going to talk."

"No one was obliging when I've been there," Sheriff Ayling put in. "All the employees were hesitant to say much. Some are probably afraid. As Jax told you, others may be involved. In any case, more interviews aren't apt to help. Miss Bounder offered scant information, and the two workers who left weeks ago have little solid evidence. Mostly guesses. We've learned all we can from them, and it isn't enough to arrest anyone. Or to locate Aaron Corning."

"Then, exactly what is Jax's role?" Alarm prickled along Bella's nerve ends. Why weren't they telling her outright?

For a long moment, Jax gazed steadily at her. "I'm going undercover as a patient."

Surprise and dismay hit Bella hard enough to drive the air from her lungs. No wonder the men hadn't presented their plan—a dangerous plan—immediately. "Go undercover in an asylum? That's what it is. An asylum. Maybe they don't do much with patients, but maybe they employ some of the horrible treatments used during the war and before it. Many mental hospitals have used torturous methods for years." As ugly possibilities rose in her mind's eye, she stared at Jax. "What an awful idea. I can't believe you'd even consider it. Your bicep and shoulder can't be any better. What if you get hurt even worse?"

Jax held her gaze. "You heard they do very little in terms of procedures. About the worst that might happen to me is getting restrained or isolated. I'll be a model patient to avoid those options." His lips quirked.

Bella didn't return what she supposed was meant to be a reassuring smile. She wasn't reassured. Not at all. "It seems very risky."

His good humor faded. "Putting someone inside is the best way, possibly the only way, to get to the bottom of the problems and prevent more deaths and disappearances. I'm a veteran and a lawman, which is the right combination for this job."

"I'm sure plenty of lawmen are also veterans." Bella looked at the other three men. "Aren't they?"

"Some are," Ayling replied, "but time is important. If Aaron Corning is still alive, we want to find him. Getting someone else might take a few days or longer. Jax can be admitted this weekend."

"I share your concerns, Bella," Jenny put in. "From what we know about the treatments, none is apt to worsen Jax's shoulder and arm issues. If I thought that was likely, I wouldn't play any role in this case."

"Neither would I," Richard added. "None of us wants him to be harmed."

"I won't be harmed," Jax said. "Other than some soreness and shrapnel occasionally coming out, I'm fine now, and I'll stay that way."

While Bella knew Jax was painting too bright a picture of his condition, she appreciated the older couple's reassurances. She was also aware her need for reassurance highlighted her deep and personal concern for him. Not that she needed to keep her feelings a secret. Both Jenny and Richard knew she and Jax planned to court when he was home for good. Derringer must, too. "Why speak with me? I only know what Jax and I learned last year, and he's probably shared all that. It wasn't much, and I don't have additional information about the sanatorium." In past cases, she'd helped with interviews, searched scenes with Jax, and participated in group meetings. If Jax was at Poplar Pines, this was apt to be the last time she met with everyone. Or saw him for some time. And what was Jenny's role? Bella didn't have to wait long to find out.

Derringer shifted to face Richard. "Why don't you explain our plan to her? Your plan, really."

Richard braced his elbows on his knees and looked at Bella. "Jenny and I will pretend to be Jax's aunt and uncle, but we won't visit often since we want folks there to think we're tired of being burdened with him. He needs a contact at other times. The receptionist position is open, and they'll hire someone quickly. From what we've heard, the first applicant gets the job almost every time. Rufus has no one who wouldn't be recognized, and Amos can't send a female agent because it's not a bootlegging case. Not that they aren't both short-handed. We want you to call about the job, Arabella. You're good with shorthand and typing, which is important." Richard paused for a moment. "You should be able to talk with Jax regularly, and you can relay information to us."

"I'd be deputizing you, too, Miss Stewart," Sheriff Ayling added.

The last statement hung heavily in the air, but sent excitement spiraling through Bella. Anticipation vanquished fear. She would be a deputy. Jax's expression gave little away, but concern darkened his green eyes. Despite that, if Jax wasn't amenable to her participation, she wouldn't be here. Bella felt sure of that. "I'd be working as an undercover deputy sheriff." She failed to keep the hope from her voice.

A low laugh left Richard. "You would. Derringer wrote up a background story already. You'd need to look it over before you call the place. If you're willing to be involved."

Her eyes widened. Derringer had supplied details for her cover? Interesting indeed. "How could I help as the receptionist? Would I be looking for clues?"

"Absolutely not." Jax was quick to reply.

The terse answer didn't surprise or discourage Bella. He wasn't enthusiastic about her participation, but he wasn't standing in her way, either. "Then, what would I do?"

"Just be a contact for me. Nothing more," he replied. "If I get information requiring quick action, waiting for Jenny and Richard to visit won't work. Especially when they won't come much. We need someone to be the receptionist, since she helps a lot. We're sure you'll be asked to assist with other than secretarial duties, too, which is how you and I would connect."

Derringer repeated the receptionist's tasks before reiterating Jax's warning. "We only need you to carry messages. As Richard said, it's entirely up to you whether or not you help. If you don't, we'll manage."

The man's cryptic caution wasn't surprising. Bella would wager he'd prefer a female agent on the job, but Jax probably would, too. Luckily, that wasn't possible. She'd been asked, and she was more than willing. She was eager and excited. "Of course, I'll help."

"Wonderful," Jenny offered the vote of confidence. Over the years, she had helped her husband on cases, and the two of them had always supported Bella's involvement.

"I have faith in you," Richard added.

"If they hire me." Uncertainty impinged on Bella's enthusiasm. "Maybe they won't."

"The place is remote. The sheriff mentioned a requirement to live on the grounds as one issue in keeping people. Not everyone wants to be there every night and day, which makes the applicant pool smaller. Of course, another is the extra duties required of everyone," Derringer said.

"I think they'll be happy to have you," Richard said.

"So do I," Ayling agreed.

Bella hoped so because, if she got the job, she was going undercover, too. And as a law officer, not an amateur detective.

Chapter Three

As he listened to the conversation, Jax couldn't shake his apprehension about Bella getting involved, but he knew someone had to be inside with him. And Richard was right. Bella would do a great job. She always did. Still, having her serve as a temporary deputy sheriff gave him pause. She had blithely accepted parameters from Derringer and him, but Jax wouldn't be completely at ease until he talked with her alone.

"We should go over some specifics." Derringer looked from Jax to Bella. "Right now, there are around twenty patients. Richard already called in regard to having his nephew admitted. He didn't get a lot of details. Mostly, generalities. Eleanor doesn't know anything about what families are told because her sister-in-law took Aaron, so the reluctance to provide particulars in advance may be standard." He pulled a paper packet out of his briefcase and handed it to Bella, along with the ones on the table. "Here are summaries of our current information, along with biographies for each of you. I did my best on short notice, so you may have to fill in a bit. Jax already has his information.

He doesn't need to have all your background. In fact, it's better if he doesn't, since the two of you will act like strangers. I don't think I need to tell you that this is purely confidential, Miss Stewart." A note of warning was obvious.

"No, you don't," was Bella's clipped reply.

Derringer pursed his lips but said nothing as he sat down again. Restraining a laugh wasn't easy, but Jax managed. Although the senior agent intimidated most of his subordinates, he wouldn't cow Bella, who was spunky and spirited. Sometimes, those qualities bothered Jax. Seeing her use them on his boss was a different story. But he couldn't dwell on his Amos's reaction. When he spoke, Jax turned back to the issue at hand. "I haven't had much chance to look at my biography. You never said exactly when I'm going to the sanatorium. Tomorrow or Sunday?"

"I called again after speaking with Rufus. They have several open beds, so I can plan for tomorrow. If Arabella gets the job right away, there's no reason to wait in taking you. The doctor indicated they'd accept you as soon as we decide," Richard replied. "Take some time to study the case and your roles."

Derringer nodded. "I'd like for all of us to meet again tomorrow. I need to leave about three o'clock to get back in time for work on Monday. As it is, I'll have to be on the road most of tomorrow evening and Sunday."

"How about one o'clock back here?" Richard asked.

After the group agreed on the time and place, Derringer spoke again. "Will you call about the job first thing in the morning and let us know what they say, Miss Stewart? Pretend you live in Karston and be in dire need of work. I put an idea in your background."

"Of course. I'll study my biography tonight and be ready early tomorrow." Bella got to her feet. "But how did I learn about the opening? I can say I'm from Karston. What if they want details?"

"Since my clerk Edna called the sanatorium to talk with Miss Bounder and was told she'd left suddenly, word has spread in the area. Edna lives between Bridgeling and Karston, so saying you heard it in your supposed hometown will cut the mustard," Ayling told her.

"All right," Bella replied. While Bridgeling wasn't far south of the sanatorium, Karston was over an hour northeast. Evidently, the clerk had a long drive to work.

"Miss Stewart, I called Boxmore Hill School after talking to Richard," Derringer said. "The headmistress understands our situation and will be a reference for you. Your story includes information on you substituting there last spring."

"I'll keep that in mind, and it gives me an idea," Bella said. "I need to have a reason for being away from the resort. I could say I'm substituting again. If Mrs. Berkey agreed to be a reference, she'd surely agree to helping a bit more. Then, if someone calls the school looking for me, she can relay the message. Maybe to Jenny? It's doubtful anyone will telephone there, but I'd rather not tell everyone at Ballantyne about going undercover. I'm afraid they'd fret."

Jax nodded. "It's a good idea."

"I agree," Derringer said. "I'll speak with the headmistress again."

Bella smiled at him before turning to Jenny. "Thank you for the tea and cookies and for going to the theater with me."

"I enjoyed it, too," the older woman replied.

All four men rose and bid Bella goodbye, while Jax fell into step beside her. "I'll walk you to your vehicle."

"Fine," she murmured.

Her one-word response left Jax feeling edgy, and he followed her to the sedan in silence. She had been enthusiastic about working at Poplar Pines, so her cool attitude seemed personal. Why? "You understand the importance of this job, don't you?" Was she upset about him getting involved?

"Of course, I do." Bella pivoted toward him. "It sounded like other patients might be in danger, and Aaron Corning may still be alive. The case is well worth pursuing."

A short exhalation left him. "I agree. Just to be clear, I've officially left the Bureau. I'm not simply taking a leave. Sheriff Ayling will be in charge, since the sanatorium is in his jurisdiction. Me being a deputy is temporary, same as you being one."

Her dark eyes widened. "You won't go back to being an agent?"

Surprise replaced the chilliness. Evidently, Bella had wondered if he was reneging on his promise to come home after the O'Donnelly case. "Absolutely not."

"And Mick understands you quitting?"

"I haven't had a chance to tell him yet, but I always said I'd leave after his wife's killers were caught." Mick had also said he'd lost the love of his life and didn't want the same happening to Jax. He brushed his errant thoughts away and focused on Bella. In the dim light from the streetlamp, her dark hair shone. Shadows kept her features from being visible, but he knew them as well as he knew his own. And if he wanted a reminder, Jax only needed to pull two well-worn photographs out of his pocket. Even when he had kept an emotional barrier between him and

Bella, Jax had looked at those pictures often. Looked and wished things were different. Now, they might be soon.

"This case seems complicated. Do you have any idea of how long it will last?" Bella asked.

"I wish I knew."

She grasped his hand. "You're taking an enormous risk."

"You are, too," he murmured, "and that worries me. Ayling intends to deputize you, but you can't be asking questions or pursuing clues. Poplar Pines seems far sketchier than we heard last year, when we investigated Mr. Monticello's death." Although the man had been a resort guest, the case had sent Bella and Jax across a wide area in pursuing his killer.

"But we weren't focused on the sanatorium. It just came up in passing." Bella let go and stepped back. "I already said I wouldn't snoop. Don't you trust me?"

"Of course, I do. There's no one I trust more." Certainty was in his tone because he meant what he said.

"Good." Her features softened, along with her voice.

"You like sleuthing, but you agreed to the undercover role quickly. Because it's a new challenge?" he asked.

Her thick, dark lashes swept down to conceal her eyes. "I do, but that's a small part of my reason. Going undercover as a patient seems perilous. If I can help speed up a solution and make your job easier, I want to do my part."

The sincerity in her tone made him gently squeeze her hand. "Thank you. As far as treatment, shell-shocked soldiers—like other mental patients—don't garner much sympathy. Not from doctors or others. It will be a very different role for me."

She looked back at him then. "Do you know any? I never thought to ask."

"I saw some cases when I was in field hospitals in France, and I visited two fellow officers when I first got home. They were in a facility back east." A shudder rippled through him. "To say the place was dreadful would be an understatement. It looked more like a jail than a sanatorium, and patients were treated like prisoners. The two of them were strapped into chairs when I saw them. They were pale and thin and listless. I contacted their families afterward. Both were married. One's wife had already divorced him and wed again. She was his only relative, but she chose not to hear about issues at the hospital. His parents left enough to cover his expenses for years. It galls me he's stuck there. The other one has parents and four younger siblings. Dealing with him at home became too much for them, and his wife wouldn't speak with me. The parents weren't amenable to discussing his treatment, either. I felt so frustrated. I wanted to help, but I couldn't find a way." Although he hadn't revealed so much to the other lawmen, Jax's troubling memories tumbled out.

"Which is another reason you're willing to risk your own health and well-being in this case."

She recognized his main motivation, which wasn't surprising since she knew him well, better than anyone else did. "It is. Please don't take any chances while you're there. While I can watch out for myself, I won't be able to protect you."

"Being the receptionist won't be hazardous." Bella spoke with certainty.

Jax wished he had the same sense of conviction. Bella would be a strong partner in the investigation, yet ambivalent emotions tore at him. Waiting to see what happened was his only option for now.

Chapter Four

First thing on Saturday morning, Bella called Poplar Pines and was asked to come that day for an interview. Before leaving for her appointment, she relayed the news to Richard, who was at the constable's office. Since Jax wouldn't need his vehicle, and hers was required at the resort, Bella had taken his Chevrolet Chummy. As she headed out of Moreley, bittersweet memories of Jax sitting in the passenger seat as she drove around town swept over her. With concerted effort, Bella pushed them to the recesses of her mind. This case was different. They wouldn't be working side-by-side.

The hour drive to Poplar Pines gave Bella time to review her fictitious background and calm her nerves. Harriet Halliday, her pseudonym, was apt to be anxious about a new job, so a little nervousness wouldn't be out of line. As Bella turned off the main road and on to the long driveway leading to the sanatorium, she released a pent-up breath. The building must have once been a lovely and spacious home. Constructed of red brick, the Georgian house boasted four white columns and a wide porch.

Black shutters framed the large windows. Large pots of mums sat on the porch and English ivy climbed the exterior walls. Towering trees, their green leaves now tipped in shades of gold and red, lined the walkways. The overall effect was one of grace and calm and beauty. But what about the goings on inside and around this place? Again, Bella felt butterflies take flight inside her. After a reassuring breath, she pulled the Chummy to a stop, climbed out, and went up the front walk. Her heart sped up as she walked into the mansion. The foyer was as attractive as the outside, Bella discovered as she stepped into the entry. A beautiful crystal chandelier hung in the middle of the coffered ceiling. In its soft light, the parquet floor shone.

"May I help you?"

Bella turned to see a gray-haired woman in her sixties descending a wide staircase. "Yes, I'm Harriet Halliday. I'm here about the receptionist's job."

"Wonderful," the older woman replied with no trace of interest or emotion to reinforce the word. As she paused at the foot of the stairs, she studied Bella carefully. "I am Mrs. Lenning. I oversee our general operations. My son, Dr. Lenning, is our medical director." She gestured toward a set of French doors off to the side of the entry. "Come into my office, and I'll go over the duties with you."

Bella followed the woman into the adjacent room. Once again, she was surprised by the luxurious atmosphere. An intricately carved desk sat facing the door. Two leather chairs, clearly for visitors, stood in front of it. On one wall was a large fireplace, where a cheerful blaze flickered. The opposite wall consisted primarily of mullioned windows looking out over a formal garden. Although summer was at an end, roses continued to bloom in a profusion of colors. Some of Bella's tension ebbed. If the patient rooms were half as nice as what she'd seen so far, perhaps Poplar Pines wasn't such a terrible place. As long as he wasn't subjected to outdated procedures, Jax need only concentrate on his job, and Bella could apply herself to helping with the investigation, when and where necessary.

Mrs. Lenning pulled a sheaf of papers out of the desk. "My son said he spoke with you this morning, and that you're proficient in shorthand and typing. Is that right?"

Bella cleared her throat. "Yes, I am." The conversation had been brief, but the doctor asked only basic questions. Evidently, he'd taken notes, too.

"You were a substitute teacher at the Boxmore Hill School?" The woman leafed through the file in a willy-nilly manner. "But you live in Karston. Is that nearby? Not that it matters."

Mrs. Lenning's scattered statements were hard to follow, and why didn't she know about a town in the general area? Bella forced her thoughts away from the woman's behavior in order to remember the story Derringer had concocted. "Yes, I'd hoped to obtain a full-time teaching position, but nothing is available right now. I was happy to learn about the job here. I really need one. My aunt, my only relative, died last winter. Keeping up her house and paying other bills is hard with no income. She was a sweet woman, but had nothing besides her home to leave me." Appearing to be in dire need of work was part of the plan. Someone who was desperate for a job would be less likely to report problems and, therefore, more likely to be hired.

"We need someone to be with us for an extended time," Mrs. Lenning observed. "Our last receptionist left abruptly, as you know if you got word about the vacancy in Karston—or wherever. When she told you about quitting, did she say why?"

"I didn't speak with her, ma'am. I heard about it through a man who got the information from someone else. I'm not sure exactly who. So many are out of work, which is why I called right off." Bella had decided on her own not to mention the clerk, since she worked in the Bridgeling sheriff's office.

"I see." The older woman gave a slight nod of her head. "She left a note and took off. If you plan to resign, I must ask you to give us notice. At least a week. It's hard to get reliable help."

Once again, the older woman's words were vague, which reminded Bella of other information in the file. Perhaps, Mrs. Lenning was rather senile. With unemployment high in the war's wake, finding employees should not be onerous. Some folks would like a place to live along with a job, and extra duties weren't uncommon. Of course, what the woman meant by *reliable help* was uncertain. "I hope this will be a permanent position."

"I do, too." She looked at the sheet of paper on the desk. "You haven't had any jobs other than substitute teaching?"

"No, ma'am. I went to business school intending to become a secretary. That's how I learned typing and shorthand. Unfortunately, my aunt became ill before I secured a position. She raised me, so I wanted to take care of her." Bella had practiced her false background story repeatedly since the previous evening, so it fell smoothly from her tongue. "The substitute teaching job was a happenstance, but I liked it there."

The woman looked pensive. "You nursed your aunt?"

"Yes, I did. We couldn't afford to hire help." Bella provided the facts in her packet. False facts, if such a thing existed.

"We may ask you to help at mealtimes and such. Some men need to be fed. Others benefit from someone reading to them or escorting them outside. A few enjoy playing games like checkers or cribbage. Would you be comfortable working with patients?"

Bella's heart sped up. The lawmen were right about her being asked to perform additional duties. Doing so would help in a few ways. She might learn more about the missing and dead patients, and she could speak privately with Jax. "Of course. I often had to feed my aunt during the last months of her extended illness. When she felt well enough, we played checkers, or I read to her."

"Our patients are not elderly ladies, Miss Halliday. Although some suffered physical wounds during the war, they are mostly strong, young men. Troubled, as well."

"Would I be in danger?" Bella asking, trying to both look and sound disturbed but not terrified. She didn't want to appear too eager to deal directly with patients or too timid to help them. Arousing suspicion was to be avoided. Jax had made that clear, and it was sensible.

"Of course not. We restrain the most difficult patients, for their own well-being and for the safety of our staff members," Mrs. Lenning assured her. A faint smile touched the older woman's lips. "Can't have them wandering off, either."

"Oh, good," Bella said with feigned relief. The idea of confining wounded, troubled veterans made her feel nauseous, and the reference to wandering was disturbing. Was Mrs. Lenning involved in the chicanery? "My aunt had a neighbor whose son fought in France." She forced a shudder. "He came home a completely different man. Sometimes, he simply stares into space. Other times, he's very volatile. His folks say he has screaming nightmares." Bella pursed her lips as if she had sucked on something sour. Being too sympathetic might evoke scrutiny.

"Didn't they seek treatment for him?" Mrs. Lenning asked. "We have men here with those issues."

"They took him to their family doctor," Bella said, making up details as she went along. This part hadn't been covered in her talk with the lawmen or in the file.

"Very few doctors can offer the help we do here at Poplar Pines," Mrs. Lenning assured her. "Of course, treatment takes time. Those with nightmares are disturbing to other patients, so we often have to place them in isolation. After your experience with your neighbor, I'm sure you understand."

The words, spoken in a matter-of-fact tone, seemed benign, but they conjured ugly images in Bella's mind. Choked with rising emotion, she had trouble forming a comment. Finally, she said, "Of course."

Mrs. Lenning offered another smile. "I think you will fit in nicely, Miss Halliday."

Bella knew she wouldn't really, but she would certainly pretend to do so. "I believe I will, too. If I get the job."

"I want you to speak with my son, but I'm sure he'll agree you are suited for the position. After all, you've already talked on the telephone with him. You mentioned living at your aunt's home in Karston. How far is that again?"

"A little more than an hour. I'm an early riser, so I won't be late." Neither Lenning had mentioned the necessity of living at the sanatorium, and Bella wasn't sure about bringing it up.

For a moment, the older woman looked blank. She rubbed her forehead and finally, spoke again. "In the winter, the roads may be bad, and we don't want to be without a receptionist for long. We have rooms here, and I'd suggest you stay during the week. You're free to go home on weekends, although we will need your help on Sunday afternoons when visitors come. You can leave early Friday evening and come back Sunday morning."

The ideas were sound and expressed coherently. Perhaps, Mrs. Lenning was simply scattered because of her workload. With papers stacked on her desk and on the small table next to it, she appeared to be very busy. Or she might put up a bewildered front to avoid coming under suspicion. Following her line of conversation wasn't easy, so Bella kept her response short. "That's fine." Bella already knew most staff members lived on the grounds and wondered why the doctor hadn't mentioned it during their telephone conversation. Perhaps, he hadn't wanted to scare her off.

"Wonderful. You'll only need to bring some clothing. The rooms have linens and such." Mrs. Lenning continued by discussing rules for dealing with the men. "If you help individual men—at meals, writing notes for them, reading to them, and such—please avoid any discussion of the war. Most find it terribly upsetting. Also, refrain from asking about their treatment and never give food or drink to a patient without permission. Do you understand?"

"Of course." Again, a brief reply seemed wise.

The woman cleared her throat. "If a patient discusses his treatment with you, immediately tell me, Dr. Lenning, or Major Billings. Also, refer all family questions to us."

Bella thought back to the file compiled by Derringer. "Major Billings is someone who lives here?"

"He does. He's an old army associate of my son. Retired with no family. He meets with patients from time-to-time, since he's a retired officer." Mrs. Lenning waved one hand in the air. "They divide some patient treatment duties between the two of them. Not my bailiwick."

Bella wanted to ask exactly what duties were split, but Harriet wasn't likely to be so bold. "I'll refer comments and queries to the three of you."

"Fine." The older woman picked up a pencil and tapped it on her desk. "Some patients have hallucinations, which can cause a ruckus. If you hear such things, come to me immediately."

"I will." What sort of hallucinations? Bella wondered, but didn't ask. Perhaps, she could glean details from other staff members.

"Excellent." Mrs. Lenning nodded. "I hope you'll be prepared to start work right away."

"I'd be happy to begin whenever you need me."

"If you can be here tomorrow, we need extra help on our visitation days. Being short-staffed puts a burden on our employees. Nurse Artem would like to take a day off, and I'd be able to allow her to do so, if you'll come in."

Since getting started soon was advisable, Bella readily agreed. "I'll put some things together later today and plan to be here in the morning, if that suits you."

"Come around ten o'clock. It will give you a chance to get settled in your room before beginning your shift. My son is busy at the moment, but he'll speak with you later. I'll show you around first."

The tour did not take long since Mrs. Lenning only presented the public and staff spaces to Bella. No patient rooms were part of their excursion. Were they more austere? Were men tied down? Apprehension remained. Exactly what was Jax getting into? "It's a lovely facility," Bella said when they were back in the foyer. Attractive landscape paintings were scattered on walls throughout the building. Perhaps, they had been left from the time when Poplar Pines was an estate.

"All mental patients deserve a pleasant environment," the older woman said. Her pale eyes darted around the main hall like she was seeing it for the first time.

"I thought you had mostly veterans here," Bella observed.

"We do now, but we could accept civilians in the future. The need for treatment of shell shock victims is so great that my son and I limited ourselves to soldiers. We can't accommodate more than twenty-five men. Right now, we have twenty."

"How long do most stay?"

Mrs. Lenning scowled. "You won't be involved in therapies or treatment, so I don't know why you would ask such a question."

Bella had thought her query was casual, not intrusive, but the woman's reaction reinforced the need to be careful. "I simply wondered because of my aunt's neighbor. Since his family is aware of me coming here for an interview, they were interested in the time and cost involved with treatment. I said I would find out."

The woman nodded. "Please tell them to call, and we can discuss their son's case. Each patient is an individual."

"Of course." Again, it seemed like the best reply.

"Now, I believe Dr. Lenning should be done with his meeting, and he wants to speak with you before you leave." The woman led the way past her own office and down a short hallway to a door with the director's name and title. She tapped on the door and opened it when a male voice called out to enter. Mrs. Lenning stepped in ahead of Bella. "Doctor, Miss Halliday, the new receptionist, is here."

Bella thought it peculiar that the woman called her son by his title, but no more peculiar than the office itself. The first thing she noticed was a buck's head above the fireplace on the wall opposite the door. Did the doctor meet with patients and families here? Did any of them find the blank, staring eyes as eerie as she did? With effort, Bella moved her attention to the tall, thin man rising from the desk. His coal black hair was slicked back from his face with pomade. The equally dark mustache and goatee seemed to be covered in the same substance. When she finally met his gaze, Bella found his eyes, rimmed in red, to be as eerie as that of the deceased stag.

"Thank you, Mrs. Lenning," he said. The older woman nodded and left the room. "Please sit down, miss." He gestured to one of the leather chairs on her side of the desk.

After taking a seat, she folded her hands in her lap and tried to maintain a casual demeanor. As she noticed the paintings on the wall opposite the desk, Bella felt more trepidation. The massive oils depicted brutal scenes of historic battles and stood in stark contrast to the pictures other places in the building. The overall atmosphere of the room was chilling. Once again, she wondered if he met with patients here. Mrs. Lenning's admonition not to discuss the war with any of them echoed in Bella's head. How could anyone not think of combat and carnage in this atmosphere?

"What do you think of our facility, Miss Halliday?" The doctor smiled as he spoke.

Bella refocused on the doctor. "It's a lovely building with a pleasant setting." She didn't mention not seeing any patients. Getting off to a good start was imperative, so anything that might be construed as criticism would be withheld. Still, she wondered where the men were. Secluded in their rooms? When did they play games, listen to books, or go outside? How often did such activities take place? And how many patients were involved? Only a few or all of them?

"Yes, it is, which is helpful to those suffering from mental conditions."

"Your mother said you have all shell shock victims now." She stuck to the basics but hoped to elicit details.

"We do. They're in dire need of care, so we focus only on them. I don't suppose you're familiar with trench warfare since you've been taking care of your elderly aunt, but it was quite horrific."

Bella tried to look suitably appalled. "No, I know nothing of it. Only that some men are tough to handle because of their experiences. Such is true of my neighbor." Feigning ignorance was her best strategy. After all, she was Harriet Halliday, homebody, not Arabella Stewart, former Signal Corps operator and current resort owner.

"You told me about him on the telephone. That's one reason I wanted to interview you as soon as possible, Miss Halliday. All our employees shoulder various duties. You seem able to do that." He continued to stroke his narrow, black mustache.

"Certainly. I don't have formal nursing training, although, as I said, I cared for my aunt."

"Rest assured, we won't ask you to take on anything demanding or dangerous. The safety of staff is of paramount importance." He sounded truly concerned.

"Good," Bella said with what she hoped was the right amount of ladylike relief. "I've heard shell-shocked soldiers can be violent."

"We have special arrangements for those who are, so they can never hurt someone here. You need not worry about that."

What worried Bella was how difficult patients were treated, but she didn't dare ask. Not after Mrs. Lenning chastised her for her earlier curiosity. "That is a relief, sir."

Lenning ran his thumb over his goatee. "Did Mrs. Lenning provide details?"

Bella ignored his formal address for his mother and concentrated on being positive. "She mentioned helping at meals, reading, playing games, and such. I'll start tomorrow, so I can be here when visitors arrive."

"Excellent. We'll ask nothing too complicated or taxing of you."

"Thank you for the reassurance, Dr. Lenning. I must seem silly, but I've led such a sheltered life." That was far from the truth, but Bella couldn't reveal her service in France or her sleuthing work.

"I understand completely. You said your neighbor suffers from shell shock. Do you know his division?"

Again, Bella was cautious. Too much knowledge about the war would undermine her backstory. "No, I don't. He was wounded in late October 1918, I believe." Maybe she shouldn't have made up a story on her own. What if she included some detail that evoked scrutiny?

The doctor leaned back in his chair. "Probably in the Meuse-Argonne offensive."

Bella aimed for a pensive expression. "Perhaps. You possess a great deal more information about the war than I do." Another misstatement for Bella, but true for Harriet.

A grin touched his thin lips. "I served as a doctor in a field hospital. I rarely talk about it, or my posting after the war. But I have firsthand experience with shell shock."

"It must have been terribly hard work in those hospitals."

"Yes, it was. We got many hopeless cases. Some men should've been left at the forward aid stations. They were hopeless cases who took much of our time, and we were often working nearly twenty-four hours straight. Sometimes, even longer. The young officers who faked serious injuries were especially troublesome."

"How awful. Officers should set good examples." Bella replied without disagreeing, even though few men had been malingerers.

"Yes, they should. However, some of the junior officers were poor at best. Not a trace of leadership or courage in many of them. Too often, they tried shirking their duty by insisting they weren't ready to go back to the line when they were. Others exaggerated their wounds. Awful examples for their men. Now, some have mental issues. Truly tragic, but we do our best to help them, as challenging as it is."

Dismay bubbled inside Bella. Matt and Jax had been junior officers, and both had showed bravery and fortitude. As Harriet Halliday, she wouldn't know such men, so Bella held her tongue. Jax had enough to handle without being subjected to poor treatment due to his rank during the war. "I'm glad you can help them."

Lenning paused. "Indeed, that's our purpose in being here. To help them return to productive lives."

Since he seemed more sympathetic, Bella relaxed a little. A knock at the door kept her from responding.

"Come in," the doctor called out.

A muscular man of above average height and middle years stepped into the room. "Sorry to be late. I was speaking with two patients."

"The patients come first," Lenning said with a nod. "You're here in time to meet Miss Halliday." Then, he introduced the man as Major Billings.

Billings took Bella's hand and bowed over it. "How lovely to make your acquaintance."

"My pleasure." When the man didn't immediately release his hold, Bella shifted restlessly in her chair and lowered her eyes. Surely, Harriet would act demure and diffident when meeting someone like Billings. Clad in a spotless uniform with shining brass buttons, the major was an imposing figure. After releasing his grip on her fingers, he took the seat next to Bella, and she covertly studied him. Although he and Lenning were close in age, Billings was tanned and clean-shaven. His bright blue eyes were clear with no hint of redness, while his mahogany hair was clipped close to his well-shaped head. In comparison, the doctor looked worn and faded. Running the facility could take a toll, and appearances could deceive, so Bella didn't draw conclusions. For now, she was observing and learning.

As the interview ended, Bella felt conflicting emotions. She welcomed the challenging undercover role for her. But she was worried about Jax. His lifelong tendency to push himself past sensible limits could bode ill for him at Poplar Pines.

After her interview, Bella headed to Moreley. Everyone else was already in the parlor of the Hastings' home when she arrived. Jenny met her at the door and escorted Bella into the room, where Derringer, Ayling, Richard, and Jax stood when the women entered. After exchanging greetings, they all found seats. Bella settled next to Jax on the sofa before revealing details about her visit to Poplar Pines, including staying there Sunday through Friday afternoons. As soon as that information was out, Jax spoke.

"Is that necessary? You can tell them you'll stay in the winter months. This case will be over long before that." Jax frowned in obvious disapproval.

Bella opened her mouth to object, but Derringer didn't give her a chance. "Having Miss Stewart on hand overnight could be helpful. She doesn't have to be out wandering the place to see or hear something worthwhile. Since she's already agreed to stay, we should stick with the plan. Besides, we knew most workers live on the grounds."

"It seems risky." Jax glanced from Derringer to Ayling, but Richard was the one who answered.

"Arabella won't tell anyone there if she witnesses something at night or any other time. Besides, she's already said she'll be careful, and we can rely on her good judgment."

"Absolutely." Bella watched Jax, who turned toward her. He looked ambivalent, so she pressed her point. "I promised not to dig around, and I won't do or say anything to make your job harder." As much as she might like to investigate on her own, Bella knew he needed peace of mind to effectively, and safely, fulfill his role. Having him fret over her sleuthing on her own wouldn't be beneficial.

Several seconds of silence ensued before Jax's handsome features relaxed. "I appreciate that."

"Now, let's move on to some details," Derringer said. "Both of you were able to study your biographies?"

"I was." Bella hesitated a moment before explaining her additions. "I needed to fill in."

"That's fine," Derringer agreed. "It makes sense, and having a neighbor with shell shock gives you an additional reason to interact with the patients. Since you're starting tomorrow, it works out well. Richard called earlier and made arrangements for Jax to be admitted today. He and Mrs. Jenkins will be the Douglasses, and he's Jack Douglass." He glanced at the Jenkinses. "Both of you are comfortable with your story?"

"We are," Jenny said. "Being concerned about Jax—Jack—won't be hard for me. I already think of him as a son."

Out of the corner of her eye, Bella saw a slight smile cross Jax's face. His own mother had died when he was only ten, so having Jenny fuss over him was a good thing.

"Just don't be too concerned," Derringer said. "Remember, we want them to think you feel burdened by having a shell-shocked nephew."

"Perhaps, I should be the one who acts aggrieved," Richard suggested. "I might be more believable in that role."

Ayling nodded. "Good idea."

"Fine, if you can manage, dear." Jenny turned to Bella. "Other than Sheriff Ayling, you're the only one who has met the Lennings. What did you think?"

With all eyes on her, Bella focused on her impressions of the pair. "Both of them seemed stiff and formal. Mrs. Lenning explained my job well enough, but didn't always answer questions clearly."

A frown furrowed Jenny's brow. "Was she confused, or was she being evasive?"

"I'm not sure," Bella replied.

"She bears watching," Ayling said.

"All the employees do," Derringer added.

"I'll be observant." Bella knew that was her primary task, and she planned to fulfill it.

"What about the son? How did he seem?" Richard inquired.

"He was ambivalent in regard to shell-shocked soldiers A little critical, but not mean-spirited. He indicated some are weak, even cowardly. Then, he called them *poor boys.* I'm not sure what to make of him. Also, he revealed he'd worked at a field hospital in France."

A scowl furrowed Ayling's brow. "I've asked folks around town about Lenning. No one had details. He never comes to Bridgeling, though. Anything else stand out?"

"He looked rather disheveled, and his eyes were bloodshot and red-rimmed. Like he hadn't slept well. Or was..." She let her voice trail off as another possibility arose.

"Hungover?" Jax supplied.

"The signs were there," Bella said.

"Something else that bears watching," Derringer said, "although it's not illegal to consume liquor, only to make and sell it. He could've had a supply on hand when Ohio went dry."

The assertion was true, so Bella went on to another concern. "Another odd thing is his mother warned me not to do or say anything to remind patients of the war, but Dr. Lenning's office has some horribly gruesome paintings, ones depicting warfare. Maybe patients don't see them, but they're awful." Bella didn't cloak her anxiety. The doctor's furnishings probably had little or nothing to do with deaths and disappearances, but they gave insight into his overall attitude. At least they did to her.

"That may or may not weigh on this case." Derringer grasped the chair arms. "We haven't discussed it, but we already know the Lennings opened the sanatorium early last year."

"They did," Ayling agreed. "Neither of them comes into town. The employees shop for the facility, and groceries are delivered. I've only spoken with the pair a few times. When they arrived and when I investigated the Falconer and Smith cases. The Lennings were dismissive, at best. As far as Miss Stewart's characterization of them, I noted Mrs. Lenning can be odd at times. She lost track of questions when I spoke with her, but she seemed bright when I first met her more than a year ago. As for the doctor, his eyes were bloodshot on one occasion. I chalked it up to being worried, but there may be another reason."

Next to Bella, Jax shifted restlessly. "What about Miss Bounder? Have you spoken with her?"

Ayling shook his head. "Still no answer. The town constable went to the house, and no one is home, but there's not any sign of foul play. The neighbors didn't know anything and hadn't seen her, so none knew she was coming home. He'll try to locate her. In any case, he'll keep me up-to-date."

"You have plenty to handle here," Jenny observed, "so it's good to have someone in her hometown watching for her."

The rest of the group concurred.

"And Billings? What was your impression of him?" Jax addressed the question to Bella.

"He was neatly attired and groomed," Bella replied, "and he seemed affable. Overall, a charming man who made a better impression than the doctor. He was wearing his uniform, which seemed strange for a retired officer."

"It does, since anything reminding patients of their service could be detrimental," Jax said. "But, if he meets with them, he might think it adds to his authority."

"Very possible," Bella said.

"Observe him, when you can. Both of you." Richard looked from Jax to Bella. "I take it none of the three mentioned patients disappearing."

"No, they didn't," Bella replied. "Maybe another employee will bring up Lieutenant Corning once I get settled."

"His status is of top importance," Ayling added.

"Just to clarify, if he's alive, getting him to safety is more important than finding out about the others or identifying those responsible?" Jax made it a debatable statement.

"Absolutely," Amos said.

Rufus nodded. "I agree. If we get him, he may have important details about who's involved and what else has happened, but young Corning him is the primary focus of this case right now. We can clean up other matters once we know about him."

Both Jenny and Richard concurred with the sentiment.

Richard put his hands on his knees. "I'd like to learn more about Lenning. The description of his office is unsettling. So is his indecisive attitude toward junior officers. Critical but somewhat sympathetic. Seems odd. I don't want him targeted Jax due to his former rank."

His concern gave Bella some reassurance. Derringer and Ayling were focused on the investigation, which was crucial. But Richard and Jenny would keep Jax's well-being in mind. So would she.

"Maybe he thinks the paintings will shock soldiers out of their troubles. It's a dubious notion, but I've heard of stranger methods to fix mental problems." Jax made the suggestions. "Many of these places don't do much for the men other than restrain, isolate, or drug them."

The last observation evoked one of Bella's concerns. "If they deem you as recalcitrant or difficult, you may be sedated. What then?" After being at the sanatorium, she wanted and needed additional reassurance from Jax.

A grin pulled up one corner of his mouth. "I won't be either one. I plan to be a model patient."

The men chuckled, but Bella found no humor in the statement. Typical of him to make light of his own vulnerability. When she glanced at Jenny, the older woman looked as solemn as Bella felt.

"You'll do a good job, I'm sure," Derringer said. "You did on the O'Donnelly case."

Bella studied the Senior Prohibition agent. With his black hair and his thin mustache, Derringer looked more like a gangster than a lawman. But his looks didn't bother her. His revelation did. "Jax has already gone undercover." When seconds of silence followed her observation, Bella stared at him. "Have you?" No one had actually said so. Now, she wanted to know.

His jaw tightened. "A couple of times, I went into speakeasies, pretending to be a customer. Someone usually does prior to a raid."

Although he made it sound simple, she was sure there was more to the story. Not that she would get details right now. Maybe in the future, when he was safely home, Bella would ask Jax about his work as an agent. Or maybe she was better off not knowing. "I see." She glanced from Ayling to Derringer. "What if they suspect Jax of being a lawman?" No one had mentioned the possibility, but it was in the back of her mind. Surely, the idea had been considered by the others.

"We don't think that's likely," Ayling replied. "Jax doesn't know any of the patients, and he's never been to Poplar Pines."

Jax shifted to face Bella. "There's no reason to worry about my cover being suspect. Or yours, either."

"Jax is right," Derringer said. "You'll be a strong contact for him, Miss Stewart. If he needs to get out, tell Richard immediately. He and Jenny can make an excuse to fetch Jax."

"We certainly can." Jenny glanced at her husband. "We can go whenever need be."

"We'll get Jax any time," he agreed. "The case isn't as important as his safety."

Bella concurred wholeheartedly with Richard, but she withheld comment. Derringer made it sound like getting Jax out would be simple, while that seemed unlikely. Even worse, he could disappear as easily and abruptly as other patients had. Bella would do whatever she could to avoid that possibility. "It certainly isn't."

Both Derringer and Ayling looked unhappy, but Richard spoke before either replied. "I'm glad you've agreed to go undercover, too, Arabella. You and Jax work well together." Richard smiled. "You're a good pair."

Jenny beamed. "They certainly are."

Warmth crept into Bella's cheeks. When she glanced at Jax, he looked equally discomfited. Only time would tell if they actually became more than sleuthing partners. Courting would move them forward. How far forward remained to be seen. So did when a courtship would actually begin. Certainly not while they were undercover. "We won't be working together like in past cases."

"No, but you'll be there, and you should find times for private conversation." Jenny focused on Jax. "If you don't have other opportunities to chat with Bella, perhaps you can ask for a reader."

"Sure," Jax agreed.

"Don't volunteer to read, Arabella. We don't want them getting suspicious," Richard said.

"I won't volunteer for anything," Bella assured him.

"Good," Derringer said.

"Do you have questions, Miss Stewart?" Ayling posed the query.

"I studied the file carefully last night," she replied, "and it was thorough."

"Is there anything else to review?" Richard asked, looking at Derringer and Ayling.

"Nothing I can think of," Ayling replied. "Amos?"

"Nope."

"Then, we need to get ready to leave." Although Jax's voice was firm, his green gaze was soft with regret when he looked at Bella.

"What time are you going tomorrow, Arabella?" Richard asked.

"Mrs. Lenning asked me to come around ten o'clock. I'll get settled in my room before visitors come."

Jenny smiled. "We'll see you when we visit."

"I'll look forward to it," Bella replied. As the group split up, she headed to the Chummy. When Jax offered to walk her out, she readily agreed. Even though she would see him again soon, the circumstances would be challenging. A few moments of private conversation in a familiar setting were welcome.

Chapter Five

Two hours later, Jax was in the backseat of the Jenkins' Winton Touring car. He had wanted to talk more with Bella, but the admission appointment was set. Before leaving, he had only a few fleeting moments to spend alone with her. Neither of them discussed the future, their future, but they exchanged a brief hug and kiss. Luckily, she had parked in the driveway between two tall hedges. Or maybe she'd chosen a sequestered place on purpose. Despite the complicated case ahead of him, Jax couldn't help but smile at the memory of having her in his arms.

Jax dozed off thinking about Bella, about them, and about their future, and woke when the vehicle pulled to a stop. He stretched his tired muscles before sitting upright.

"At least you got a little rest," Jenny said, as she shifted to look at him. Concern darkened her blue eyes.

"But not enough to seem hale and healthy, which is good," Richard said.

"You're right." Jax rubbed his stubbled jaw. "I probably look scruffy since I haven't shaved in a couple of days. Too busy."

"Or had a haircut lately," Jenny said with a trace of teasing.

A rueful smile tugged at his lips. "I planned on going to the barbershop this weekend." All his plans had disintegrated after Derringer called.

"A fresh trim and recent shave would make you appear too normal. So would neatly pressed clothing. Your overall look is fine for the role." Richard turned into the sanatorium driveway.

Jenny, her expression still troubled, spoke again. "You need to take time off after this case. Richard and I can stay on for another week, even two or more."

"We certainly can." Richard puled to a stop, climbed out of the driver's seat, and peered at Jax. "Ready to go in?"

Jax nodded, even though more than one issue plagued him. With one death, a mysterious disappearance, another missing patient, and an at-large employee, a lot was on his shoulders. Since he could do nothing about finding Miss Bounder, Jax focused on his immediate role. In his assignments with the Bureau, he'd worked with a group of agents. While in his job as a town constable, he'd relied primarily on those in his own office. With murder cases, Richard, and Bella helped. Sometimes, Jenny pitched in. They were a good team, as good as any he'd been on lately, but solving the current case would have a different path. He hoped he was up to the challenge, especially when Bella was taking on a new and hazardous task.

Within moments, the trio was in the hospital's expansive foyer. A wide staircase rose to a second-floor balcony where several doors were visible. Landscape paintings adorned dark panel walls. An ornate desk sat to one side, while a settee and two chairs were on the opposite wall. All-in-all, the entrance was pleasant, even welcoming. It was nothing like the facility where his former comrades-in-arms were. This place didn't look like a jail or even an asylum. But looks could be misleading. A voice broke into Jax's perusal.

"Good evening. I'm Mrs. Lenning."

The woman moved toward them. Her gray hair was pulled into a tight bun and spectacles perched on her ample nose. She wore a tailored suit with a pristine white shirtwaist. He immediately noticed the buttons weren't in the right holes, which made the garment pucker in front. The skirt grazed her ankles but revealed scuffed, dirty shoes. He'd seen a garden as they drove up to the building. Had she just been out there? The rest of her clothing wasn't suited for outdoor chores, or indoor ones, either. Bella hadn't mentioned Mrs. Lenning's attire, or her son's. She had only noted Billings' neat uniform.

Jax forced his thoughts to the scene before him. As the older woman's gaze ran over him, he noted disapproval and possibly disgust. Did she share her son's view of shell-shocked junior officers? Not that the doctor's view was particularly clear. Why had they opened a sanatorium to serve them? Simply to make money? The idea seemed quite plausible, since understaffing and poor care would not be as costly as running the facility well.

Jenny and Richard introduced themselves and Jax. Jack, he reminded himself. Until this assignment was over, his name was Jack Douglass, not Jax Hastings.

Mrs. Lenning pursed her thin lips. "The lieutenant is in dire need of a haircut and a shave."

Definitely disgust in the words and tone, but she sounded well-balanced. Not flighty or confused.

"We tried to persuade him to have it trimmed," Jenny put in, "but he's had a terrible spell recently. Mostly sitting in his chair, day and night."

Jenny was good, very good, at playing a role. Jax's confidence went up a notch as he watched her. He had reliable people working with him. They would get to the bottom of the case in due time. With luck, not too much time.

"That's why we brought him here," Richard said in a curt tone that Jax had never heard him use. "We can't cope at home anymore. My wife is worn out with the boy, and so am I."

Jax stared at the far wall and schooled his features. Reacting to anything being said wasn't wise. He needed to look detached.

The older woman's expression softened. "I understand. Now, come along. Dr. Lenning is in my office waiting for you," she said before leading them down a short hallway to a set of French doors. She rapped before opening it. "Jack Douglass, his aunt, and his uncle are here."

"Bring them in."

Mrs. Lenning and Jenny entered first, while Richard gestured for Jax to precede him. The sign indicated the office belonged to the woman, and he wondered why they weren't going to the doctor's bailiwick. And why had Mrs. Lenning knocked on her own office door? Bella was right about the pair acting oddly.

"I'll leave the four of you to talk," Mrs. Lenning said after Jenny, Richard, and Jax were seated in chairs facing the desk.

"I'm sure we can help you, lieutenant. We've had good luck with many others in your predicament." Dr. Lenning, a tall man in his late forties, said with a reassuring smile.

Jax, schooling his features, merely nodded in response.

"We certainly hope so," Jenny said, with just the right touches of anxiety and hope. "Jack is nothing like the young man who sailed for France in 1918."

"That's not unusual, according to what we hear from families," the doctor replied. "Of course, I can't promise he'll be exactly like himself after a stay with us. Some men simply couldn't handle battle and are never quite right."

The man's offhand dismissal of the real suffering experienced by those in the trenches infuriated Jax. His mind went to all the brave young officers and soldiers he'd fought beside in France. American, British, French, Australian, and more. Almost all had shown tenacity and bravery. Only the greatest self-discipline kept Jax from telling the doctor as much.

"We understand," Jenny hurried to say. "What type of treatments do you use? You told my husband modern ones, but what are they?"

Lenning smiled again. "We don't share medical procedures with relatives. We need your trust in our ability to properly care for your nephew."

Jax wasn't relieved by the weak reassurance. A glance at Jenny revealed anxiety flashing in her blue eyes. She quickly controlled her reaction, but Jax knew she wouldn't desert him if he was truly shell-shocked. Others might be desperate enough to leave relatives to uncertain care, which increased his resolve to get answers.

"We have complete faith in you and your staff," Richard put in. "My wife feels motherly concern for the boy."

Jax noted Richard didn't say he felt the same sort of parental worry, which was his role.

"Of course," Lenning replied. "Now, as I said during our call, we require our patients to stay a minimum of two months. Fees are paid upon admission. If he leaves sooner, there's no refund."

Relatives had to be at wits' end to agree to such restrictions. Jax remained impassive, but he was grateful he wouldn't be staying a month or more. At least, he hoped the case would be solved long before then.

"We understand. It'll be worth every penny, and I can assure you that he'll be here for at least two months," Richard Jenkins said.

While her husband spoke, Jenny wrung her hands. "That's such a long time."

Richard patted her arm. "We need some rest, dear. We can't continue to have our lives turned upside-down with the boy's troubles."

Jenny nodded. "Can we see his room, doctor?"

Lenning shifted his gaze to the woman. "When I spoke with your husband on the telephone, I said we would see to all the lieutenant's care—physical and mental—while he's with us. He'll be sharing a room, and I'd rather we didn't disturb the other patients, which could happen if they see you and your husband."

Beside Jax, Jenny stiffened. "I see."

"That's fine. We understand." Again, Richard appeared to be ready to leave his troubled nephew and not look back.

The doctor smiled again, but it didn't quite reach his eyes. "We know what's best for our boys."

"Of course," Richard said.

"I suppose so." Again, Jenny twisted her hands in her lap.

Jax noted she sounded less than certain. But, so was he. Bella's gut feelings and worry, seemed on target. As usual. The place looked pleasant at first glance, but what was really going on?

"Perhaps, we can see the room when we visit tomorrow." Richard spoke again.

Lenning frowned. "You won't be able to come back so soon. We like to have our boys get acclimated before they have visitors. We'd be happy to see you on Wednesday, if all goes well and your nephew adjusts properly."

"And if he doesn't?" Jenny asked. Concern was etched on her face.

"You'll need to wait until next Sunday. After a week, the lieutenant will probably be able to cope with a change in routine. He won't be sitting and staring into space here." The doctor maintained his brittle smile.

Apprehension filled Jax and, when he glanced at Richard, he saw the same emotion flash across the older man's face. If Jax got any information in the next few days, or needed help, he'd have to rely on Bella. Thank heaven she was starting work tomorrow. Frustration and dismay warred inside him. The investigation wasn't off to a good start. Not at all.

"How many visitors may come?" Jenny asked.

"Two at most. More overtaxes our patients." Again, Lenning looked at the papers in front of him. "According to your application, the lieutenant has no family other than the two of you."

"That's right. We'll come when we can, but it may not be often," Richard said.

"I understand," the doctor replied. "A fair number of our boys don't get many visitors. Friends and relatives find it difficult to see them suffer mental impairments."

Jenny wiped at her eyes with a handkerchief. "I'm sure my husband told you, but Jack's major problem is not sleeping, and he lacks energy and stamina due to his insomnia and nightmares."

Lenning frowned. "So, it appears."

Jax felt the sting of criticism although the physician maintained a concerned expression.

"Now, if you'll sign the admittance papers and provide the check, you and your wife are free to go." Lenning pushed a form across the desk. "We'll get the lieutenant settled right away."

Jenny perched on the edge of her chair. "You have his file, and we've spoken with you," she began, her tone tentative. "Jack has had a few tough days. Patience is important at these times."

A glance at the woman made Jax realize she was fighting not to reveal deep apprehension. He wanted to offer reassurance, but the situation wasn't exactly what they had figured. Despite his worry about involving Bella, having her in the receptionist job might prove crucial. To the case and to him getting out, if necessary.

"We've dealt with many men like Lieutenant Douglass. You needn't fret about him, ma'am."

"Easy to say, doctor," was Jenny's response. She turned to Jax. "It will be difficult for us to come often, but we'll be here Wednesday evening."

"It might be best to wait until next weekend." Lenning's words seemed to be a suggestion.

Jax took a covert glance at the Jenkinses, who both looked anxious. Only a moment of silence before Jenny spoke up. "My husband and I are taking a trip starting next Friday. If we don't see Jack this week, I don't know when we'll be back."

Her husband patted her hand, but kept his attention on the doctor. "She won't rest easy if we can't see him on Wednesday. Nothing was said about not being able to come tomorrow when you and I first spoke. Now, you're saying we should wait weeks? I understand procedures, but I don't want my wife upset."

The senior constable's tone hit a balance between plaintive and belligerent. Jax waited and wondered about the medical director's response. As the silence stretched out, his uncertainty grew.

Lenning offered another brittle smile. "Plan to come on Wednesday. Then, you'll feel better about not seeing him for a while."

What would happen in *a while*? Jax wondered if someone would offer to get rid of him when Jenny and Richard returned. Probably not this soon, and they wouldn't agree to such a scheme anyhow. He focused on the doctor while the man's attention was on the Jenkinses. His eyes were still bloodshot and red-rimmed, as Bella had observed. Now, dark stubble shadowed his cheeks. The combination gave him a seedy, worn appearance. Did he always meet with patients and families in this condition? If so, weren't they concerned? Again, Jax figured people were grasping at straws to leave a loved one in this place.

A tap at the door preceded a muscular man in uniform stepping into the office. He immediately introduced himself as Major Curtis Billings, shook Richard's hand, and bowed to Jenny. "I hope I'm not too late. I like to greet our families and new patients, but I was running an errand. You're somewhat of an unexpected arrival, lieutenant. We usually hear about prospective patients well in advance of their arrivals."

Jax nodded but remained silent.

"The Douglasses were about to leave," Lenning said. "Perhaps, you'd see them out."

Billings beamed. "Happy to do so."

Jenny stood. "We'll be back in a few days." She gently squeezed Jax's arm as she spoke, which had him swallowing hard over the lump rising in his throat. Richard patted his shoulder. Maintaining an impassive demeanor proved difficult. The couple had become like second parents to him, and their concern deeply touched Jax. The emotions threatening to swamp him—homesickness, duty, and uncertainty—were much like his feelings when he and Matt had left for France. But he wasn't an inexperienced young man leaving home for the first time. He'd been a soldier, a constable, and an agent. Evidently, none of those roles kept strong feelings at bay.

"We'll get the lieutenant settled," Lenning said. "We'll see you again on Wednesday evening."

The last statement, clearly a dismissal, was punctuated by the doctor rising to his feet. Since they had won a main point, Jax wasn't surprised when Jenny and Richard accepted it as such. "We'll see you soon," the older man said.

Jenny's farewell consisted of a big hug and a little sniffle. Then, Billings escorted the pair out.

Dr. Lenning turned back to Jax. "Let's go to my office and finish our discussion."

With little choice, Jax followed the man to another room. As soon as they entered, he recalled Bella's description, which had been accurate. The overall atmosphere was oppressive, even morose.

"Sit down, lieutenant. I don't know how much your aunt and uncle shared with you about our facility, but we've changed our procedures lately—something I didn't have time to explain to them. Keeping our new patients isolated is the main one."

What had provoked a change and why hadn't the Jenkinses been told? Jax let his attention rest on the physician but, caught off-guard, he didn't reply.

"Your hearing isn't impaired, is it?" The question was asked in a gruff voice, unlike the one Lenning had used with Jenny and Richard.

"No, sir." Jax kept all inflection from his voice as fresh dismay crept through him. While he had known Poplar Pines wasn't an innovative mental facility, Jax hadn't worried about the policies and procedures for most patients. Bella had. But she often got intuition about situations.

"Then, answer when I speak to you."

With effort, Jax kept his voice bland. "Yes, sir."

A knock at the door interrupted. "I brought coffee and cake for you and the new patient." A young redhead deposited a tray on the desk and handed a cup to Jax. Her hazel eyes briefly met his before darting away. "I already added cream and sugar."

"Thank you, Anita," Lenning said. "You may go."

The girl nodded and scurried out.

Lenning looked back at Jax. "You're too late for supper, so this will tide you over until morning."

Jax preferred black coffee, but he accepted the beverage and a slice of cake. Something was better than nothing.

"Go ahead and eat," the doctor said. "I had a meal, so I'll save my refreshments."

Since he was hungry, Jax took several bites before speaking. "Thank you, sir. It's very good." Being submissive didn't come easily, but he was playing a role.

The doctor looked at the papers on his desk. "You'll be isolated for a time. Probably a few days. Maybe longer. It all depends on your progress."

After eating half of the cake, Jax took a long swallow of coffee before nodding. "I understand." Except he didn't. Would he be trotted out of isolation when his supposed aunt and uncle came on Wednesday, only to be returned when they left? Didn't patients tell their family members about being stuck in solitary confinement? Didn't relatives object? Probably not if they were terribly desperate to get help for their loved one. Or to get relief from caregiver duties. But the isolation was new. How new, Jax didn't know. Maybe Bella could find out.

"Troublesome patients may require a longer term apart from others." The man's dark eyes narrowed on Jax. "Your aunt and uncle indicated your biggest problems are nightmares and insomnia. Is that right?"

"Mostly." Since his mouth felt dry, Jax drank more coffee. "I don't sleep well due to the nightmares, which are terrible." He struggled to reconstruct his planned description, but his mind felt muddled and his eyelids drooped.

"Have you been drinking, lieutenant?"

The words floated to Jax through a haze. "No, sir. That's illegal."

"It is, but folks still imbibe. We have a nice supply left from before Prohibition." A humorless laugh left the doctor as he pulled a flask out of his desk and lifted it to his lips. "Finish your coffee and cake. That might help you."

Confused, Jax tried to focus on the doctor, but doing so proved to be impossible. He leaned forward to put his nearly empty plate and cup on the desk and almost fell to the floor. Dr. Lenning said more. A lot more, but Jax lost track of the words.

As he slid off his seat, realization hit him at the same time he hit the floor. He'd been drugged.

Sunday, people began to arrive around one o'clock. Since dinner coincided with the start of visiting hours, some of the staff needed to supervise patients and their families while they enjoyed the garden. Other workers helped prepare for the midday meal. As part of the efforts, Mrs. Lenning asked Bella to leave her post, although she had only been at work for a short time.

Upon her arrival at ten o'clock, Bella had carried her carpetbag to her room on the third floor. While small, the accommodation held all the necessary accoutrements: a narrow bed, a faded armchair, a vanity table with a stool, and a battered dresser. Several hooks hung on one wall. Bella had put her jacket, shirtwaists, and skirts there. She kept her knickers in the bag, since she didn't want others questioning why she owned a pair. The attire had become popular sportswear in the past couple of years, and Bella wore them more often now, but they weren't common garments. After locking the door behind her, she hurried back downstairs, per Mrs. Lenning's orders.

Little of note happened at the start of her shift. Bella saw only two employees, an older woman in a nurse's uniform and a burly man who must be an orderly, come and go. Neither stopped to speak with her. When Mrs. Lenning approached the desk, Bella offered a smile and a greeting. The woman nodded in return.

"I'll be in the foyer to greet relatives as they arrive, but we could use your help with meals. We have two new patients who aren't eating in the dining hall yet." She grimaced. "Because they have issues, we can't give them access to knives and forks. Nor do we want them with the others. Some visitors do not understand recalcitrance or outbursts, but you do. After all, you have that troublesome neighbor."

"Of course," Bella agreed, but anxiety filled her. If the two were new patients, Jax must be one of them. Her pulse pounded in her ears, but she maintained an outward calm. She hadn't expected to see him so soon. Not that she wasn't happy about the prospect, especially after talking with Jenny and Richard last evening. The three of them had met after the Jenkinses' return to Moreley. Jenny had expressed her concerns, which echoed inside Bella. Thank goodness, the couple had insisted on visiting Wednesday.

"Come along, Miss Halliday. Arnold Drier, one of our orderlies, will carry the food up for you. He'll stay in order to make sure the boys cooperate."

Bella's anxiety increased as the stocky man surveyed her. The icy glare in his eyes chilled her to the core. Although not much taller than she was, the orderly had broad shoulders and beefy arms. As Drier led her to the uppermost floor and down a narrow, dim hallway, he maintained the same frigid expression. "I thought patients were on the second floor," Bella observed.

He didn't bother to look at her when he replied. "Them's regular rooms. Up here is isolation for the new ones and for the troublemakers."

The knot of apprehension inside Bella tightened. Jenny and Richard had mentioned nothing about Jax being stuck in the attic. Did they know? As she and Drier walked down the narrow corridor, Bella noticed every door was shut. "This area must have been staff quarters when the place was a home."

"Some of us lives up here." He jerked one thumb to the left. "Over that way. There's a locked door between this side and the men's quarters."

"What about these doors? Are they closets?" She gestured toward several closed rooms lining both sides of the hall.

"Nope." After the terse reply, Arnold continued on.

His terse replies kept her from asking more questions. When they finally reached the far end of the corridor, Arnold faced her. "The two new ones are here. Start with whichever one you want. Makes no difference."

Although the man was an orderly, he spoke with an air of command Bella found imperious and improper. She was tempted to tell him he was not her boss, but thought better of it. If Jax was in one of these rooms, and he must be, she needed to see him and didn't want to be relieved of her assignment. Nor did she want patients to forego their meals. But would Drier listen in?

"We need to be snappy or I'll miss my dinner."

"I can feed them, and you can go downstairs." Bella tried not to sound too eager to get rid of him.

For a moment, he stared at her. Then, he nodded before jerking his thumb at one door. "The one here, Phinney, ain't bright. Don't say nothing. The other's got injuries and ain't able to feed himself too good. He's in bad enough shape that he won't be no threat. His name's Douglass."

The orderly spoke in a harsh tone, completely lacking concern. Fresh anxiety curled in the pit of Bella's stomach. Jax—Jack Douglass—had suffered two war wounds to his right arm, but he could eat easily enough. What had happened since yesterday? "Let's begin here," she said, nodding toward the left.

Drier opened the door and went in. Bella, blinking at the sudden darkness, slowly followed him. When her eyes finally adjusted, shock hit her. A man, clad in loose pajamas, sat on a narrow bed. A quick glance around the room added to her dismay. With no windows, it was more closet than room. The bed, a cot really, took up most of the floor space, leaving a gap for one wooden chair. Nothing adorned the beige walls, which gave it a stark, sterile appearance.

Finally, her gaze fixed on the unfamiliar, thin figure. "We're here with your dinner."

The dark head came up. The eyes looking at her were bottomless pools of emptiness. For several moments, Bella wasn't sure he even understood her. Then, he murmured his thanks, and she went to sit on the chair. He acted insensible, which meant Jax was the one who couldn't eat alone. Was he pretending the debility to get help? Bella pushed the question aside and focused on the pale man in front of her. She would find out about Jax soon enough.

"This one can feed himself. The other one can't, so let's get going."

The man's complete lack of empathy disgusted Bella, but she merely nodded and trailed him across the hall. As she did, cold sweat broke out across her forehead. What would she see?

Drier opened the door to a similar room—dark, tiny, cramped, and cool. This time, however, the patient wasn't sitting on the bed. He was standing at the far side of the space, staring back at them. In the dimness, Bella couldn't make out his features, but she knew in an instant it was Jax. Her heart constricted. He was clad only in thin pajamas, his feet were bare, his right arm was in a sling, and his left hand was bandaged.

What had happened since yesterday afternoon? With effort, she fought to keep her terror from showing.

"Arnold, I don't want you to miss dinner," she said, trying to keep her voice well-modulated, "and there's no reason for you to stay. I can handle this alone." Why was the man hesitating? He clearly wanted to get downstairs and eat. And Bella wanted him to go.

Several seconds of silence passed before the orderly looked at Jax. "Don't give the lady no trouble or you'll regret it, lieutenant. Understand?"

"I understand." Jax's voice sounded gravelly.

"Good." Then, the orderly was gone.

When the door closed behind Arnold Drier, Bella put the plate on the small table next to the cot. "Are you all right?"

For several moments, he gazed at her. Finally, a long exhalation left him. "I've been better." The hint of humor in his ragged whisper made Bella smile. "I'm sure you have." She moved her attention from his heavily shadowed eyes to his bandaged left wrist and on to the sling. "What in the world happened to you? Yesterday, you were fine."

His shoulders slumped. "Evidently, I fell and sprained my wrist on the way up here. The tumble didn't help my shoulder and arm." He touched the sling.

"*Evidently?* Don't you know?" Bella felt another stab of apprehension.

"No, I don't because I must've been drugged while I talked with Dr. Lenning. A young woman brought coffee and cake. I didn't stay awake long after I had them."

"Are they still drugging you?"

"Since early this morning, I get pills every few hours. There's a younger nurse who isn't vigilant. She's been up twice today.

I've been able to keep them in my mouth both times. When she left, I spit them out and ground them into the dust under the cot. No one's cleaned up here in an age. As long as I act groggy, I won't fall under suspicion. It's almost time for more. I think." He pressed the fingers of his right hand to his head. "I'm not sure how long I've been here. Maybe I slept a day or longer instead of only one night. What day is it?"

"Sunday." Bella tried to not look as worried as she felt.

A frown furrowed his brow. "Then, I've only been here one day." It was more a question than a statement.

"Not an entire day," she said. "You came late yesterday, and it's only early afternoon."

"I've slept most of that time, which is making it impossible to get any information."

He sounded put out, while Bella felt more worried about his condition than the case. "Since Richard and Jenny are coming Wednesday, you'll have to be in a regular room by then. Of course, they thought you would be now. I spoke with Jenny last night, and she told me about your admission. At least the part she and Richard saw, including meeting the major."

"What did Billings have to say when he escorted them out?" Jax asked.

"Mostly the same as what was in the file. He understands the difficulty in caring for a shell-shocked relative, and how you'll get the best care here. He also mentioned the cost, mostly to commiserate on how expensive it is." Bella chewed on her lower lip. "I asked Jenny if he tried to emphasize the problems and a solution."

"Like getting rid of the troublemaker permanently."

She shook her head. "Nothing so bold. I wonder if he feels people out about how frustrated they are. Jenny said Richard acted overwrought and disgusted. Billings simply expressed empathy."

"It could be an implied suggestion. Or he's just trying to make families feel better. I only saw him in passing, so it's hard for me to say."

"We'll both find out more, I'm sure." She paused before returning to his earlier comments. "You think someone comes every few hours to give medication to you?"

"Yep. The young blonde today, and I have a vague memory of someone older with frizzy gray hair coming last night. Neither had much to say, but an orderly was with them."

"Was Arnold the one who came during the night?"

Jax's brow wrinkled. "Arnold?"

"Arnold Drier. He was with me just now."

"He was here this morning. Last night, it was someone else. I didn't get a name. He was a wiry guy with a scraggly salt-and-pepper beard. Gray hair needing a cut. I think the description is right. Or I dreamed all of it."

Under the circumstances, his bewilderment was understandable. "I haven't been here long enough to find out about shift assignments but, if the other orderly worked last night, he's probably off now." Since Jax seemed to have trouble sorting out actual events from dream images, Bella mentally reviewed information gleaned from yesterday afternoon's meeting. She chewed on her lower lip and considered how to reveal the sparse information she'd gotten from Drier. Not by saying she'd posed queries, as few as they'd been. Jax would have to be in a fugue state not to question her means and methods, if she admitted them. "Arnold mentioned his quarters, and those of other male employees, are at the other end of this hall. There's a locked door between the sides, though."

Jax's gaze narrowed. "As far as I recall, he wasn't chatty with me."

The statement, while not clearly disapproving, held a note of dismay. "I got that impression from what he said to you." The orderly had tacitly threatened Jax. She moved to a new topic. "I saw the young man in the room next to you. He's evidently new, too, but he looks wan and frail."

A half-shrug lifted one of Jax's shoulders. "His physical condition could be related to shell shock. Or from being stuck here."

"I suppose so." Jax's condition had deteriorated since yesterday afternoon, which didn't bode well for his stay at Poplar Pines. Solving the case quickly had become even more imperative.

With the fingers of his bandaged hand, Jax rubbed his forehead. "Some male employees living on this floor means I probably can't get out and look around at night. They can most likely come and go freely from their side."

Alarm hit Bella full-force. Was he seriously entertaining the idea? "No, you shouldn't try, since I'm sure that's the case. Besides, the night nurse could come up any time during her shift. And getting out of here wouldn't be easy."

"Good points," he admitted. "Tell Richard about me not going straight to a regular room and get his view on it."

"I will." Bella perched on the edge of the cot and patted the space beside her. "Sit down. I don't know how long Drier will take for dinner, but we likely don't have a lot of time to talk."

"Probably not."

When Jax sat next to her, Bella let one hand rest on his left arm. "Are you hurting very much? The medication is meant to knock you out, but it would ease the pain. Maybe you should take half of it."

"I'm okay. What about the other officer you saw? Other than him looking rough, did you notice anything else?"

Bella wanted to find out more about how Jax felt, but he wasn't apt to admit more, so she answered his question. "He's heavily sedated."

"Do you have any idea how long he's been here?"

Bella shook her head. "No. Just that he's new, too."

"We can eliminate him as being involved or seeing anything useful. But he might be a target. Any patient could be."

A new knot of dread formed in Bella's throat. "I hope some patients talk freely with you. They might have suspicions about what's going on and who's involved."

"We can hope. Other than the Lennings, Billings and Drier, have you talked to others here?"

"I met the cook, Mrs. Barley, in passing when we got your food just now. There was a young woman, who must be her assistant, loading trays, probably for the dining room. I didn't get her name."

Jax's brow furrowed. "A petite redhead?"

"Yes. Is she the one who brought cake and coffee when you were meeting with Lenning?"

"It had to be her. He called her Anita. She didn't stay long."

"I wonder if she knew the food was drugged."

"So, do I. But Rufus knows her, since she's from town. He didn't have anything bad to say," Jax said.

"She may just follow orders. I'll talk with her since most of the female employees have rooms close together. Maybe I'll get a feeling about her involvement."

"Where is your room located?"

"On the third floor. The main steps go that far, but not up here. Drier and I took a back stairway from the kitchen. There's access to every floor from it. This floor and the third one evidently housed staff when the place was a residence."

"Can anyone go from the kitchen to the women's quarters?"

"The men workers would use that staircase to come to their rooms."

He frowned. "There's no locked door to keep them off your floor?"

She shook her head. "My room has a lock, so the others must, too."

"Is it a sturdy lock?"

Jax's tone and question revealed alarm, which made Bella give careful consideration to the situation. Had someone accessed the women's quarters, harmed Miss Bounder, and left a fake note? The possibility was unnerving. If she was a victim, someone else could be, too. What if both employees and patients were targeted? She stowed the idea in the back of her mind and went on. "Not really. I was only in my room for a short time when I arrived this morning. I'll be sure to keep the door locked at all times."

"Please do."

"You agreed I could play a role in the investigation. Are you having second thoughts?"

"Second, third, fourth, and so on." Jax pressed his bandaged hand to his forehead. A rueful grin tugged at one corner of his mouth. "I'm sorry. I don't like you being in danger, which I've already said more than once. I understand you don't care to hear my worries repeated."

Although Bella disliked being coddled, she understood his concern. After all, she fretted over having him in harm's way.

"I'm already involved, and I'll be careful, just as I promised."
She paused for a long moment. "Keep in mind, I don't like you
being in danger, either."

With his right hand, he reached out and took hers. "Thank
you." His voice was barely audible. "We both realize this case
differs from the others we've worked. You aren't an innocent
bystander, notetaker, or driver this time. If someone figures out
you're checking on me or you're not who you say you are..." As
his voice trailed off, his fingers tightened on hers. "I couldn't live
with myself if something happened to you."

Warmth spread through her. Was the aftermath of the drugs
loosening his tongue? They'd had a serious discussion about the
future in April, but everything was put on hold when he left to
join the Prohibition Bureau. And all was still on hold. "Nothing
will happen." When he leaned toward her, Bella followed suit.
His lips brushed hers, but he pulled back quickly. Too quickly.

"As much as I'd love to continue, we need to talk more about
the case before Drier returns." His green gaze gleamed.

Resignation filled Bella, and she scooted back. "You're right.
He's harsh and uncaring, and I don't want him to overhear us.
I didn't let on that I found his attitude to be appalling."

"With your sympathetic heart, that had to be hard."

"I didn't want to make anyone suspicious by seeming to know
too much or be too concerned."

"Very wise." He winked.

Bella beamed in return. "See, I can be restrained."

A low laugh left him. "Good to know."

She wanted to ask him again to be careful, too, but belabor-
ing the point wouldn't help. Undercover roles were inherently
chancy, which they both realized. Neither needed a reminder.

"We probably don't have a lot more time, and you need to eat. I'm afraid it's only a meatloaf sandwich and cabbage slaw."

His amusement disappeared. "I hate cabbage, and cold meatloaf sounds dreadful. Besides, I'm not hungry."

He sounded like a petulant child, which made Bella grin. "I admit it doesn't look very tasty, but you have to eat something. It's bad enough you're cooped up in a tiny room."

His eyebrows rose a fraction. "But it's on the water side of the building, which is helpful."

Bella frowned as she looked around the room. One small window was set high on a wall, too high to see out. "How did you discover that?"

"Early this morning, when the first round of drugs wore off, I dragged the bureau beneath the window and stood on it. With the full moon, the river was visible, but everything else was pitch-black. I don't see how a patient could get out and down to the dock in the dark. Even last night, it would've been impossible to navigate the garden and the area beyond it."

Bella studied the piece of furniture. "That's decrepit. I'm surprised it didn't collapse. Not to mention moving it surely didn't help either of your arms." Did he want to cause more damage? Surely not.

"It's sturdy enough." Again, he sounded grouchy.

"And I'm sure you will use it, in any case, but what about your arms? You must've taken the right one out of the sling to move furniture."

"I was careful." After the curtailed reply, he picked up the sandwich and avoided her gaze.

Following an interlude of silence, Bella went to the import of his statement. "You didn't see anything other than a glimpse of the river?"

"A few gas lamps in the garden. Everything beyond there was completely dark. A flashlight or lantern would be necessary to get around. Even then, Falconer getting very far from the building had to be difficult. If he was alone."

"Now, you're sure he didn't go on his own."

"My observations confirmed what we all discussed already. Falconer had to be taken out there by a person, or persons, with a light. The same must be true for Smith and Corning. I don't believe any of them wandered off alone."

A shiver of dread rippled through Bella. "It's awful to think about."

"I agree, but it seems plausible."

"It definitely does," Bella replied. "I'm more and more convinced relatives paid to get rid of Falconer and Smith. Aaron Corning, too, but we need to find out for sure."

"We do, because the most obvious answer isn't always the right one."

Bella smiled. "A sleuthing fundamental." When Jax grinned in return, she relaxed a little. "We also have to figure out which employees are involved."

"And see if any patients might play a role."

She gnawed on her lower lip. "What would another patient do?"

"Look the other way when men are taken from a room. Maybe help move someone out." He shrugged. "I just don't want to overlook anything or anyone."

"That brings up another point in the back of my mind. Miss Corning mentioned Aaron's wife complaining about the cost of his care. She also said caring for him was a sore trial. Maybe Falconer's and Smith's relatives told similar stories. That could've given someone here the idea of providing a permanent solution.

Who knows? A family member might've dangled the idea first instead of someone here." Speaking the suggestion made Bella sick at heart. "I can't imagine doing such a thing, but others might."

"You couldn't do it. You'd go without to ensure a loved one had proper care. Not everyone is as kind and caring."

"You would, too."

He nodded. "But some people are selfish. Like my buddy's wife. She divorced and remarried. Divorce alone is scandalous, but when I talked to her, she wasn't bothered at all. She said his parents left enough for him to stay at the asylum for a few years, and she doubted he'd live much longer. There wasn't a trace of regret or sadness in her voice, and she ended the conversation saying she had a tennis match."

"How horrible," Bella said. "Is the new husband wealthy?"

"Wealthy and powerful, from what I gathered." Jax laid down the partially eaten sandwich. "My other friend's family is overwhelmed. They can barely cope with the children still at home, so caring for him themselves is out of the question. His wife inherited a lot of money, but she didn't want to pay for his care any longer. The amount is high, and a burden to his parents. I'm not saying they'd entertain getting rid of him, but others in their shoes might, especially if they don't have to be directly involved."

"At least we can make sure no one else here is harmed."

He bowed his head and rubbed his neck. Because the effort seemed difficult for him, Bella took over the massage.

"Thanks, Bella. Even though I worry about you being part of this investigation, I'm glad to have you on my side."

Her breath caught in her throat. "I'll always be on your side, Jax."

"Same with me." He winked. "Now, we've gotten sidetracked again, and time is going quickly."

With reluctance, Bella returned to their discussion. "Richard and Jenny revealed what they paid to supposedly keep you here for two months, and it's significant. Those with limited means have to feel a lot of pressure." Bella continued to gently rub his neck. Beneath her fingers, she felt the taut muscles relax. "Other than what I've said, I haven't discovered much at all."

He lifted his head and met her gaze. "You only got here to-day."

"True." The comment reminded her of the reason she had been sent to the attic. Bella stopped the massaged, grabbed the fork, and speared some cabbage slaw. "Try a little of this." She lifted the dab to his mouth. "You need to eat more."

"I don't want to be hand fed like an infant, and cabbage isn't a favorite of mine." He pressed his lips together.

Again, he sounded like a cantankerous toddler. "You realize someone will have to help you when you're in the dining room, right? That person can be me, if you cooperate now. If I take this plate back almost full, Mrs. Lenning might see me as a failure and assign someone else. Then, how will we talk?"

For a moment, he looked mutinous. Finally, he nodded. "All right."

After Jax took several more bites, Bella laid the fork down. "Have a little more of the sandwich." When he did, she returned to the case. "What did you think of the Lennings? Richard said you met both of them."

Jax nibbled a little before putting the food down. "He and Jenny probably told you Mrs. Lenning took the three of us to her office."

Bella nodded.

"She was civil, but reserved. A little disheveled, though. They both seemed professional. After Richard and Jenny left, he escorted me to his office."

The memory of seeing the room made Bella grimace. "His dreadful office."

Jax made a sour face. "Very dreadful."

"I can't imagine how any man who actually had shell shock would react. It doesn't mesh with Mrs. Lenning ordering me to never discuss the war with patients. Like they might become upset. Doesn't she realize her son's office has depictions that could cause more problems than simply mentioning the war would?"

"It makes no sense. The paintings are gruesome enough to cause nightmares in a normal person."

"They certainly are, and that deer's head." Bella shuddered. "I felt like the poor thing was constantly staring at me."

"The eyes are disturbing."

"So are Lenning's eyes," Bella observed. "What happened then? Besides, you being drugged."

"It's not all that clear to me. Once I ate and drank the tainted stuff, I had trouble following him. But he pulled out a flask and took a long gulp. Said they had plenty of booze from the pre-Prohibition days."

The revelation gave Bella pause. "That would explain his bloodshot eyes."

"And his messy appearance. Billings was certainly a contrast. Before Lenning and I went to his office, Billings came in. He introduced himself and escorted Jenny and Richard out."

"They mentioned as much. He seems more amiable than the Lennings, and that could be a good thing." She clasped her hands together and held them to her chin.

"Be careful talking to him. Still wearing his uniform strikes me as odd."

"I agree, but I may learn something in casual conversation. The same with talking to others."

"I hope I can get some information," Jax said. "Then, we can exchange details like we have in the past."

His words were a bittersweet reminder of previous cases when they hadn't been handcuffed by being apart so much. "When you get downstairs, I hope I can read to you. That seems like the best way to speak privately."

He grinned. "I haven't been read to since after my tonsillectomy."

The memory evoked an answering smile. "I promise to read whatever you choose, not one of my favorite *little girl* stories, as you called them back then."

He snickered. "I was afraid your brother would tease me."

"About not being manly?"

"Not exactly," Jax murmured. "As far as the good doctor, I didn't learn much from him before I passed out from the drugs."

Bella wondered why Jax had quickly changed the subject. Since Arnold could return any time, she followed the new line of conversation. But what had he worried about when she read to him years ago?

"I'll tell Richard what Lenning said to you, and about him drugging you."

"All right. As for slipping me the sedative, I suppose it was to ensure I didn't complain about being isolated up here. Or put up a fuss on the way."

"Possibly." Uneasiness once again assailed Bella, and her mind turned back to a myriad of risks. "Is it possible Lenning suspects you're a lawman?"

"I don't think so. If that was the case, I'd likely be missing, too."

The assertion, while probably accurate, chilled Bella to the core. Missing or dead. "That seems probable." Despite her best efforts, she couldn't keep the tremor from her voice.

A moment of silence preceded his next comment. "If you feel uneasy at any time, walk away."

"I couldn't leave you here with no contact." The very idea appalled her.

"You'd need to tell Richard after you're out of here. He and Jenny will come for me, as they promised." Jax released her hand. "But I don't think we need to worry about that prospect. If I thought we did, I'd say so."

Bella knew he would. Because time was passing far too quickly, she said, "Now, let's see if you can stomach more of this food."

Jax gave a shake of his head. "I've had enough, but thanks."

"I wish I could bring you something better."

"Me, too. Some of your muffins sound wonderful."

"I'll bake a whole batch just for you when you're out of here," she promised.

"Sounds great," he replied with a grin. "With some luck, I won't be up here too long."

"I hope you won't." Bella didn't like him being isolated, especially with someone like Arnold Drier around. "Even though my normal schedule will put me here Sunday through Friday afternoons, I'll make an excuse to leave tomorrow. I can say I forgot a few items at home. Then, I'll head to Moreley. I'll share what happened to you after the meeting with Lenning and anything else I've observed. Is there more you want me to tell Richard? Even though he and Jenny are coming on Wednesday, they're both worried. I'd like to ease their minds." And her own.

"Tell him I'm all right, but be very cautious after leaving. Take the long way back to Moreley, just in case someone is watching you. We don't want anyone associating you with Ballantyne or any of the cases you worked on in the past," Jax replied. His lips quirked into a smile. "And remember, Harriet. No snooping around the place."

Bella only had the chance to nod because Arnold was opening the door. "Let's go. Mrs. Lenning wants you back at the front desk."

"All right." Bella picked up the plate and followed the orderly out of the room. It took all of her self-discipline not to look back at Jax.

For the rest of the afternoon, Bella stayed at her post. Although some visitors passed by, few gave her more than a nod of the head. The telephone rang periodically, but little else provided distraction, which gave her far too much time to think about Jax. By late afternoon, she had reviewed their conversation multiple times. Being stuck in an attic room, Jax hadn't learned much. But neither had she.

Chapter Six

Eight o'clock had come and gone before Bella retired to her room. Visitors left by six, but plenty of work remained, so everyone pitched in to restore the guest areas to normalcy. Bella learned names, but the conversation focused on what needed to be done, so she got no helpful clues. Supper was catch-as-catch-can with sandwiches on trays being the main meal. A few cookies and partial pitchers of lukewarm tea, left over from refreshments for guests, rounded out the offerings.

After the chores were done, Bella encountered Anita Little, the cook's assistant in the hallway outside her room. Earlier, they had met in passing, but hadn't chatted. She had to be the one who had taken coffee and cake to Jax, and the case file mentioned her as a local girl. Sheriff Ayling had no qualms about her. Even so, Bella remained skeptical.

The young redhead offered a weary smile. "How was your first day?"

"Fine." Before saying more, Bella considered Jax's admonitions to be cautious. She also thought about Richard's long-held and oft-repeated guidance about gut feelings. "I spent most of my time at the front desk, although I went to the top floor with Arnold to feed two new patients. Neither was too interested in the food. Lieutenant Phinney's plate was virtually untouched. Lieutenant Douglass ate a bit more."

Anita's smile faltered, and when she responded, her voice was hushed. "Mrs. Lenning don't want us sending the regular meals to the ones in isolation. I got no idea why. They get leftover food and not enough for grown men. Some up there are almost ignored. It's not right, but I'm afraid to say anything. I need this job and the room and board that goes with it." She scanned the hallway before looking back at Bella. "Some patients get put in the attic if they've got troubles, and new ones do, too."

The young woman's soft voice and furtive glances telegraphed anxiety. Since Bella didn't want the conversation to end, she proffered an invitation. "Would you like to come in and have a muffin? I made some before leaving home this morning."

Pleasure blanketed Anita's face. "That sounds very good."

Bella led the way into the small room, now serving as her home away from home. The narrow bed provided one seat, and the armchair was another. "Please sit down."

"Thank you," Anita replied.

While the young woman settled into the faded chair, Bella retrieved the tin and took out several muffins. She handed two to Anita, along with a napkin. Then, she did the same for herself before perching on the bed. "I imagine you had a busy day, what with some visitors eating here, too."

"We did. Wednesdays and Sundays is the worst, but we don't have enough help at no time. Just Mrs. Barley and me to do all three meals, all seven days."

The information backed up what Bella already knew but added nothing, so she tried another query. "Have you worked here long?"

"Since the place opened. Before then, I worked in my folks' diner in Bridgeling. When they both got Spanish flu, I kept it going. But it got harder and harder." Tears filled her eyes, and she brushed them away with the back of one hand. "After they passed, I couldn't do it no more. I got a little money from selling, but not enough to keep me going for long. They was hiring here, so I come about the cook's job. Mrs. Lenning said I were too young, but I could be the assistant. Mrs. Barley was taken on to cook. I've known her all my life. A bit stern but goodly, and it's nice to know someone."

"Mrs. Barley is from Bridgeling, too?" Bella knew the answer but hoped for more details. Until Jax got to a regular room, he wouldn't gain many facts, which put added onus on her.

"She is. Her husband died a couple years back. Didn't leave her nothing, so she's got to work. Having room and board helps the both of us. She lost her house, and my folks lived upstairs from the restaurant so, when I sold the place, I didn't have no home, neither."

Bella's heart clenched. Her parents had also died from influenza, but Harriet Halliday's folks hadn't, so she made a broader reply. "I'm so sorry. It was a terrible ailment."

"It were. I never got it, but lots of our customers did. My ma took food to some, which is how she come down with it." She swiped at her eyes again before finishing one muffin and starting the other.

"How kind of her." Bella's mother had often taken meals to neighbors who were ill or injured. Had she caught the flu that way? Bella didn't know, but she wouldn't be surprised. "If you don't have an automobile, do you ever get away on your day off? If you get time off."

"My half-day is Monday after the noon meal. Supper is always a cold collation then. Most weeks, a friend from town drives out for me. We take in a moving picture and get dinner. In summer, we sometimes swim in the river at her folks' farm."

"How nice."

Anita offered a wistful smile. "It is, but I haven't been able to go for a while. Course, I have to do supper dishes when I get back. No matter what time."

"Do you return late?"

"Not past ten o'clock. The Lennings don't like the help coming and going late."

"I'll keep that in mind." Bella wasn't sure what to make of the information, but she tucked it away as possibly significant.

"If you want to keep your job, don't do nothing out of line."

The advice provided an opening for Bella to commiserate with Anita. "I really need the job," she said before drawing from the biography created by Derringer to provide more details.

"Since you lost your auntie, are you all alone?"

"I am. For now, I won't sell, but I need income to keep the house up." Bella broke her second muffin into pieces while considering how to glean details without being obvious. Conducting straightforward interviews, as she and Jax had done in the past, was easier than this. "Mrs. Lenning made it sound like the job would probably be long-term, but I wasn't sure and didn't want to ask a lot of questions."

Anita toyed with the napkin. "I wouldn't ask no questions, neither, but you'll probably be staying. The other receptionist quit sudden-like. She didn't tell no one, just left a note."

Bella tried to look baffled. "I see."

"Just be careful. Cora, Miss Bounder, were too snoopy all along." Anita put another piece of muffin into her mouth.

"I don't suppose most other workers are." Bella used the statement as a lure and hoped to snag something useful.

A half-shrug moved the kitchen aide's narrow shoulders. "I dunno. Most stick to their own business like I do."

Since Bella didn't want to ask outright about various workers, she tried a different avenue. "You said there's not enough help. It shouldn't be hard to find more employees, since so many folks are looking for jobs."

"I don't think the Lennings want to pay anyone else." Anita toyed with her napkin. "The missus pinches every penny twice."

"Isn't it hard to treat patients with so few employees?"

Anita broke her other muffin into pieces. "Not sure about any of that."

Frustration gnawed at Bella. She needed more information. Was the young redhead afraid to reveal too much, or was she hiding the truth? Bella tried another idea. "I only saw ten who had visitors. Is that typical?"

"Pretty much. I seen the ones who got company. Some do okay."

Bella's stomach knotted. Evidently, those without visitors didn't. "Do you know much about the patients?"

The color drained from Anita's face. "I work in the kitchen, so I only see them in passing. I didn't know nothing about shell-shock and crazy people when I come here. I'd heared this place was to help soldiers, but it don't seem like many get better. When I take trays of food to the dining room, some stare into space. It's no wonder their folks don't come."

The young woman's words and reactions indicated tension. Why? Not only that, she had taken the coffee and cake to Jax

Had she been aware drugs were in the refreshments? Pressing for more might cause Anita to withdraw, so Bella shrugged. "I just wondered. I've only heard a little about what's done to help soldiers. My neighbor has shell-shock, and his parents are struggling to keep him at home. I thought I'd tell them about Poplar Pines."

Anita clasped her hands together and stared down at them. "Maybe they should try another place."

The reply was disturbing. "How long do most patients stay?"

After a moment, Anita met Bella's gaze. "The ones who get regular company go home within a couple of months. Folks got to pay for two in advance. Sometimes, the relatives who visit lots don't wait that long to get their boys out."

Finally, more information. "They must miss their sons, brothers, or husbands. It's sad some get few guests. The limited visiting hours may make it difficult for people to come often."

"I suppose."

When Anita took another bite of muffin, Bella continued. "I just wondered. The one patient, Lieutenant Phinney, was very withdrawn. I thought company might be good for him, and for Lieutenant Douglass, too. He was also quiet, but perhaps he was given medication to ease the pain in his sprained wrist and other arm, which was in a sling. He didn't even remember how he got hurt." Bella injected a note of derision into her voice and rolled her eyes. Both should camouflage her concern for Jax.

"I heard he fell down a few steps," Anita murmured. "He's lucky not to get injured no worse."

Only the strictest self-control kept Bella's sympathy in check, as she considered how much damage might have occurred if he'd tumbled all the way down one of the long staircases. "Are falls and such common among the men?"

A half-shrug lifted one of Anita's narrow shoulders. "Not that I know."

"That's good. I caught glimpses of the men with visitors, but I haven't seen any patients up close other than the two upstairs. I suppose a few have physical wounds from the war."

"Some do."

Again, the young woman's comment provided nothing of significance. Bella was considering what else to say when a tap on the door interrupted. "Come in."

"I just wanted to see if you were getting settled. I'm Marjorie Mayfair, one of the nurses. I'm sorry we didn't have time to talk earlier." The slender blonde's smile faltered when her gaze fell on Anita. Abruptly, she looked at Bella. "Sorry, I didn't realize you weren't alone." Disapproval emanated from her.

Anita flushed and rose to her feet. "Thank you for the muffins, Miss Halliday."

Before Bella could do more than utter a *you're welcome*, the cook's assistant was gone. For a long moment, she stared at the doorway. Finally, Marjorie's voice broke into Bella's thoughts.

"I'm sorry if Anita made herself a pest. She desperately wants attention."

Once again, Marjorie's delicate features formed an amiable expression. Bella wasn't sure what to make of the nurse's attitude toward Anita. Was there some impasse between the two? Anita had delivered adulterated food to Jax. Was she involved in the nefarious doings? If so, did Marjorie realize or suspect? Uncertain, Bella offered a benign reply. "Since I ate lunch alone after feeding the men upstairs, I saw her in passing. Of course, I've met the Lennings, Major Billings, and Arnold Drier. I saw you while we cleaned up."

"I wish we could've talked, but Mrs. Lenning had me checking the patient rooms, since Nurse Artem is off today." The blonde rolled her eyes.

"She mentioned one nurse wanting the day off when she asked me to start this morning."

"There are only three of us, so getting free time isn't easy. Wanda, Nurse Artem, always asks for a Sunday off and gets it." Marjorie tsked, tsked. "Twenty patients may not seem like many, but we have our hearts and hands full."

Bella gestured to the chair vacated by Anita. "Please sit down."

Marjorie took a seat. "I won't stay long. You must be tired after helping with patients, getting settled, and such."

"A little tired. I took food to two of them. Both are new, from what Mrs. Lenning told me." The comment revealed little and asked nothing, but Bella hoped it elicited additional information. Finding out why Marjorie and Anita weren't friendly was near the top of Bella's list. Although it might have nothing to do with the deaths and disappearance, it could be a clue.

"Did you talk with them at all?" Marjorie inquired.

Bella replied carefully. She wanted to get details, not give them. "Not really. Both seemed withdrawn. Maybe sedated."

Something flickered in Marjorie's gaze before she shrugged. "New patients can be hard to handle, so they're given mild medications."

Marjorie must have been the young nurse who visited Jax. Evidently, she was unaware he'd ditched the pills. While Bella yearned to query the other woman, she forced herself to make the most tepid of remarks. "That's understandable." Bella shared the story of her fictitious neighbor and hoped Marjorie was more garrulous than Anita. She ended with, "His carrying on upsets his parents and the neighbors. Sometimes, he wanders outside at night. It's sad and scary."

Long moments stretched out before a reply came. "I'm not directly involved in treatments, and we're provided little information." She chewed on her lower lip. "Before I took this job, I knew a bit about procedures at asylums. Some are dreadful. When I started here, I was told modern methods were used."

"I heard the same thing." Actually, Bella had been told very little, but she'd learned a lot from the lawmen. "That's the case, isn't it?"

Another long pause ensued. "Some men are restrained. They put others in isolation, if they create a disturbance. Just recently, new patients are separated for several days."

"How are patients restrained?" Bella's stomach roiled as she considered possibilities.

"Strapped in wheelchairs or on their beds. The latter happens if they're up and complain to the night nurse. Artem is usually on duty then. She hates being bothered."

"How would the men bother her?"

"By wanting water, another blanket, anything. She makes one check when she goes on duty and another right before the day nurse takes over. In-between, she sleeps."

The revelation took Bella aback. "What if a patient needs help when she's resting?"

Marjorie made a dismissive gesture with one hand. "She doesn't care, and Mrs. Lenning doesn't, either."

"That's sad." It was much worse. It was awful. Did Poplar Pines primarily exist as a moneymaker? Several things pointed to that probability and made Bella more determined to get justice for all the patients. And the families who paid hefty fees in hope their relatives got much needed help.

"It is, but I try to make them comfortable when I start in the morning. Sarah Bailey does the same in the afternoons."

"I haven't met her yet," Bella observed.

"Sarah's an excellent nurse. She works tonight, since Artem won't be back until late tomorrow. Her day off usually ends up being almost two days. Anyhow, since only a few patients had visitors, Sarah had to stay on the second floor with the others. She went to bed after that." Marjorie looked at her watch. "By now, she's back at work."

"I see," Bella murmured. "Are there only two orderlies?"

"Yep. Arnold, who you met, and Warren Starling. He helped us clean up. Scrawny, scarecrow-like man. Scraggly beard." Marjorie shook her head, which sent her blonde bob swinging like fringe in a breeze.

The description, as unkind as it was, fit Jax's account and matched the man Bella had seen in passing. "Of course. I met Mrs. Barley, but not the housekeeper." She wasn't actually sure such a position existed. The case files hadn't named one, but how was the place kept clean?

A low laugh left Marjorie. "There's no housekeeper or maid. A couple of girls from town come out twice a week, always right before visiting hours. They were here very early this morning. The patient rooms get short shrift, and we have to tidy up our own quarters. We take turns scrubbing the lavatory at the end of the hall." She made a face. "We're always very short-handed."

Once again, Bella voiced her observation about jobs. "Many people are out of work. It seems odd, so few are employed here."

The young nurse gripped the chair arms. "I had trouble finding a job in the city. Not sure about other folks getting work."

Bella tried more questions. "What if patients complain about being restrained? Don't their families object?"

"The men who get regular visitors aren't tied down very often. Some relatives get upset over that. Others are weary of dealing with problems and stop coming altogether. A few drop the men off and never return."

Useful details were slowly emerging. "That's sad for the patients. I imagine the ones who see and hear from relatives and friends do better."

"They usually don't stay as long, so that's probably true. I wouldn't stay, either, if I could get a decent job in Toledo or Cleveland or Columbus."

"You don't like it here?"

A half-shrug lifted one of the younger woman's slender shoulders. "The pay is fair, and I have a pleasant room. Bigger than this one, since I got to pick when I was hired." She sighed. "My parents didn't approve of me taking nurses' training. They think I should already be married with a passel of children, so if I moved home, they'd be trotting out potential suitors constantly. I don't even want to live in the same city, since they kept at me to step out with one, in particular. He's twelve years older than me, and a dead bore. He didn't even serve in France. Too sickly or something. I would've joined the nurse corps if I'd been qualified then."

Bella gauged Marjorie's age at twenty-one or twenty-two. If so, she'd been eighteen or nineteen when the war ended, which made it unlikely she could have served in France or in a military hospital at home. Early on, the age requirement for members of the American nurse corps was twenty-five to thirty-five.

"You don't want to marry?"

"Not to someone old and not to a man who is dull. Some of my nursing school classmates live in cities. When I save enough, I want to do that, too. A lot more fun things happen there.

I should have the money to move soon." Marjorie grimaced. "Don't tell anyone, especially Anita. The little busybody would report to the Lennings right off. She always wants to curry favor."

Was this a sign that Anita had crucial information? The girl seemed lonely and innocent, but previous investigations had proven appearances were often deceiving. "Don't worry. I won't breathe a word to anyone." Except Jax and the other lawmen.

"Thank you." Marjorie jumped to her feet. "Now, I need to get to bed. I have the early shift."

The young nurse wasted no time in leaving. Once she was gone, Bella sank into the faded chair and thought about what she had learned. Nothing major, but plenty to prove the investigation was imperative.

Chapter Seven

Monday morning, Bella dressed and hurried downstairs. Although she had seen some workers in passing the previous day, she wanted to get to breakfast early and observe more. A small group of employees had already gathered at a table in the far corner.

"Good day." Marjorie was the first to speak when Bella stopped by an empty chair. "Sit down."

"Thank you," Bella said as she took the seat next to the young nurse. After being passed dishes of eggs, toast, potatoes, and ham, she glanced around the group. She felt all eyes, curious eyes, on her. Before she could introduce herself, Marjorie filled in.

"This is Harriet Halliday, our new receptionist, but she hasn't officially met the group." Marjorie gestured to the woman next to her. "This is Nurse Artem. She's back early from her day off."

The gray-haired woman nodded but didn't stop eating. "You've already met Arnold Drier."

"Of course. He helped me take food upstairs yesterday," Bella said, but Drier didn't react. She also noted the implicit criticism in Marjorie's comment about Wanda Artem, who remained impassive.

Before Marjorie could continue, the wiry man next to her chimed in. "Good morning, Miss Halliday, and welcome. I'm Warren Starling, one of the orderlies."

Bella exchanged greetings with him, while wondering about Marjorie's disparagement of Anita and Artem. Were both other women somehow involved in the perverse doings?

Starling jerked his thumb at the man to his right. "This here's Ian McNulty. Gardener and handyman."

"I've seen the garden from the building. I hope to get out and walk through it soon," Bella said with a smile. "It looks lovely."

The gardener, a good-looking man in his early thirties, glanced at Bella. "Good morning and welcome to Poplar Pines." When he grinned, his hazel eyes sparkled. A wink set off his bold demeanor. "Let me know if you want a private tour."

"I'd be happy to show you around," Marjorie put in, her voice sharper than seemed appropriate.

Was the young nurse critical of everyone? Bella wondered.

"Just don't wander in the garden at night. Ian is very particular about his plants and such." Nurse Artem made the remark.

McNulty chuckled. "Not to worry, Harriet. I don't mind pretty ladies picking a few blooms—day or night."

Beside Bella, Marjorie went rigid. When a harrumph left Nurse Artem, Bella turned to her.

The older woman's frizzy hair was swept into a bun. Fine lines edged her mud brown eyes and the corners of her mouth. Gauging her age wasn't easy. She might be in her forties or fifties.

"If you're wise, you'll take my advice." Nurse Artem went back to her meal.

"Of course. I certainly wouldn't want to damage any plants." Bella found the exchange odd, but she had no opportunity to mull it over since Marjorie went back to making introductions.

"Last, but not least is Nurse Sarah Bailey. Sarah, this is Harriet Halliday." As she spoke, Marjorie sent a quelling stare at McNulty, who was again grinning

The newcomer nodded. "How lovely to meet you," the woman said. A smile enhanced her warm greeting, but fatigue lined her face and dark circles ringed her quicksilver eyes. Her dark auburn hair was swept into a long braid. Despite her weariness, Sarah was a beauty.

"I'm happy to meet you, as well." Bella went back to eating, while the others did the same with a few bits of conversation here and there. She listened with one ear but continued to consider what she had heard so far. Nothing useful, but plenty that seemed strange.

Arnold Drier finished first and rose to his feet. "I'll get one bunch of boys from upstairs." His attention went to Artem. "You check on all of them before coming down?"

"Most were awake, and I told the others you'd be up shortly to bring them to breakfast." The older woman's tone showed little interest, and Artem returned to her meal immediately.

Drier gave a brief nod. "You coming to get the rest, Star?"

Bella started at the nickname, which didn't fit the thin orderly. When Starling stood, the ill-fit of his uniform was obvious. Not only did the attire hang on him, the pant legs ended above his ankles. His hair, lank and listless, brushed his collar. Bella never judged people on appearance, but she wondered how he'd gotten the moniker and hoped it wasn't someone's idea of a jest.

"Ready to go." Starling gave a slight bow to Bella. "See you later, Harriet. If you want a tour of the garden, I get off work later. I'd be happy to show you around."

Uncertain about the idea, Bella offered a wan smile. For now, she'd take a wait-and-see attitude.

Drier and Starling were barely out of the dining room when the gardener, issuing a jaunty farewell and broad grin, got up. "If you'd really like a garden tour, Harriet, I'm always happy to show a pretty girl around my place." After repeating his earlier invitation, he winked in Marjorie's direction. "Isn't that right, Nurse Mayfair?" Amusement put a lilt in his voice.

Marjorie lifted her chin in an imperious gesture totally lacking in humor. "Indeed, it is, but you wouldn't to spread yourself too thin."

Deep masculine laughter escaped McNulty. "I'll never do that." He put one forefinger to his brow in a casual salute before turning to leave the room. He was closely followed by Nurse Artem, leaving Sarah, Marjorie, and Bella at the table.

"Warren may have a crush on you," Marjorie said before Bella could comment on the gardener.

"I hardly know him. He was just being friendly." What an odd remark for Marjorie to make, especially when McNulty had been the one being flirtatious. Bella sipped her coffee and glanced at Sarah, who was focused on her food.

Marjorie shrugged. "He's friendlier than Arnold overall, and he's been very attentive to Anita."

"He's a good deal older than she is." Although Bella wanted to ask about the gardener, she didn't want to abruptly change the topic.

"Almost twice her age," Sarah put in, "but she has no family, and his attention makes her feel better. She may see him as a big brother or uncle."

"Sarah is kind. Both Warren and Anita like attention and can be pests. She trails after Ian as much as possible, too. He flirts too much, but it's not serious in her case." Marjorie gestured toward a small table set in an alcove at the far end of the dining room. "Plus, she toadies up to the Lennings and Major Billings, too. They all eat together, and Anita waits on them like it's a fancy restaurant."

Sarah shook her head. "The Lennings own the place, so it's natural for her to cater to them."

"You and I don't." Marjorie's blue eyes became slits.

"We're nurses, so we aren't called to wait on them," Sarah replied.

"No, but we get summoned to do a lot more than nurse." Marjorie pushed her plate away and leaned back in her chair.

Before the young nurse could offer more complaints, Bella posed a question. "Do the Lennings usually eat with Major Billings?"

"Usually. Sometimes, he's away," Marjorie told her. "He comes and goes at will."

"Then, he isn't a regular employee?" Bella asked.

With one forefinger, Sarah traced the rim of her coffee cup. "We don't really know. He may be more of a partner. No one ever says, but he has a lot of authority and, as Marjorie said, freedom to come and go with no set duties."

"What is his role when he's here?" Bella tried to sound like the average interested new employee, not like a temporary sheriff's deputy.

"Talks to the patients," Sarah replied. "Tells them to buck up and be real men." Her lips pursed as if the words tasted bad in her mouth.

"Which is ridiculous," Marjorie murmured.

Their observations confirmed the material in the case file. "Is he a physician?" Bella knew he wasn't, but what was the man doing here?

"No, he's a retired army officer." Sarah provided the information. "That's how he met Dr. Lenning."

Bella nodded. "Did the major serve in France?" Dangling known information was a tried-and-true sleuthing method. She hoped it proved successful now.

"He did, but back at headquarters. Not at the front." Sarah's gaze grew clouded, and she bowed her head.

Since Nurse Bailey was close to thirty, Bella wondered if she had been near the line. "Were you in the Nurse Corps during the war?"

Before meeting Bella's gaze, Sarah put one hand to her heart as if it pained her. "I was mostly at a clearing station. We saw many gravely wounded men. Most in body, others in spirit. One reason I came here was to tend those who suffered so badly overseas. I try to help them." Her attention moved to the other nurse. "Marjorie does, too."

The last statement lacked the conviction of the previous ones. Bella tucked the detail away for future reference.

After a quick look at her watch, Marjorie got to her feet. "I need to see about getting the men settled when they come for breakfast or Mrs. Lenning will be angry."

When the other nurse was out of earshot, Bella turned to Sarah, who seemed sympathetic to the former soldiers. Bella again relayed the story of the fictitious neighbor. "I told his folks I'd find out about treatment here, but I've gotten no details. Just that modern methods are used, along with isolation, restraint, and sedation. I'd like to find out more."

A troubled expression crossed Sarah's face. "I heard they used modern methods, too, but it's not exactly the case." A faint smile, one that didn't reach her pale eyes, touched Sarah's lips. "We don't have enough help, which is an issue."

"A lot of folks are out of work. Both Anita and Marjorie mentioned badly needing their jobs." Bella stated simple facts and waited for a reaction.

Sarah glanced around the room before looking back at Bella. "I suppose most working folks need their jobs, but my situation is unique. My fiancé is here." She bit on her trembling lower lip before continuing. "He was leading his men over the top and into No Man's Land when several of them were hit. Dalton tried to get his sergeant, who was mortally injured, back to the trench, but a German sniper pinned them down. Dalton was stuck in the mud with a dead man overnight."

"How awful." Bella had heard of such cases but couldn't say so. After all, Harriet Halliday wouldn't know those details.

"It was terrible. Dalton only had a flesh wound but, when he came to the clearing station, I could see he wasn't right. I begged the doctors to not send him back to the line. We all knew the Armistice was coming, and it did within a few days." Sarah's troubled expression softened. "One finally agreed Dalton could be sent to a field hospital. Although he healed physically, he was never right in his mind. He still isn't." Once again, she looked around the room before slightly lifting one hand. "He's in the far corner. The one with auburn hair."

Bella shifted to see Sarah's fiancé. Only one man in that direction had the right color, a lighter shade than Sarah's own. Even from a distance, his slack jaw and blank stare were obvious. Sympathy washed over her, and Bella had to fight to hold back tears. "I'm so sorry."

"Thank you." Sarah's voice was a hoarse whisper. "He doesn't recognize me anymore and hasn't for a long time. He has barely spoken in almost three years. For a while, his folks cared for him at home. They hired help, and I pitched in. Finally, they grew weary of the situation and brought him here. When I visited, they needed another nurse, so I took the job. I was grateful, since I also have lodging here. If his mother and father stop paying, I could afford his care because the rate would be reduced."

"I see." Bella understood the issues involved in caring for a shell-shocked relative. Although she had no personal experience, several friends from her Signal Corps days did.

"I doubt if you do. How could you? How can anyone who doesn't have a loved one in Dalton's condition?" She swiveled to face Bella. "It kills me when he's restrained or isolated, but at least I'm around to make sure nothing really bad happens."

The last phrase put Bella on alert. *Nothing really bad* could mean different things. Since she wouldn't ask outright, she nodded. "That's good."

Sarah's shoulders relaxed. "I'm sorry. I shouldn't criticize you. We've just met. It's hard to see him like he is now. His folks can't accept it, so they don't come. They'd like to forget he's still alive."

Was Sarah afraid Dalton's parents would be open to having him killed? After another quick glance at Sarah's betrothed,

Bella wondered if the victims had been in similar conditions. Had their loved ones justified getting rid of them because of that? "Perhaps, as time goes on, he'll get better."

A wistful look came over Sarah's face. "I hope so. I really do."

Before Bella could reply, Anita appeared and began stacking dishes. "Got to get the table ready for the men," she muttered. "Some's here already, and we use this table, too."

"Of course," Sarah said. "I should wash out a few things this morning. Clean clothes are essential. It was good to meet you, Harriet."

Bella watched as the nurse left without stopping to see her fiancé. When Anita reached to pick up her plate, Bella rose from her chair. "I'll get to work a bit early."

"Always better than being late. Then, the big boss won't find fault with you." Anita kept working as she spoke.

"Good advice," Bella replied. But she wondered who the big boss was. Dr. Lenning, Mrs. Lenning, or Major Billings?

At noon, Bella was once again summoned to take food upstairs. This time, Warren Starling met her in the kitchen. When he nodded a greeting, a shock of his hair fell forward. Although it covered his right eye, the orderly didn't brush it back. "Nice to be working with you, Harriet." A grin split his face and revealed a few missing teeth.

"Thank you." Bella made a bland reply. She didn't want to be too friendly, since she hoped Warren wouldn't want to stay while Jax ate.

"You need a haircut," Mrs. Barley said in a tart tone. The cook's lined face settled into a frown. "Better see to it on your next day off or the Missus will be after you."

Another grin kicked up one corner of the man's mouth. "She can yammer all she wants. She ain't gonna fire me." With that, Starling turned to Bella. "If you can handle the two new ones, that would help. Both are sedated, so you won't have no trouble with them. Then, I can grab a bite. That's what Drier did yesterday. Right?"

Bella smiled in relief. "I'm happy to do that. Everything was fine yesterday, and I'm sure it will be today, too."

"Then, let's go, Harriet."

Starling let Bella precede him on the stairs. When they reached the top floor, he paused. "Lieutenant Douglass is the only one who can't feed himself. With his left wrist sprained and a bad right arm, he struggles. But you know that from yesterday. Heard he was wounded in France and has some dreadful nightmares and insomnia, too. It's a shame he fell here. He didn't need no more problems."

"No, he doesn't." Warren Starling was more sympathetic than Arnold Drier. The attitude might not represent his true character, so Bella wasn't making a final judgment. His comment about Mrs. Lenning not firing him created skepticism. Was he instrumental in the odd goings on? And how had he gotten so many details about Jax? Simple gossip or something else?

Starling unlocked the door to Phinney's room and let Bella take the tray inside. Since the young officer was sleeping, she left it and returned to the hall. The cold meal wouldn't be affected by sitting for a time. After the orderly unlocked Jax's door, she entered the small room.

"I'll have to lock the door, but you should be safe." The orderly glanced inside and back at Bella.

"Of course."

Starling gave her a nod before shutting the door. When the lock engaged and his footsteps faded away, Bella turned toward Jax. "Good afternoon."

A slight smile turned up the corners of his mouth. "Is it good? Hard to tell up here."

The underlying note of amusement in his voice heartened Bella. Being undercover was tricky, and being unable to get information, which was nigh on impossible in the isolated attic space, had to be frustrating. Maybe Jax would feel better if she shared her findings. Before embarking on a discussion, she put the tray on the table. "This doesn't look any more appetizing than yesterday's meal, but you need to eat."

After picking up the ham sandwich, Jax took a bite. "I hope the staff gets fed better."

His comment opened an avenue to talking about the two women and what Bella had learned. "Our food is fine. Anita says patients in the attic get worse fare than the others."

The sandwich froze partway to his mouth while Jax stared at Bella. "Did you ask?"

Bella shook her head. "You're very suspicious."

"I'm aware of your propensity to poke around, even when you shouldn't and even when you say you won't." His wry tone sapped any real criticism.

"Anita stopped by my room last night, and we got to chatting. She shared a few things with no prompting from me." Mostly true.

Jax swallowed another bite before replying. "What else did she say?"

Bella summed up the cook assistant's background and revelations. "From how she acted, I think she knew you were getting
cake and coffee laced with a sedative. But I'm not sure."

"The girl acted anxious when she came to Lenning's office
with the refreshments, but that doesn't mean she's not an active
participant. Rufus Ayling thinks both local women are nice, but
he's had little contact with them recently. Besides, money can
make good people do bad things. As for the rest, it's mostly
confirmation of what we already knew, but even that is useful.
Any other interesting details arise?"

"When Marjorie Mayfair, that's the young blonde nurse,
stopped by, Anita left. Marjorie was rather abrupt with her, like
Anita had overstepped her position by coming into my room."

Jax's brow crinkled. "Did this nurse have much else to say?"

"She sat down and talked for a few minutes last night. She
confirmed you and the other officer up here are sedated. The
first night, I'm guessing someone gave you an injection, as well
as whatever was in the refreshments."

"Nothing was really clear for a long while, so that seems
right." He rubbed his stubbled jaw. "I need to keep acting like
I'm drugged or they may switch back to shots."

"Marjorie wasn't at all suspicious about you when we spoke."

A smile kicked up one corner of his mouth. "That's good."

"I didn't get much more from her last night, but I got to the
staff table this morning in time to chat. Marjorie introduced me
to everyone." Bella summarized the gist of the conversation and
finished with Sarah's revelations.

"I'd like to know what she meant by protecting her fiancé,
too," Jax murmured.

"She seems desperate for him to get better. I only got a glimpse, so it's hard to say if that's a real possibility or a futile wish."

"What about the other nurse? The older one. What did you think?"

"She said very little. Marjorie was critical of her for taking time off, but Nurse Artem didn't respond. However, she mentioned not going into the garden at night because Ian, the gardener, wouldn't like it."

"Not sure if that's significant or not. It's unlikely I'll see someone who works outside, so what's your opinion of him?"

"He was friendly, overly so. Around thirty. Good looking and aware of it. He's flirtatious, like a lot of handsome men." Bella couldn't repress a grin. "Luckily, you and my brother weren't in that category."

Jax chuckled. "Thanks, but I imagine I look pretty rough around the edges right now." He ran one hand over his face before giving his hair a tug.

"I've seen you look nattier, but we're off the topic," Bella said. "Marjorie said Anita seeks Ian out often."

"Hmmm. That and the warning to stay out of the garden at night could be related to the case."

"I thought the same thing," Bella agreed. "McNulty offered to give me a private tour twice, which seemed to upset Marjorie. She said he's a flirt, but he seemed to want to make her jealous."

A troubled expression fell over Jax's face. "She could be smitten with him, and he may like to flatter all the pretty ladies."

Jax's implicit assertion about her prettiness made Bella smile. "Maybe so, but it's not apt to be important to the whereabouts of Aaron Corning or the rest of the case."

"Let's not dismiss it, though. Anything else?"

"Another interesting point is, Nurse Artem sleeps away most of her shift."

"That could be useful going forward."

His comment evoked apprehension. "The doors to patient rooms are kept locked, so you won't be able to roam around."

Jax nodded. "A lock pick would be useful. Richard might bring one on Wednesday."

Suspicion crept through Bella. "Did you ask him to do that?"

His gaze shifted away from her, and he didn't reply.

"Jax, that's risky. Nurse Artem could check on you any time. Besides, what would you look for and where would you look?"

"Forget I mentioned it. Like you say, maybe it's not a good idea."

The word *maybe* failed to ease her worry, but Bella let it pass. Arguing with him wouldn't help, and she could talk to Richard first. "I'm planning to go home tonight. I'll use the excuse that I didn't have time to pack everything, but I want to tell Richard what we know now. That will ease his mind, and Jenny's, too."

"Jenny is motherly." A slight smile played across his lips.

"You've been without maternal fussing for a long time."

Jax's smile broadened. "Your mother spoiled me after my mom died, especially whenever I got sick. It was nice she always insisted I stay at Ballantyne to recuperate." Jax took her hand as he spoke.

Memories of his bouts with measles, mumps, chicken pox, and tonsilitis rose in Bella's mind. She'd had to keep her distance when he'd had the first three, but Bella had made it her mission to fetch and carry various necessities to the sickroom when he had his multiple throat infections followed by surgery. "I remember."

A low laugh rumbled out. "I bet you do. You made my stays more pleasant, especially the one after I had my tonsils out. I watched the clock all afternoon because you always came up after school with a big bowl of ice cream for me."

Pleasure rippled through her. Talking about happy memories lifted her spirits and strengthened the bonds between them, ones that had weakened after her brother's death. "And another one for your supper."

"I was as glad to see you as to get a frozen treat. Your parents and grandparents checked on me often, but I looked forward to you coming up. Being spoiled was nice." Amusement twinkled in his green gaze.

"I enjoyed doing it," she admitted. Some of her lightheart-edness dissipated. "I wish I could've been there both times you were wounded in France, but I didn't hear about either until you were already back on the line."

His grin faltered but didn't completely disappear. "I would've enjoyed seeing you, although you were busy with your work as an operator." He gently squeezed her hand. "We'll make up for lost time after this case."

"We will." The certainty in her response surprised Bella. Far too often during the last three years, the two of them had either been at arm's length or tip-toeing around each other. Although the current circumstances were far from ideal, they were in a better place again. A promising place.

Jax released her hand and leaned back, but his good humor returned. "Do we need to go over anything else?"

His use of *we* made Bella's spirit soar. Being fellow deputies, even if only temporarily, revealed a lot about his willingness to accept her on equal footing. "I wish I had more details, but I don't. I'll keep my ears and eyes open. Sometimes, folks give dribs and drabs of information in casual conversation without realizing it."

His features relaxed into a smile. "You're good at picking up subtle hints, so you may get details that way. Any bits would help. All cases are puzzles, and this one is mostly missing pieces."

"You're good at recognizing undercurrents, too. Richard is right about us making a fine team."

"He is. We're a team in unusual circumstances at the moment."

In her reply, she focused on the path ahead. "Because I've helped you eat up here, I'll probably continue to do that when you go to a regular room. Most meals served downstairs require cutlery, so you might need me even more." Bella beamed at Jax.

Displeasure clouded his eyes. "I'm to be fed like a baby indefinitely?"

The note of chagrin in his deep voice echoed inside Bella. "You're playing a role, remember?" she asked with a trace of humor. "Jax Hastings wouldn't need to be fed. Jack Douglass does."

A rueful grin played across his lips. "Both of us have a sprained wrist and an arm in a sling."

"Which wouldn't be the case if you weren't undercover."

"True."

Bella would have liked to talk longer, but time was passing quickly. "Before I go, is there anything else for me to relay to Richard?"

"No, just that I'm looking forward to seeing him and Jenny on Wednesday. And remember to take the long way home. We can't be sure you won't be followed."

"I will," she agreed although being trailed seemed unlikely.

Jax paused for a moment. When he spoke again, his voice dropped a note. "And I'll look forward to seeing you when you can manage it."

"I'll try to manage it as often as possible."

Chapter Eight

After taking food upstairs, Bella returned to the front desk. She was reviewing her duties when Dr. Lenning appeared.

"How is your second day going, Miss Halliday?"

The man, wearing a dapper serge suit and highly polished shoes, looked far more professional than he had during her interview. Perhaps, he had simply had a bad day, although Bella couldn't shake the feeling that he had been hungover when she last saw him. "Very well, thank you."

"Good, good. It's important for us to have a reliable, skilled receptionist. Visitors see you first, and we want to make a good impression." A broad smile curved his thin lips and moved his narrow mustache.

"Of course," Bella replied, although her initial impression of him hadn't been positive, he was more genial now. Before she could say more, Major Billings appeared.

"It was good to see you chatting with some of our families yesterday," the military man observed. "And I heard you're taking meals to our two new patients."

Nothing in Billings' statement was accusatory, but Bella felt like she was on the defensive. "I wanted to welcome people yesterday. Some chit-chatted more than others. As for going upstairs, Mrs. Lenning asked me to deliver food."

"I see," the major said.

"I've spoken to my mother about an orderly staying with you," Lenning added. "She thought one always was, but it seems both Drier and Starling came back and ate while you were left alone with Douglass."

Anxiety made Bella's mouth go dry. She swallowed hard. "The lieutenant didn't give me any trouble."

"Was he talkative?" Billings asked.

The query escalated her apprehension. "No, not at all." Surely, she and Jax hadn't been overheard. Not when there'd been no sign of anyone else in the attic. As she spoke, Bella glanced from one man to the other. "I tried making small talk but to little avail."

A period of silence ensued. During it, Bella smiled. Or tried to. Her nerves threatened to get the better of her.

"Patients can get confused, especially when they first arrive," Lenning said. "Don't take anything they say to heart. As far as families, send them to one of us, if they have questions."

"Your mother mentioned sending people to her with questions, as well." Bella spoke in a benign voice.

The doctor scowled. "She gets confused at times, so she isn't the best source."

Billings nodded, but his expression was more benevolent. "She's a lovely lady but getting up in years, and her mind isn't always sharp. I'm sure you noticed already."

"I'll send folks to the two of you, if they need information." Bella by-passed responding to the criticism of Mrs. Lenning.

Was the woman running the business end? Or was Billings? Did it matter to the case? Bella's current concern was not coming under suspicion, or having Jax be more closely monitored.

"Excellent," Billings replied before turning to Lenning. "I have a couple of things I'd like for us to discuss."

Lenning hesitated briefly. "Of course. Let's head to my office."

After the pair moved on, Bella slumped back in her chair. Both men made her uneasy, but so did Mrs. Lenning's inconsistent behavior. Were they all involved in the evil doings?

The remainder of the day passed slowly. Relief filled Bella when she got into the Chummy and headed away from Poplar Pines. With Jax's warnings in mind, she chose a turnoff leading in the direction of her fictitious aunt's home, not Moreley. She stayed on the route for twenty minutes. When she was certain she wasn't being followed, Bella took a crossroad winding back toward her destination.

Over an hour later, she pulled the automobile to a stop in front of the Hastings house. Twilight was falling, and a lamp glowed in the front window while another lit the porch. For a long moment, Bella gazed at the familiar home. Jax's home. Would it someday be hers, too? The question, one held at bay for years, burst forth with surprising strength. Although courtship didn't always lead to marriage, wouldn't it in their case? If so, would they live here? Or at Ballantyne? They could take a suite in the inn or choose one of the cottages. As far as Bella knew, Jax planned to return to his position as town constable, not try to revive his dream of being a golf professional. But he was still considering surgery on his right arm. He might play golf again if it was a success. Would he reconsider working at Ballantyne? If not, could she continue running the resort without living there? She supposed so, but the idea of making her home elsewhere gave Bella pause. For months, she'd figured they were past their main issue—Jax's guilt over Matt's death. But they hadn't discussed details of a shared future. She chuckled to herself. As Jax said, they would have time to talk when they were stepping out. And they'd start courting sooner, if they solved the current case quickly.

She went to the front door, which opened before she could knock. Richard welcomed her. "Nolen called to say he saw the Chummy heading up Main Street in our direction. Come on in."

Nolen Rogers, a deputy constable, had been Jax's sergeant during the last weeks of the war. Naturally, he would be interested in the case on more than one level. After taking a seat in one of the fireside chairs, Bella leaned back. "I don't have a lot to report."

"No news can be good news." The senior constable's tone was hopeful, if restrained. "Did you have trouble getting away? I know they want you to stay Sunday morning through Friday afternoon."

"I only took a small bag yesterday morning. I said I didn't have time to get the house in order and had forgotten to pack a few things, which gave me an excuse to go back—supposedly—this evening."

"Smart."

Jenny's appearance with a tray interrupted their exchange. Richard took the load from her and put it on the table in front of the fireplace. While his wife sat in the chair across from Bella, he pulled another one up. After Jenny poured coffee and distributed sandwiches, she smiled. "We waited supper, since I wasn't sure you'd eat before leaving Poplar Pines."

Bella gratefully accepted a cup and plate. "You're right. I left as soon as I finished work. Thank you so much for thinking of me."

"We can't have you go hungry," Jenny replied.

"Jax appreciated you fussing over him while he was here." Bella made the comment without forethought, but it was true.

"He needs a little pampering," the older woman replied.

Bella smiled. "I agree. He's been on his own for a long time. Even when his dad was still alive, Jax always stayed with us when he got sick."

"He'll need someone to look out for him after surgery," Jenny said.

Surprise hit Bella hard. "He hasn't mentioned much more about an operation since June. At least not to me. Has he definitely decided on it?"

"Richard and I pressed him when he was here Friday night, and he's going to see the doctor in Toledo after this case is over." Jenny gave Bella a reassuring look. "I doubt if he had time to tell you. Everything was rushed."

"He's been considering it." Maybe Jax hadn't told her because he still might change his mind, but Bella hoped he would go through with the procedure.

Richard's voice interrupted her reverie. "If he has the surgery soon after this investigation is done, I can stay on while he recuperates."

If the Jenkinses remained in town, Jax would undoubtedly recover in his own home. Disappointment filled Bella, but she fought it down. His well-being was the main issue. Where he convalesced was a lesser concern. "That would work well."

"Indeed. Now, we only have to clear up the current case," Richard replied with a twist of irony. "You've spoken with Jax?"

Bella nodded. "Twice." Briefly, she reviewed the highlights of their conversations. When she revealed his injured wrist and the additional harm to his right arm, Jenny and Richard exchanged solemn glances.

"He's sure it's only a sprain and not a break?" Richard asked, his brow furrowed with anxiety.

"He is. I'm no expert, but that seems to be the case." Bella summarized her Sunday night conversations with Marjorie and Anita. She included Anita serving the adulterated refreshments to Jax.

"She bears watching, but I wonder why the nurse referred to the cook's assistant as a pest. Did you feel like Anita was a nuisance?" Jenny posed the question.

"Not at all. She seems lonely, and working in the kitchen isn't an easy job," Bella observed. "With twenty patients, the Lennings, Major Billings, and some employees, they have a lot of mouths to feed."

"Plus, it's hard work in a hot room," Jenny said in agreement.

"Did either Anita or Marjorie mention Miss Bounder?"

"Only in passing. They didn't seem to be aware she'd spoken to Miss Corning," Bella replied, "or didn't want to say so. Marjorie was more talkative at breakfast this morning, and she introduced me to everyone."

"Good," Richard said. "Any thoughts about the employees?"

"Yesterday, Arnold Drier, an orderly, went upstairs with me. He seems to be a harsh sort. Not interested in the patients' welfare. Today, the other orderly accompanied me. Warren Starling. He's more pleasant, but both of them were eager to eat their own meals, which is why I had chances to speak privately with Jax." Bella went on to discuss Nurse Artem and Ian McNulty.

"It's interesting Nurse Artem warned you to avoid going into the garden at night," Jenny commented.

"I wondered about that, too." Bella laid down her sandwich, which she had been nibbling off-and-on.

Richard took a swallow of coffee before chiming in. "I have to wonder if Aaron Corning is still on the grounds. They might be holding him some place. A shed perhaps?"

"I've only seen part of the garden. No building is near the main one, but it's large with lots of trees around it. A boxwood hedge, too. There's a gazebo, but it's open, of course." Bella tapped her fingers on the chair arms. "Jax noticed the garden has a few gas lamps but, beyond there, it's pitch-black at night. Anyone going to the river would need a light."

"Does he have a view of the river from his room?" Jenny asked.

Bella simply nodded, since she didn't want the older couple worrying about Jax taking a tumble off the rickety dresser. "Mine does, too. I looked out last evening, and it would be very hard to see without artificial light. I'm planning to stay at Ballantyne tonight, but I can watch when I'm back at Poplar Pines."

"Don't sit up all night," Jenny, her motherly tone evident, said.

"I won't," Bella assured her before turning to Richard. "Jax thinks he can sneak out of a regular room once he's in one. The doors are kept locked, but he mentioned a lock pick."

As soon as her observation was out, Bella saw Richard bend his head as if something on his plate was of the utmost interest. Then, he took a big bite of sandwich. Unsure if she should press him, Bella waited. After a moment, Jenny spoke.

"You're very quiet, dear."

Richard kept chewing and pointed to his full mouth. Neither woman said anything. A charged silence followed before he spoke. "Lawmen sometimes use picks."

Jenny pursed her lips. "Bella and I are aware of that. Before we took Jax to the sanatorium, you warned him not to put anything in his bag that might create suspicion. A lock pick falls into that category, so how would he obtain one? You two exchanged a few private words Saturday afternoon before we left."

As his wife's last statement hung in the air, Richard shifted in his seat. "He asked if I could bring him one, and I agreed. We can take it on Wednesday."

Bella shook her head. "From what I've observed, patients don't wear anything with deep pockets."

Richard's brow furrowed. "I didn't consider that. Are visitors searched?"

"Not that I know of," Bella replied, "but Jax won't have a place to hide a pick."

After a long inhalation, the senior lawman focused on Bella. "If you wear a skirt with deep pockets, you could take it to him. In fact, you could unlock the door. Then, he won't be rambling around on his own. Less likely to get in trouble that way."

"That seems rather risky," his wife said.

"Arabella has good sense. Besides, neither of them needs to be searching without a solid reason." Richard paused briefly. "They've gotten some bits. Maybe looking around at night will add to the pile. We have to find out if Aaron Corning is still alive and being held on the grounds."

Jenny moved to perch on the edge of her chair. "It's possible, but why not kill him right off? I've been thinking about that when I wake up and can't get back to sleep."

A shrug moved his broad shoulders. "Aaron was seen in his room only hours before his sister called from the Bridgeling hotel. When she got the runaround, she drove to Poplar Pines. Whoever is involved in getting rid of patients probably didn't want a body being found on the day she got there. Or have anyone get caught in the act of killing him. Besides, the moon will start waning soon. Less natural light means it'll be easier to get him out—if he's still around."

"That makes sense," Bella murmured, "but he could be dead. There are a lot of places to hide a body on the grounds."

"Very true, and I may be engaged in wishful thinking, but it's a gut feeling that I can't shake," Richard said.

Bella grinned. "And we never overlook our hunches." Richard had said as much many times.

Laughter left Jenny. "We certainly don't."

Richard chuckled. "The two of you have instincts and intuition as good as mine. What do you think?"

"I agree, dear. Odds are fair he's still alive."

Uncertainty held Bella momentarily mute. Were the odds really in Aaron Corning's favor? She figured everyone was guardedly optimistic, so she didn't comment. Instead, Bella focused on breaking Jax out of his room at night. It had merit, although he wouldn't like her being involved. "I could take the pick with me tonight."

Richard shook his head. "Nolen borrowed it because his mother locked herself out. I'll get it back and bring it Wednesday."

"All right," Bella replied.

"Just be careful, Bella." Jenny once again sounded motherly. "We don't want you getting caught with a lock pick."

"I will," Bella assured her. "I definitely will."

"Any additional important information? Other employees stand out in any way?" Richard asked. "I'll speak with Rufus again in the morning, so I can update him."

"Like I said, everyone was at breakfast, except the cook, Mrs. Barley, and Anita. I've seen the cook briefly. A bit of a curmudgeon."

"And they all live on the grounds?" Jenny asked.

"Yes. Most in the house. There's a cabin near the dock, where Ian McNulty, the gardener, lives." Bella provided a thumbnail sketch of the man.

"That, combined with Artem's warning, makes him interesting to me," Richard observed.

"To me, too." As Bella glanced from Richard to Jenny, she thought about previous investigations when Jax was always present at such meetings. Instead, he was in a perilous position, which only made her more eager to get back and help him. "I won't leave the sanatorium again until late Friday. I don't feel good about being away at all, though."

"We need reports," Richard reminded her. "You're the only one who can carry word to and from Jax."

Warmth crept into Bella's face. "Of course. That's why I was asked to be involved."

"You're in a tenuous spot with this case," Jenny said, "but your work is crucial. You've already gotten new information."

Bella shook off her anxiety. "I have a little more to share before I go. I didn't mention Major Billings. From what Marjorie and Sarah said, he's in a position of authority, so he may be a partner. He comes and goes as he pleases."

"Does he perform actual work of any kind?" Jenny asked.

"So far, I only know he meets with patients and tells them to buck up and such. He and Dr. Lenning stopped by the receptionist's desk today. They were concerned about me spending time alone with the patients in the attic and mentioned Jax." She repeated their assertions. "I told them he didn't have much to say, and Phinney barely talked at all."

A look of alarm crossed Richard's face. "Do you think someone listened in on you and Jax?"

"No, I don't. The floors are creaky up there. I would've heard footsteps." Bella took another bite of sandwich. "Jax is apt to be in a regular room soon, but I may not speak privately with him until then."

"Keep being cautious." Richard laid his plate aside and picked up a pad and pencil. "Anything else?"

"I told you I met all three nurses. Sarah Bailey, who works the afternoon shift, and I were the last ones at the table, and she has an interesting situation." Bella shared what the woman had revealed.

"How awful about her fiancé," Jenny said, her voice rich with empathy.

"Her comment about protecting him is interesting." Richard spoke without inflection.

"And rather troubling," his wife added.

"It bothered me, too," Bella said.

Jenny leaned back in her chair. "Her fiancé is very vulnerable, which means they could pressure her to ignore, or take part in, getting rid of patients."

A sick knot formed in Bella's stomach. Sarah had evoked deep sympathy, but maybe she didn't deserve it. "Would she be in trouble if she didn't report the crimes?"

"Not nearly as much as if she's involved," Richard replied. "She may not be. Remember, I'm a long-time lawman, and I get suspicious more easily than the two of you. That's one reason I value your involvement. Us coppers sometimes see guilt where there is none."

His wife offered a slight smile. "You're very astute, dear, but Bella and I will keep you from leaping to unwarranted conclusions."

"Thank you." A chuckle escaped him as he jotted something on his notepad. "I'll call Amos and get him working on some information about Major Billings. Rufus has already looked into all the staff, along with Samuel James. Did you see him?"

Bella shook her head. "He must not be an employee, so he may be a patient. I don't know any names except for Phinney. I should've asked for the name of Sarah's fiancé. She called him Dalton, so I suppose it's a first name."

"That's not of immediate importance. Finding out about James is more imperative." Richard grimaced. "If Rufus could get in touch with Miss Bounder, it'd be a big help."

"No one answers at her aunt's house?" Bella asked.

"Not even the housekeeper. I don't like that, either," Richard said.

"As far as James, isn't there a list of men in the sanatorium?" Jenny asked.

"Not that I've seen. I looked through all the unlocked desk drawers at the receptionist's station. There has to be one, and it ought to be readily available." Bella turned to Richard. "Do you think it's a bad sign or a simple coincidence?"

"I don't believe much in coincidence, especially when crimes are involved," he replied. "You've only been there a short time, but doesn't the receptionist sort mail? That might provide some clues."

"Supposedly, yes. Today, Mrs. Lenning did it, since it arrived when I was upstairs feeding Jax and Lieutenant Phinney." Bella finished her sandwich and laid the plate aside. "I don't feel like I've made much headway. Of course, Jax is very frustrated since he's isolated."

"You've had a busy two days and learned a lot," Jenny said. "Jax should be in a regular room soon. For now, he needs to rest and let his new injuries heal."

The older woman's admonition rang true to Bella. "I'll tell him what you said."

"Tell him I second Jenny's wisdom," Richard said. "It's only been two days. Finding out Aaron Corning's fate is the most pressing matter. If he's still alive, the guilty parties likely got spooked when his sister showed up. Murder for hire is serious business, and they'll be cautious longer. Of course, that's an opinion."

"A professional, experienced opinion," Bella said with a smile.

Richard's nod acknowledged her compliment. "You have a long drive in the morning, so we should wrap up our discussion. Any other details come up that we need to know on our end?"

"Not really. I haven't asked many questions, certainly none that would cause suspicion. I've mostly observed the staff and the patients who came down yesterday. It seemed odd only a few had visitors on Sunday. Some families live at a distance, and I expect fewer will come Wednesday evening."

"As long as we can see Jax, I'll be happy," Jenny said.

"I will, too." Richard focused on Bella. "Were families allowed to step outside on Sunday, or did they have to stay in the guest areas?"

"Most went out to the garden. Since visiting hours begin at four o'clock, you could go outside with Jax. That would give you almost three hours before darkness sets in," Bella replied. "I don't think there's a time limit on your stay."

"Good. We'll need some privacy. I'll also call Amos Derringer in the morning. I can relay what we know and see if he has news. Unfortunately, I won't get word to you until we visit on Wednesday." Richard picked up his coffee and took a long sip. "I hope we can chat with both you and Jax then."

"We'll need to arrive at the start of visiting hours because you'll be getting off work around five o'clock, won't you?" Jenny asked Bella. "With luck, we may have a few moments of privacy to chat with you, too."

Bella chewed on her lower lip as she considered possibilities. "Mrs. Lenning told me they expect everyone to help, as needed, because of staff shortages. She's asked me to assist already, like on Sunday. If she doesn't on Wednesday, I'll say I can pitch in. After all, I'll be staying there anyhow, so it's not like I have to get off work at a certain time."

"Wait to see if she asks you to help. That'd be better, since it wouldn't alert anyone to you having a questionable interest in what happens there," Richard said.

"I'm being careful not to be too inquisitive," Bella replied. Richard wasn't as hovering as Jax, but he repeated his warnings, too.

"Good," Jenny said. Her blue eyes focused on Bella. "You and Jax are in sensitive positions. I won't rest easy until this case is closed, and the two of you are back in Moreley."

"I hope that will be soon," Richard added.

Bella silently agreed with both of the Jenkinses because getting home, and having Jax nearby and safe, was always on her mind.

Tuesday proved to be long, mostly because Bella left Ballantyne before seven in the morning in order to be at the Poplar Pines front desk by eight. Her story about substitute teaching evoked no curiosity at home, which was a relief.

After rushing into the foyer, she saw Mrs. Lenning standing, arms across chest, as the clock struck the hour. Bella offered a smile. "I was able to pick up some items I needed." She lifted the bag in her hand.

"Put it in the corner, since your work day has started." With that, the woman turned on her heel and walked away.

Bella gritted her teeth. Thank goodness she didn't need this job and would leave soon. As a Signal Corps operator, Bella had strictly adhered to rules and regulations, but she'd never been chastised by her superiors. None had been as inconsistent as Mrs. Lenning, though. Imperious at times and rambling at others.

After quickly stowing her belongings, Bella took a seat at the desk. The morning went smoothly, with no further visit from the woman, but Bella was happy to see Marjorie enter the reception area. She wanted to maintain a cordial connection with the nurse, in the hope of learning more.

The other woman smiled at Bella as she paused at the front desk. "Did you enjoy your evening at home?"

Bella shrugged before shaping her answer as Harriet. "Mostly, I packed more things and made sure everything was in good order."

"If I can get a Saturday off, I could go home with you. A change of scenery would be pleasant."

A knot of anxiety formed in Bella's stomach. Inviting any-one to her fictional home was impossible, but quelling the idea might create suspicion, so she responded with care. "Do you often get Saturday off?"

Marjorie frowned. "No. Mostly, I try to save up and take off both Friday and Saturday. Of course, we're always shorthanded, which means I've had to cancel plans at the last minute. Any time one of us nurses gets a day off, someone else has to take extra shifts. Sarah is very good about pitching in, but she has more reason."

The comment piqued Bella's interest. "She told me about her fiancé being a patient here. Such a sad case."

"It is. He isn't responsive, but Sarah is open to any sort of treatment even though none has worked in the ten months he's been a patient. Desperate, I suppose. I feel sorry for both of them."

"Sarah has worked here for all ten months?"

"About that long. His parents admitted him right before last Christmas, and she started a week later. His mother and father came to fill out the paperwork and haven't been back. Sarah makes all the decisions about Dalton's care, and she meets privately with Dr. Lenning and Major Billings periodically."

Another interesting tidbit. "I don't see much of either man." After yesterday's encounter, Bella preferred to avoid the pair.

"Billings rarely interacts with the help, which is fine with me." Her voice lowered a fraction. "As for Dr. Lenning, he spends a good deal of time in his office. But I didn't come over to chat. Mrs. Lenning wants you to help in the dining room. We have a couple of patients who have trouble feeding themselves, as you already know."

"What about the ones upstairs? I've helped them the past two days." Even if an orderly stayed in the room, Bella wanted to see Jax and make sure he was all right.

"They moved to regular rooms late last night. They're the ones who need help in the dining room today."

Relief filled her. Jax was out of that tiny, dark, dusty space. And she could talk with him. "I'm happy to assist them."

"Mrs. Lenning will be in her office with the doors open, so she'll keep an eye out for deliveries and such. I'll walk down with you, since I pitch in where needed, too. Once I make sure everyone is settled with their meals, I'll head back upstairs. I need to get medications ready."

"Are drugs stored on the patient floor or does Dr. Lenning have them in his office?" Bella posed the question as she fell into step beside Marjorie.

The nurse sent her a sidelong glance. "Nurses can administer medicine." Her clipped tone matched her faster stride.

Bella fell silent until they entered the sun-filled dining area. At each of the four large oak tables, placed in the corners, sat a handful of men. For a moment, she scanned the faces before recognizing Jax. "I see a patient over there who may need assistance." Bella gestured toward his table. "I helped him upstairs."

"Lieutenant Douglass definitely can't cut his food or probably butter bread." Marjorie once again sounded open and friendly.

The urge to hurry over warred with the need to maintain her cover. After yesterday's conversation with Lenning and Billings, Bella was even more intent on being circumspect. "He seemed cooperative when I was helping upstairs."

A smile touched Marjorie's lips. "Very much so. I haven't had a lot of contact with him, but he's quiet and pleasant. From looking at his file, it seems his biggest issues are nightmares and insomnia. Since he sleeps poorly, the lieutenant was dozing at home during the day. According to his aunt and uncle, who brought him, he can't hold a job. Naturally, they want him to be productive, which is why he's here."

"Because he's in poor shape, I'll start with him." Quickly, Bella made her way to Jax's table. His blonde head was bowed, but she took the empty chair next to him. Once again, she focused on playing her role as Harriet Halliday, a challenge when she was with him. "Hello, lieutenant. You might not remember me, but I brought you meals when you were upstairs." His green gaze flickered over her face without revealing a trace of recognition. Was he more heavily sedated? The glazed look in his eyes most likely resulted from drugs, but how many more had he been given? And how often? Why wasn't he continuing to avoid swallowing the sedatives? Was he getting injections? Uneasiness crept through Bella as she glanced around the table. The three others looked as dazed as Jax.

"I remember you."

His voice sounded rusty but, when Bella turned her attention back to him, Jax winked. A genuine smile curved her lips as relief flooded her. He was acting out his own role, although how he made his eyes look glassy, she couldn't fathom. "I thought I'd help you with your meal. Butter your roll and cut your meat?"

His green gaze twinkled before he replied, "Yes, I could use help with both."

"I'd be happy to do that for you." Bella took the fork and knife and began slicing the chicken into bite-size chunks." Finally, he was getting hot food.

"Thank you," he said.

While Jax ate, Bella looked around the table. None of the men made eye contact with her, nor did they talk to one another. When she glanced at the other clusters, she noted some patients were chatting, although none appeared animated. Again, she wondered at the efficacy of the treatments, such as they were. As she briefly focused on each face, Bella noticed some familiar ones—men who'd had visitors on Sunday. They looked livelier, but what did it mean? Anything of importance? This case was completely unlike others she had worked with Jax. Were they doomed to fail due to the complicated circumstances? Bella shook off the negative notion. The dead deserved justice, and Aaron Corning's fate had to be determined soon, especially if he was still alive and on the property. But where? She glanced around the table again. "Does anyone else need help?" They didn't seem to, but Bella wanted to appear unbiased.

"No, thank you, miss," one replied. The others shook their heads.

Bella offered what she hoped was a reassuring smile. "Tell me if you do." She turned back to Jax, who was awkwardly trying to feed himself. "Do you need more help, lieutenant?"

He shot her a glare, but his verbal response did not show displeasure. "No, thank you, Miss..."

"Miss Halliday," she supplied. "Harriet Halliday." He was struggling to eat, but Bella didn't offer to assist him again.

"Of course." Jax spoke without inflection or interest.

After he finished his food, Nurse Artem came by the table. She glanced around the group before addressing Jax and Lieutenant Phinney. "You're scheduled to meet with Major Billings in the side parlor at two o'clock. Don't be late." She turned to Bella. "You can take Douglass out for a short time, Miss Halliday. He's been inside ever since he arrived, so a bit of fresh air might do him good." The woman looked directly at Jax. "Would you like that?" Her tone sounded like she was addressing a small child, not a war veteran.

"Yes, ma'am," he replied in a flat tone.

"Miss Halliday will take you. Be good for her," the woman said.

"We could sit in the gazebo. I saw it from the windows, and it looks charming." Bella offered the idea because the structure not only reminded her of a similar one in their town center, it was far enough away from other seating that they wouldn't be overheard.

Nurse Artem scowled at Bella. "You can't sit there. Someone should have told you that, since we've all been warned. There's dry rot, so it isn't safe."

"We'll find another place," Bella readily agreed.

"See that you do," Artem said before moving on.

Bella withheld comment to Jax but again asked if any of the other men needed help. None did, so she rose from her seat while Jax did the same.

Once outside, she led him to a bench at the far end of the garden. Two other patients were already enjoying the day, so Bella nodded as she and Jax passed them. When they were settled, she turned to him with a smile. "I'm glad we can talk in relative privacy."

"Me, too, but I'm surprised the nurse suggested you bring me outside. She's been terse with me, and this seems like a special privilege."

"The first one you've had since you got here. But it surprised me, too. I haven't heard anything about Nurse Artem's position being superior to the other two nurses, although she evidently has more leeway in taking time off. Maybe one of the Lennings directed her to let you come outside. Or Major Billings. Her warning about the gazebo seemed harsh. It looks sturdy. Freshly painted, but maybe that hides the rot." Bella gestured toward the structure. "The rope would keep anyone from going up the steps."

"I agree. I'll keep my eye on her, as much as I can."

Bella would, too. "How are you feeling?"

One corner of his lips moved into a half-smile. "Somewhat groggy. Before I moved to a regular room, I got an injection."

"That explains why your eyes look slightly glazed."

He grimaced. "I feel somewhat off-kilter to go with it."

Uneasiness filled Bella. "Do you think you'll be given shots now?"

He shook his head. "Nurse Artem came with the syringe last night. I was out until this morning, when Nurse Mayfair came in with pills. I ditched them when she turned her attention to Dalton Miniger, one of my roommates. In any case, I doubt if I'll get regular injections." Jax paused briefly. "You're right about Miniger's demeanor. No outward signs of awareness. Really tragic, but not unusual. The other bed is empty, although Mayfair said the man should be back from treatment later today or tomorrow."

"I wonder where the treatments are carried out. When Mrs. Lenning gave me a tour, I didn't see any exam rooms or even the patients' quarters. I haven't asked, and no one has volunteered information."

"Don't ask." Jax looked into the distance. "Since Phinney and I are meeting with Billings later this afternoon, treatment may be mentioned then."

Although Jax maintained a calm tone and expression, Bella felt a surge of anxiety. Only strict control kept her from letting it show, since he didn't need to bear her fear along with everything else. "I haven't seen the private areas, either. The Lennings reportedly have large suites at the north side of the building. Billings has a small suite there, too. I got that from the staff dining table."

"Where does Mrs. Barley stay?"

"Her quarters are near the kitchen at the back of the place." Another discovery, made since she had last seen Jax, surfaced. "There's a little library off that hallway, too. When this place was a residence, it was used as a schoolroom for the help's children. Or so I was told. A large pantry is next to it. Both are kept locked, but the library door was ajar earlier today, so I asked about the room. I got a terse reply and a suggestion—almost an order—to move on. I saw enough to know Aaron Corning can't be in there." Bella chewed on her lower lip. "Do you think he might be held in the pantry? It's also along that hall. Richard has a gut feeling he's alive and here somewhere."

"It's possible, but a room by the kitchen? That seems too close." Jax looked around the garden and beyond.

"Could he be in McNulty's cabin? It's near the dock. You can't see it from here, but the place is visible through the window of my room. After I met him the other morning, I looked."

"Maybe. From the attic, I could see a boathouse. It wouldn't be the best place to hide someone, but it is a possibility."

Fresh frustration filled Bella. "The main building is enormous, and the property is expansive. A shed could be in the woods, and there must be a storm cellar some place. We have one below the inn in case of a tornado. Most old homes do."

Jax sat up straighter. "The door to yours at Ballantyne is accessible only from the outside, but I've seen houses that had access from the interior. Some had a tunnel to the cellar. What if that's the case here?"

"I've seen a couple like that, but where is the entrance? The two houses I was in with interior access had an entry from near the kitchen. I didn't see any extra doors there."

"Same with the ones I've seen."

As Bella drummed up mental images of the sanatorium's back hallway, she had another idea. "The little library is close to the outside exit."

"And it's never open?"

"Only the one time that I've seen. It's been locked otherwise."

A sigh of frustration left him. "A pick would come in handy."

Bella grinned. "Richard plans to bring one. If we can manage, he'll give it to me since you have no decent pockets."

Jax glanced down at his hospital attire. "You're right." Once again, he met her gaze. "How will you get the pick to me? I'll always be wearing this awful garb while I'm here."

A heartbeat passed before she responded. "I'll bring it to your room at night."

His gaze narrowed. "All right, but how will I get it back to you?"

Bella didn't hesitate a moment in responding. "I'll go with you."

"Oh, no." His answer was quick and sharp. "If I get caught, I don't want you around."

"We won't get caught." She made her reply just as firm and pointed. "I won't bring the pick to you if I can't go along."

His jaw set in a stubborn line, while his eyes flashed with dismay. "We'll see what Richard says about that."

A triumphant smile surfaced. "Richard already agreed."

Jax shook his head, but his expression relaxed. "Of course, he did. Just be careful."

"Always." Out of the corner of her eye, Bella saw Mrs. Lenning on the veranda. "We better go in. I already got chastised for arriving this morning right at eight o'clock. I felt like an errant child."

Low laughter escaped Jax. "Is she such a harridan?"

"She's inconsistent in her attitude. Sometimes, she seems flighty. Other times, she's alert. This morning, she seemed put out, but I wasn't late. I was right on time."

"Maybe she didn't like you asking to go home yesterday when you're only supposed to take off Friday evening through Sunday morning."

"I suppose that could be the reason. But it doesn't have much to do with the case, except this isn't a pleasant place to work."

"Luckily, neither of us will be here for long."

His comment should have evoked relief, but uneasiness stalked Bella. Their other cases had been solved relatively fast. This one posed more complications and additional danger. Those worries never left her mind. She got to her feet, and Jax followed suit.

"I've got that meeting with Billings coming, so I should go inside myself."

"When you'll be lectured about *bucking up.*"

Jax grinned. "Probably so. I'll make an effort toward that end, just to avoid getting shots every few hours."

"Smart. You don't want to be difficult."

His smile widened. "Am I ever?"

Bella shook her head, but she couldn't help but grin in return. "No comment."

"You wound me." He laid his wrapped wrist over his heart.

The gesture reminded Bella that he'd already been injured at Poplar Pines, and a shiver rippled through her.

Jax's humor faded. "Are you cold?"

"No, I'm fine." She hoped he would be, too.

Mrs. Lenning, her voice rife with annoyance, called out. "Harriet, bring the lieutenant in. Major Billings is ready for him, and you need to return to work."

"We'll be right in." After watching the older woman retreat into the house, Bella turned back to Jax. "I'll see you later. I'm interested to learn more about the major."

"I am, too."

Jax braced himself before entering the parlor. Billings might only lecture, but he could mandate treatment. While he wasn't afraid of discomfort, Jax needed to investigate. Being subjected to electric shock or more isolation would throw a wrench into that.

"You're Douglass."

Jax's attention went to the figure by the mantel. Clean-shaven and square-jawed, he had an erect posture marking him as career military, as did his uniform. Medals, polished to brilliance, bedecked the left chest area of his tunic. Jax hadn't noticed details at their initial, brief meeting, but he'd wondered about the man always wearing his uniform. It still seemed strange.

"Did you hear me?" Billings asked.

The major hadn't actually posed a question, but Jax gave an answer. "Yes, sir. I'm Jack Douglass."

The other man's dark gaze narrowed. "Sit down. We're wait-ing for Phinney."

Jax took a chair. Billings said nothing more, so an uncomfort-able silence developed. Part of the problem for Jax was wanting to make progress in the case. Going undercover had seemed like a fine strategy, but he hadn't considered how much it would limit his exchanges with others. Team meetings, interviews, and crime scene perusals had been the stock in trade of other inves-tigations, as had Bella being his partner. More often than not, she got important insights that he missed. Although her original task had been taking notes and playing chauffeur, because of his war wounds, Bella had quickly done much more in several cases. She still was. He just wished they could talk any time, not in fits and starts. Almost unconsciously, he massaged his right bicep with his bandaged left hand. Both ached intermittently. Abruptly, Billings' voice broke into his thoughts.

"Are you clumsy, Lieutenant Douglass? I heard about your tumble after arriving and about your injuries in France. Getting shot twice within a few weeks is cause for concern."

The major's harsh tone and haughty expression were at odds with other people's impressions of him. But those people weren't patients. Evidently, Billings was affable with outsiders, but tough with men who were hospitalized. When the man spoke again, Jax's assessment was confirmed.

"I knew of more than a few junior officers who wanted to get off the line for a while. They thought being wounded would make them heroes. Tin heroes. Genuine leaders want to be in the thick of battle."

His initial reaction was to defend his fellow junior offi-cers, most of whom had been courageous and selfless. But he couldn't afford to be at odds with Billings, not when the man might have leeway to stick Jax back in the attic—or worse.

When Jax didn't reply, the major released a harrumph. "Nothing to say for yourself? Not surprising. There's no excuse for cowardice."

Jax ground his teeth until he thought they might crack, but he kept silent. Finally, Phinney appeared in the doorway, and Billings turned his attention to the newcomer.

"You're late. Sit down so we can start." Billings scowled, as if tardiness was a personal affront to him.

Phinney blinked in confusion.

"I said, sit down, lieutenant." The major barked out the order.

A tremor rippled through Phinney's thin frame as he shuffled across the room and took a seat. His gaze, heavily shadowed, briefly rested on Jax before skittering away. The young man seemed to be in poor shape, or he was an excellent actor. If the former was true, men like Phinney needed and deserved proper treatment. If the latter was the case, Jax needed to find out why quickly. Phinney hadn't been at the place long enough to take part in disappearances. Could he know anything useful? Jax doubted it but he wasn't dismissing the idea.

Billings didn't take the third chair. Instead, he stood in front of the fireplace with his arms crossed over his chest. Jax noticed the gesture didn't cover the medals, which was surely intentional.

"Gentlemen, you are relatively new to Poplar Pines. It's important you follow the rules and not cause trouble. Your families are paying good money for your stays here, and you'd be wise to keep that in mind."

The warnings created more curiosity. Richard had indicated his nephew was a problem, which could make him open to leaving *Jack* indefinitely, or eliminating him. What had Phinney's family said? Something similar?

After staring daggers at both men, Billings continued. The orientation, such as it was, continued for another hour. The major repeated the need to be strong and not give in to depression. Jax made mental notes to tell Bella. Not much pertained to the case, but she might have a fresh slant on the lecture. He hoped so and, with some luck, they'd have a few private moments during dinner to talk again.

Chapter Nine

Luck proved to be on their side. As Bella was wrapping up her stint at the front desk, Mrs. Lenning approached her. Her expression wasn't as severe as earlier, but the words were more order than request.

"You're probably ready to go to your room, but you've been such a help with our patients who can't eat on their own. Lt. Douglass is a particular problem, what with two bad arms. You've dealt with him already, so I hope you'll consider doing so again. I've enlisted Marjorie to assist another one of our most crippled boys."

The words *crippled boys* made Bella's skin crawl. So did the older woman's cloying tone. None of them were boys. They were men wounded in spirit. "Of course, I'll help."

"Come along then. Patients are already coming down. You can eat afterward."

Bella followed the other woman into the dining room. A few men were seated and platters of food were on the tables. Almost immediately, she caught sight of Jax sitting alone at the farthest end of the space. Perhaps, they could have a few moments of privacy before others joined him. "I see Lieutenant Douglass. I'll go over now." Mrs. Lenning nodded, and Bella hurried to Jax's table. "Good evening."

He rolled his eyes. "For some, I'm sure it is." The indistinct murmur didn't carry far.

With a chuckle, Bella sat down. "Let me cut your meat up."

"I saw you walk in with Mrs. Lenning. I assume she asked you to help me."

"She did. You have her convinced that your arms are badly damaged." Bella didn't share the woman's characterization of him as one of the *most crippled*. Instead, she finished her task and put the plate back in front of Jax. "Are they bothering you a lot?"

"Not really."

The nonspecific answer and stiff posture gave her pause. "One is in a sling, so you must still have some trouble." A long, low breath escaped her. "Your right shoulder hurts? Or your bicep? Or did more shrapnel work its way out?"

After taking a bite and laying the cutlery down, Jax exhaled sharply. "You know me too well."

"I wouldn't say *too well*, since I'd like to know you better." As soon as the words were out, heat scorched Bella's cheeks.

"Good to hear." A laugh rumbled out before Jax quashed it and schooled his expression. "As much as I want to learn more, let's stick to the case right now."

"Yes, let's," Bella replied, embarrassed by her outburst. Good heavens, she sounded like some flirtatious flapper, not a lifelong friend. But friendship might be on the way to becoming more. She cleared her throat. "I haven't seen much of the major. What did you think of him?"

"He was career military, and it shows. *Buck up* was only part of his spiel. He definitely believes soldiers with shell shock are weak and cowardly. Real men go through battle without mental problems, according to him. He wasn't as pleasant with us as with you, Miss Corning, or Jenny and Richard."

"Probably wants to make a good impression on workers and relatives, which is interesting. Underneath, he may be different," she murmured.

"I don't believe he's different than he seemed today with Phinney and me. His nicer attitude is the façade. He indicated we need to avoid causing problems, overcome sad thoughts, and realize our families are paying dearly for care. He didn't mention specific procedures other than isolation, but we knew about that. Phinney went ashen. I don't know if he could handle being in the attic again, and I have to wonder if that's a step toward getting rid of problem patients."

Revulsion swept over Bella. "What about other treatments?"

"Right now, I'm not sure. Sticking troublemakers away is the cheapest, easiest way to deal with them."

"Rufus is trying to contact families who took their sons out quickly, since he has two names from the employees who left." She had learned as much before leaving Ballantyne early that morning, since the senior constable had spoken to the sheriff around dawn and then, called Bella. Luckily, she had answered the call, so no one at Ballantyne was suspicious about her current job.

"That would be very helpful, so I hope he hears soon."

"Maybe Richard and Jenny will know tomorrow." She chewed on her lower lip. "So far, I haven't heard about actual procedures, either."

Jax rubbed his bandaged wrist. "Like we've discussed, not much is done here. My other roommate will be back from wherever he is today, I think. That's a puzzle."

"It is," Bella agreed. "If he was in the attic, I didn't see any trace of him." But Arnold hadn't answered her question about the closed doors.

"I hope he returns," Jax said. "As for most of the activities, they seem to be talking with the major, isolating troublemakers and new patients, heavy sedation for the unruly, lighter medications for everyone else. I haven't witnessed or heard about anything else. That gives us three reasons to solve this case. Solving the deaths, finding Corning—hopefully alive—and getting all these men appropriate help."

Bella looked around the room. "They deserve that, especially the ones whose families may resort to extreme measures to rid themselves of a burden." After she cut the snap beans to manageable size, she glanced back at Jax. "It infuriates me to think the place is a money-making mill."

"Me, too." His nostrils flared with a sharp intake of breath. "This is one of my most complicated, pressing cases."

While Jax spoke, Bella cut up more of his food. "It's a conundrum. What about Phinney? You said he was anxious, but how did Billings treat him?"

"Phinney was quiet during the orientation, and, other than to shoot him an occasional glance, Billings ignored him. Of course, he didn't say anything directly to me once he launched into his lecture." His brow furrowed. "I found out Phinney only got here a few days before I did. I doubt if he knows anything useful, although I can't be sure. Of course, there's very little that's certain in this case."

The exasperation in Jax's voice made Bella offer reassurance. "It's always that way for a while. More clues will come out, and we can piece them together."

"I'm depending mostly on you this time."

Bella's heart stutter-stepped. Jax's attitude toward her involvement in his cases had transformed over the past two years and, most especially, over the last few months. Although he'd issued a warning early on, and mentioned his continuing concern on Sunday, he wasn't fussing over her. "I won't let you down."

"I know." He winked.

For several seconds, silence ensued. Abruptly, it ended with the arrival of Drier and another patient. "Sit here," the orderly said in a harsh tone. Then, he turned away without a word or a glance for Bella.

The newcomer—tall and lean—nodded before helping himself to food from the platters. A lot of food. Bella stared as he shoveled it in. After a moment, he shrugged.

"Sorry, but I'm starving," the man said. "I've been in isolation for four days. Bread and water would've been great. Just got water, though."

The revelation sent dismay hurtling through Bella. Four days without food was punishment, not treatment.

"You wouldn't be Dalton Miniger's roommate, would you?" Jax asked.

"Sam James," he replied, but didn't look up, "and I'm in the same room as Dalton."

The revelation piqued Bella's interest, since Miss Bounder had mentioned this man to Miss Corning. What was his significance?

James' gaze narrowed on Jax. "Who are you?"

"Jack Douglass. I arrived Saturday and just got put in a regular room. Your room." Jax jerked a thumb at Bella. "This is Miss Halliday, the receptionist."

James nodded at Bella. "They replaced Miss Bounder fast."

Unsure what to make of the man's attitude, Bella smiled. "I was happy to start right away. I really need a job." She wanted to ask where James had been held but resisted. While patients weren't apt to be involved in the dirty doings, it was possible. It was even possible James wasn't actually a patient. Perhaps he was a plant to make it easier to get rid of people. Despite his voracious appetite, he could be lying about being in isolation for several days.

"Desperation seems to drive many folks around here." James returned to his food with zeal.

"My aunt and uncle were at wit's end, which is how I ended up as a patient," Jax said.

James glanced up. "Do they have money?"

"Some. Why?" Jax acted innocent.

For a long moment, the other man held Jax's gaze. "No particular reason."

Bella felt sure the response wasn't true. James knew something, but what? "How long have you been a patient, Mr. James?"

"They use military titles here," he replied, "so it's Captain James. I got here two weeks ago. Spent several days in isolation, got put in a room, and sent up to the attic again."

"May I ask why you were upstairs a second time? I'd like to avoid that." Jax looked suitably uneasy. "It wasn't a pleasant experience."

A harrumph left James. "It'll be less pleasant if you go again. Like I said, no food and one pitcher of water all day. You won't have my problem, so don't worry about it."

The cryptic comment served to further unnerve Bella. Unable to hold her tongue, she asked, "What problem?"

"None of your business, Miss Halliday," Captain James said.

The arrival of several others prevented further comments. Bella cut up food, buttered bread, and added sugar to coffee. Not all the newcomers required help, but they seemed to enjoy attention. Except to murmur their thanks, the men spoke very little. While she wanted to ask pertinent questions, as she and Jax had done during previous cases, Bella avoided being intrusive. Getting information while maintaining an undercover role wasn't easy, and the excitement of the new responsibility was gone. Determination and anxiety had taken its place.

As each patient left the table, she bid them *good evening*. She hoped Jax would linger, but he left amid the others. James fell into step behind him. The man had must have information, which he wasn't sharing with her. Bella hoped he was more forthcoming with Jax.

After helping clear the tables, Bella headed to her room. Marjorie was coming off duty at the same time. "It's been a long day," the young nurse said. "I suppose Mrs. Lenning roped you into helping at dinner."

"I didn't mind," Bella replied. "Some men have trouble handling cutlery. Even getting a spoonful of sugar into coffee was challenging for a couple." Their tremors had made the task difficult and embarrassing. Two had strained to get cups to their lips, but they soldiered on. Jax had, too, but he drank very little of the hot brew. After other men joined them, he'd avoided accepting her help. Male pride, no doubt.

"It's sad. Some will never be back to normal." Sympathy joined the fatigue on Marjorie's youthful face.

"Time and treatment can work wonders, from what I've heard." Bella made a statement but hoped Marjorie would expand on the comment, as if the words made up a question.

The other woman shrugged. "Some spend weeks here. A few stay for months. I'm guessing a handful might not leave at all. Three have been here ever since the place opened. They get company, and they're no trouble."

While the reply wasn't as communicative as Bella wished, it was revealing since the nurse didn't mention therapy at all. "That must get expensive for families."

"I'm sure it does, and it's often like pouring money down an open drain." Marjorie put one hand to her mouth as if that would hold back the words. "Don't repeat that."

"Don't repeat what?"

Bella looked up to see Anita staring daggers at Marjorie, who quickly replied.

"Don't repeat how long this day has been. I'm sure you feel the same way, since you've been in the kitchen for hours."

Anita looked skeptical as she glanced from Bella to Marjorie and back. "Every day is the same. We all knowed when we started here that hard work and long hours was expected."

The response surprised Bella. During the previous encounter between Anita and Marjorie, the nurse had sounded harsh. Now, the kitchen assistant did. Turmoil among the staff wasn't necessarily related to the case, but Bella noted such exchanges before focusing on the moment at hand. "Would the two of you like to come in and chat? I still have a few muffins." Her gaze went to the large flask in Anita's hands. "Maybe you'd share your tea or coffee with us?"

Anita fell silent but, after a long moment, Marjorie spoke. "That sounds lovely."

The nurse's expression didn't match her words, and Bella held her breath. She would love to observe the pair and see if they revealed anything useful. Sometimes, how something was said was as important as the actual words.

Long moments passed before Anita nodded. "That would be nice."

"Come in." Bella opened the door and led the way into the small room. "I haven't really gotten settled yet."

After Marjorie sat on the sole chair and Anita perched on the bed, the cook's assistant spoke. "You don't have no pictures of your family. You said your folks died when you was little, but don't you got no photographs?"

For the first time, Bella realized not putting homey touches in her room might spark curiosity. Unwanted curiosity. In France, she'd always had three photographs at hand: two of her with Matt and Jax, and another of her parents. She couldn't put out a picture of Jax, but she could bring a family shot. If the case wasn't wrapped up before Friday evening, when she went home again, she would. "I'll still be spending a couple of nights a week at my aunt's home, but a few photographs and such would make the space more cheerful." Bella pulled two cups, left by a previous occupant, off the shelf as she spoke. Then, she retrieved the tin of muffins.

"We should meet in my room sometime. I brought everything I could from home," Marjorie said. "It's comfortable and pretty, with a quilt and nice pillows. I have framed needlepoint and photographs, too."

"Sounds very pleasant," Bella replied.

Anita handed the thermos to Bella, who opened it before pouring coffee into the cap and the two cups. When each woman had the beverage, she offered muffins. Several moments passed while they enjoyed their snack. "We should invite Sarah to join us some time, although I suppose she's on duty now." Bella offered the suggestion.

A frown pulled down the corners of the young nurse's pink lips. "She is. I don't see much of her. Often, she spends free time with Dalton. Nurse Artem welcomes the help when she comes on duty. Not that she ever puts herself out."

But the woman had suggested Bella take Jax outside. Why? Disquiet beset her. Were they under suspicion? Another potential pitfall was Sarah spending time at night with her fiancé, Jax's roommate. They would need to be cautious in moving about after hours.

Marjorie, getting to her feet, interrupted the troubling thought. "I'm exhausted, so I really must get to bed. Thank you for the refreshments."

Bella had barely bid the nurse good evening when Anita rose. "Thanks. I need my sleep, too. You can bring the thermos down in the morning."

With that, Bella was alone in her room. Alone with a few additional details and less confidence about wrapping up the case quickly. After stowing the muffin tin and flask, she went down the hall to the lavatory. Following a sponge bath, Bella returned to her room, put on her nightgown, and climbed into bed. But sleep was a long time coming.

Chapter Ten

Wednesday proved to be frustrating. Mrs. Lenning didn't call on Bella for help at breakfast or lunch, which added to Bella's anxiety. What if she couldn't speak with the Jenkinses or Jax today? How would she obtain the lock pick? What about Samuel James? What was his role? Had Jax learned more about the man? Too many questions weighed on her mind and dragged down her spirits. Typing letters for Mrs. Lenning proved to be tedious, as did sorting the mail.

When visitors began to arrive around four o'clock, Bella was glad for the diversion. Since dinner coincided with the start of visiting hours, some of the staff needed to supervise patients and their families as they enjoyed the garden, while others helped prepare for the evening meal. As part of the efforts, Mrs. Lenning again asked Bella to leave her post and help. Some of her worries dissipated. At least she would see Jax and probably Jenny and Richard.

"I'll be in the foyer to greet relatives as they arrive, but we could use your assistance with the evening meal. Some guests will eat with us, along with the patients. It creates more work, but we have to cater to those who pay the way." Mrs. Lenning looked and sounded professional and controlled.

"Of course," Bella agreed. "Do you want me to come right away?"

"No, later on. For now, chat with the visitors and lead them to the back veranda, if they don't know the way."

Before Mrs. Lenning could say more, Richard and Jenny Jenkins entered the foyer. Relief flooded Bella, but she reminded herself not to show any trace of recognition. As she did with other visitors, she smiled and said, "Good afternoon. Are you here to visit a family member?"

The couple stopped in front of her desk. "Yes, our nephew Jack Douglass is here," Jenny replied in a suitably pleasant but benign tone.

Mrs. Lenning offered a bright smile. "It's nice to see both of you again."

"We're looking forward to being with Jack." Jenny sounded enthusiastic.

"I hope he hasn't been too much trouble," Richard said in a less positive tone.

A sigh escaped the older woman. "Before you see him, I want to remind you that patients sometimes create stories out of whole cloth. Most don't want to be here, so they make up tales about mistreatment, odd goings-on, and such. That may be the case with Jack."

"I wouldn't be at all surprised," Richard said in agreement. "Don't worry, Mrs. Lenning. We won't take anything he tells us to heart. He's been a sore trial, to be sure."

Bella watched the exchange in dismay. The woman had skillfully and easily offered an excuse for any complaints Jax might make, something she probably did with every patient. No wonder families didn't become alarmed or suspicious. They were predisposed not to believe the men.

A smile wreathed Mrs. Lenning's face. "He's outside enjoying the lovely weather. The last time I saw him, he'd chosen a place at the far end. I can escort you."

The words were barely out of her mouth when Nurse Artem came scurrying down the hall. "We need your help in a room, ma'am," she said to her supervisor.

The older woman grimaced but nodded. "All right," she said before looking back at Richard and Jenny. "Miss Halliday will have to escort you to the garden." The woman turned her attention to Bella. "Don't take too long, but make sure they're settled with the lieutenant. Of course, be certain he's comfortable, too. Sometimes, our boys feel uneasy when relatives visit."

"Certainly," Bella assured her. Once the two women disappeared, she smiled at the Jenkinses. "Please come with me."

None of them spoke until they were on the wide veranda. Bella glanced around before saying in a whisper. "He must be in the little alcove down there." She gestured toward a niche in the far brick wall where two benches were barely visible. "I won't be able to stay, but he's really looking forward to seeing the two of you."

"We feel the same way about seeing him," Jenny replied.

The trio made their way to Jax, who sat staring into space. When he turned toward them, a smile lifted his lips. "Welcome, Aunt and Uncle."

"It's good to see you, son," Richard replied with sincere enthusiasm. Gone was the dismissive uncle who tried to highlight his impatience—and possible openness to getting rid of his nephew permanently.

Jenny, her expression troubled, was slower to respond. "How are your wrist and arm?"

"A little sore, but nothing serious," Jax replied. His gaze traveled to Bella. "How did you get to escort them out here?"

"Mrs. Lenning was called to some emergency. Otherwise, she would've come along."

Jax rolled his eyes. "A lucky break to avoid chatting with her." A smile curved his lips. "And to chat with you instead."

Warmth rose in Bella's cheeks. "I'm afraid I won't be able to stay long. I have to get back to the front desk in case I'm needed to help others."

Something akin to disappointment darkened Jax's green gaze. "I hoped we could all talk."

"Have you learned something new?" Bella asked.

"A little, and I wanted your opinion." Jax ran one hand over his face. "Maybe we can speak later."

"Is it something we need to discuss today?" Richard's tension was obvious in his tone and posture.

Bella watched as Jax glanced around them. No one was within earshot, which might be his concern. Her pulse sped up as she considered what he might have discovered since being in a regular room. A few minutes wouldn't hurt, so she perched on the edge of the bench while the Jenkinses sat on the matching one across from Jax.

"First off, Bella and I met Samuel James last night at dinner." Jax summarized the conversation for the older couple.

"If he's only been here a couple of weeks, he isn't apt to be part of the plotting," Richard said.

"Probably not, unless it was as an outsider," Jax agreed. "But, on the way to our rooms, one of the other men welcomed James back. No response from James, but when he got ahead of us, the other guy warned me to be careful. Evidently, James and Miss Bounder were seen chatting in private a few times before she took off."

"I wonder why," Bella said.

Richard ran a hand over his face. "I wish we could've talked to that receptionist."

"She's still out of touch?" Bella asked.

"Yes, she and her aunt are both still away. The other Bounder relatives don't have a telephone. The local lawman has been good about staying in touch with Rufus, and in seeing about another way to check on the women."

"Good. It's not likely I'll get much out of James. He isn't talkative, so I haven't gotten any place with him," Jax said.

"Does he have family?" Richard asked.

"Evidently, his brother drove him here, checked him in, and left," Jax replied.

"What about this man who approached you last night? Do you think he just wanted to warn you?" Jenny asked.

"Yep. I didn't see an ulterior motive. We were together slightly ahead of the others and the orderlies, so no one else heard us. I'm keeping the warning in mind. James might've been an outside contact and, instead of being in isolation, he could've taken off some place." Jax frowned.

"That scenario bodes ill for Aaron Corning," Richard put in. "If James left the place, even for a short time, he might've taken Corning with him."

A taut silence followed the statement. When Bella glanced from Jenny to Jax, she noted they looked as worried as she felt. Aaron Corning's fate was their top concern. Was it too late to help him?

"That's what disturbs me," Jax said after a moment.

"If James has been involved, maybe Miss Bounder was, too." Bella put both hands to her face. "Her offer to meet with Eleanor could've been a way to allay fears."

"But why did Miss Bounder mention Samuel James?" Jenny asked.

A harsh breath left Jax. "That's a good question, and I've got no answer. I don't feel like we're any closer to a solution. We've got vague ideas about who might be involved. As for why and how, I'm still stumped."

"Just observe James. He might give something away by accident," Richard said. "As for anyone suspecting you and Arabella of talking too much, aren't you still being asked to assist?"

"I am," she replied.

"Then, it should be fine," Richard said. "Anything else to share?"

"Unfortunately, no," Jax replied.

The senior constable turned to Bella. "Have you learned anything new?"

"I found out a few things, but I'm not sure any are especially valuable." She began with the previous evening's conversation with Anita and Marjorie, and her discussion with Jax about a hideaway. She summed up by saying, "The two are at odds, but I'm not sure why or if it means anything. Same with the little library by the kitchen. It could be important."

"Keep your eyes and ears open for now. I know you will." Richard turned to Jax. "Are you given free rein during the day?"

Jax shook his head. "When we come down for meals, they lock our door behind us, and we don't go back until evening. There's a day room, and some patients spend mornings there. One orderly is with us at all times. Not much conversation takes place, although I tried to chat with several men. Arnold made sure he stood within earshot when I did. Some play cards, which is how I can get away first. They usually wrap up a game before going to meals, so I go to the dining room as soon as possible, hoping to see Bella."

She smiled. "A clever strategy."

"It's one way to communicate. I don't have many others." His jaw tightened until a muscle twitched. "My past undercover work didn't prepare me for this. Nothing has."

"You're the one in the toughest spot," Jenny observed.

"You are," her husband agreed. "It's harder for me, too. One of the hardest in my experience. As Jax pointed out early on, it's a whodunit, howdunit, and whydunit. And he's right about having a few folks in the *who* category. Too many people."

Bella nodded. "That's a great summation. I feel like that, too, but I have a lot fewer experiences. I haven't seen lights or people at night. As for good clues, I'm not sure I have many." She described her most recent exchanges with other workers. "Not much of use. Has Sheriff Ayling spoken with any of the families who took relatives home?"

"No luck yet," Richard replied. "We could use some fresh information."

"Bella had another idea," Jax put in. "One about a possible escape route."

"We both had the idea," Bella said. "Jax and I wondered about a storm cellar with access from the building. It's not common, but we've both seen them."

"I have, too," Jenny said. "An interior door is very likely in a mansion, which Poplar Pines was. I suppose you have an idea about where the entrance might be."

Bella smiled. "The little library I mentioned could house a doorway. I've only seen the door ajar once. The back wall is all bookcases."

"A bookcase could hide a door." Jenny made the suggestion.

"My thought exactly," Bella said. "Another suspicious point is Nurse Mayfair was in there when I passed by. She noticed me, said it was a private area, and closed the door, but I got a quick glimpse before she did. I saw enough to know Aaron Corning isn't there."

"More and more interesting." Richard ran one hand over his face. "There's a good deal to consider."

"I sure wish I could check it out." Jax's attention went to Richard. "Bella said you might bring a lock pick along."

The senior constable beamed. "We did. Jenny has it in her pocketbook. Bella will take it, since you don't have deep pockets."

"Be careful, both of you," Jenny said. "We don't want you getting caught."

"We will," Jax assured her. "The last two nights, I didn't see Nurse Artem or Arnold after she brought the sedatives, which were in pill form. I held it in my mouth until they were both gone."

"They only administer sedatives once? Did the others sleep all night?" Jenny asked.

"I believe so, but we didn't get the medication until ten o'clock. I dozed off after that and woke before dawn. The other two slept another hour," Jax replied. "Nurse Mayfair came in then. In any case, I have plenty of time to look around, and I'll be careful."

If Jax thought he was investigating without her, he was wrong. "*We'll* be careful." Bella said. Jax looked like he would offer another objection, but he finally nodded.

"We will," Jax agreed.

"I'll put the pick in my skirt pocket and get it to Jax later tonight." Bella turned to the older couple.

Jax's green gaze narrowed on her. "How much later and how?"

Bella pursed her lips. After explaining the logistics, she said, "I'll wait until one o'clock, and I'll make sure Nurse Artem isn't out and about. She isn't apt to break her routine of snoozing every night."

"You're most likely right," Jax admitted. "Few of the employees seem concerned about patient welfare."

"Neither do the Lennings or Billings," Bella added. "In any case, we'll look around the library."

Jax studied her face for a long moment. Finally, he gave a slight nod. "All right. I can't say I like the idea of you coming to my floor and unlocking the door, but we have few options and, the sooner we figure out what's going on, the sooner we'll both be out of here. Hopefully, with Corning."

"I agree," Richard said.

"Let's tentatively plan on one o'clock tonight. Tomorrow morning, that is. I won't knock, but you'll hear the pick in the lock," Bella said.

Jax pressed his lips together, as if to halt further warnings. A moment passed before he nodded. "I'll sit close to the door, so I hear you."

"That sounds like a good plan," Jenny said, but her face was pale.

The older woman's reaction was a reminder of the danger involved. But solving the case was of paramount importance, and their options were few.

"A sound plan," Richard agreed, although his expression held more concern than confidence.

Bella appreciated the older couple's support and friendship. After swallowing the lump of emotion in her throat, she spoke again. "Aaron Corning could be hurt or drugged. What then?"

"I've been mulling that over since last night," Jax said. "None of us is armed, and I doubt if I can carry him out."

Dismay filled Bella. "Of course, you can't. You shouldn't try."

"I agree," Jenny said in a firm voice.

"If he's not mobile, you'll have to leave him. Arabella can make an excuse to go home tomorrow and come to us." Richard turned to Jenny. "Perhaps, your mother would make a call from Karston to report an emergency at Harriet Halliday's home. A fire or break-in, maybe."

"She'd be happy to help," his wife said.

"That would give me a reason to leave," Bella put in.

"If that's what happens, come to Moreley, but take the long route so no one gets suspicious." Richard spoke to Bella and then, to Jax. "We'll set up a raid, if you two find Corning but can't bring him along."

Jax nodded. "Locating him would be a big step forward."

"It sure would," Richard said.

"What if Corning can walk out himself?" Jax asked. "That's been our primary goal, but what about the rest of the case?"

"I'd like more evidence to solve the deaths, but his safety and yours is the top concern. Besides, once we have him, we'll find out who's involved. At least we'll find out who snatched him.

That could lead to all the suspects." Richard drove his fingers through his hair. "If you can get away with him, go ahead."

"The Chummy is parked about fifty yards from the building," Bella said. "On the north side of the property. There's an old apple orchard. We could slip through it without being seen."

"All that hinges on finding a hidden door and passage," Jax said. "What if the men were taken out through the back door and garden? Bella and I talked about Corning possibly being held in the gardener's cabin or even the boathouse."

Richard shook his head. "Don't go that far. It's too risky."

His wife looked around before speaking. "That gazebo in the middle could hide a trapdoor beneath the raised floor. Have you gotten close enough to see if the panels could easily be moved, Bella?"

Bella followed Jenny's gaze. The lovely white structure, raised three feet off the ground, had two paths leading to it—one on the side of the building and the other leading toward the back of the garden. Both were lined with shrubbery. For the first time, Bella noticed the bushes along the trail leading toward the river were nearly six feet tall. "The part going east is pretty well obscured. The lattice work around the bottom is in sections, so one could be taken out and replaced, as needed. Getting down the path without being seen wouldn't be difficult."

The older man shifted to look in the same direction as Jenny and Bella. "The river isn't visible from here. How far is it?"

"About two hundred yards from the gazebo, as far as I could tell from my room," Bella replied.

"The gazebo would be the perfect place for an underground tunnel to end," Richard observed.

"Very much so," Jenny agreed. "If there's a hidden corridor from the little library, they could spirit men out of the building through it, to the cellar—maybe beneath the gazebo. Then, on to the dock when it's safe to do so."

As Bella listened, she considered how to move forward. The full moon would wane over the next few days. By then, the conspirators would likely feel safe in getting rid of Aaron, if they hadn't already. She wanted to inspect the river side of the gazebo, but not in the middle of the night with Jax. Having him wander too far from his room seemed risky. Could she do it alone? Should she? More thought was required. For now, she would plan on meeting him and checking the little library for a secret door.

"You'll be able to see about a passage if you get behind the locked door tonight," Richard said.

"With a little luck, we'll also learn something about Aaron Corning," Jax said.

"And about his abductors," Bella said.

"We've got several suspects." Richard drummed his fingers on his legs. "It could be Billings and the doctor involved in nefarious activities. The mother may know, but not participate. Or she may be confused often enough to not realize what's going on."

"She's sharp at times, so the confusion may be an act," Bella said.

"Hard to say for sure." Jax met Bella's gaze. "Nurse Artem also interests me. Are we certain she sleeps most of her shift? Couldn't she go downstairs? Maybe to the little library?"

Bella pondered the point. "She could."

"Which means she and Billings might be among the guilty parties," Jenny suggested.

"Or both Lennings, the major, and Artem are involved." Richard made the observation.

"We can't forget about Samuel James, either." Jax released a pent-up breath. "We're not narrowing down the number of suspects."

"In this case, we may have to do that after we find out what's happened to Corning," Richard said. "Others could be involved, too. You've noted that the gardener's place is nicely isolated, so he could play a role."

Before anyone could comment, Mrs. Lenning appeared on the veranda. "I have to go." As Bella rose, Jenny reached into her voluminous pocketbook and pulled out the pick. Bella quickly shoved it into her skirt pocket before glancing back at Jax. "See you later." A brief nod was his only response.

When Bella got close to the veranda, she caught sight of movement in her peripheral vision. She turned in time to see Arnold Drier and Mrs. Lenning engaged in conversation. Their voices didn't carry, and their faces weren't visible. The two of them being together shouldn't be a cause for alarm, but Bella's nerves were constantly on high alert and seeing the pair together only increased the level.

Jax watched Bella go with conflicting feelings. When Richard commented, he realized those feelings must be on his face.

"I'm sure you still have misgivings about Arabella being involved in digging around with you, but she's a skilled sleuth and an intelligent person." The older man maintained a steady gaze.

Contradicting honest, astute observations would be foolish, so Jax didn't. "I don't disagree. In the past, she's had crucial insights in all our cases." He idly massaged his left wrist. "This is a thorny situation. Far more so than others I've investigated. I'm edgy due to that and because I haven't learned much worthwhile."

"Both you and Arabella have gotten some details that fill in the puzzle. We can't expect a lot more so soon. Not under these circumstances." Richard ran one hand over his face. "Being undercover and not able to meet with the rest of us regularly has to be tough, but I still believe having you here as a patient is the best strategy."

Jax shifted on the hard bench. "I know it is. We wouldn't get far interviewing people, and watching the place is virtually impossible, since it's so isolated."

"But you wish those strategies would work because that would be safer for Bella," Jenny observed.

A glance at her made him shake his head. The empathy etched on her face cut through his defenses. What was the sense of pretending Bella wasn't always on his mind? "I'm dealing with my worry, but it's still present."

"Understandable," Richard said. "This case won't last forever, and you'll be home to stay soon."

After a long moment, Jax agreed. "It just seems like I've been here for weeks instead of days. You're right, of course. Besides, something could happen any time. Tonight or tomorrow even."

Richard grinned. "You know what I always say about gut feelings."

Jax smiled in return. "I do." And he hoped they were both right.

Chapter Eleven

That evening, Bella got into her knickers, but kept the rest of her work outfit on. After the change, she tried to relax on her bed. An impossible task.

Every few minutes, she looked at her watch. The hands crept slowly around the dial. After ten o'clock, all activity in the hallway ceased. By eleven, silence filled the women's quarters. At midnight, she perched on the edge of the bed and waited. Intermittently, she gazed out the window.

Shortly after twelve, a lantern shone at the far end of the garden. Her heart banged hard against her ribs while her gaze riveted on the sight. Soon, a flashlight beam came from closer to the river. Two figures—one taller and broader than the other—were barely visible but, when the pair merged into one, Bella wondered if she was observing a clandestine tryst. The tall person had to be a man. Since Ian McNulty lived in the cabin, he was the most likely candidate. But who was the woman? Marjorie and Anita had similar builds, so it could be either of them. The nurse had mentioned Anita chasing after Ian, but he had winked at Marjorie who had smiled back. Not to mention the young nurse's reaction to the gardener's flirting. They seemed like a more likely pairing to Bella.

After the couple broke apart, they turned toward the cabin. Within a moment, they disappeared from view. Warmth surged into Bella's cheeks. Definitely an assignation, which meant the gardener's quarters weren't apt to house Aaron Corning. Unless, the lovers didn't mind company. That thought had Bella's face flaming hot.

Finally, at one, Bella tiptoed out of her room. For a long moment, she stood outside the door. No light peeked out from other quarters along the corridor, and no sound reached her ears. None except her racing pulse. Was it drowning out everything else? It certainly seemed loud enough to do so.

She took a long breath to steady herself. Then, she snuck toward the staircase. When a board creaked beneath her feet, Bella went stock-still and strained to hear any movement in the other rooms or in the hallway. Not much time had passed since she had seen the couple in the garden, but she needed to be cautious. The woman would return at some point, and Bella didn't want to encounter her—whoever she was. Following a long pause, she crept to the far end. One-by-one, Bella descended the steps. As she reached the second floor, she again looked around. The mansion had electricity, but only one lamp was on, leaving most of the hall in shadow. Bella reached into her pocket and pulled out a flashlight, one she had brought from home on Monday. The beam lit her way, and she was able to reach Jax's room with no problem. Thank goodness, she didn't need to go far.

At his door, Bella listened carefully. When not even a whisper reached her ears, she extracted the pick from her other pocket. Since she'd never undone a lock, Bella had practiced on her own door several times. Even so, her hands trembled as she slipped the device into the keyhole. Long moments passed before a click indicated success. After a deep exhalation, Bella slipped the tool back into her pocket and turned the knob. A beam of moonlight shimmered through the window, while heavy shadows filled the room. Why wasn't Jax up and ready? Was he still sleeping? Had he been drugged?

A sick, sinking sensation roiled her insides as she looked around. All three beds were empty. Bella snapped the flashlight back on. Sheets, blankets, and pillows were strewn across the floor. One mattress was half off the frame. Obviously, a struggle had taken place. Wounded and hurting, Jax would have been vulnerable, and Dalton Miniger had shown no ability to defend himself. What about James? Had he helped capture his roommates or was he another victim? Bella searched around but found no clues. Had someone suspected Jax of being a lawman? Maybe recognized him? But why were the others gone? Her mouth went dry while her palms got slick. After wiping one hand on her knickers, she swung the light around the room again. No one was there.

Another query hit her. How long had they been gone? Bella went to the disheveled beds and ran her hand over the sheets. No warmth remained, so the fracas hadn't occurred in the last few minutes.

What should she do? Where should she go? Up to the attic, down to the kitchen, to the little library? Outside? With no idea of where Jax and the others were, Bella was all at sea. A sound in the hallway abruptly broke in her thoughts. When Bella spun to look, she saw Sarah silhouetted in the door.

The young nurse glanced around the room before turning to Bella. "What happened?" Her voice sounded weak and thready.

"No idea." Bella swallowed hard over the arid lump in her throat. "What are you doing down here?"

"I come to check on Dalton some nights. Most nights, actually."

"I see." Uncertain about Sarah's role in, or knowledge of, the reprehensible goings-on, Bella halted. What should she say? Jax was gone, so she was on her own. Rescuing him was her first concern. But how? Would the nurse be an impediment? Or could she help?

Sarah braced one shoulder against the doorjamb. "I'm not sure you do. He's very vulnerable, and I fret about his safety."

"If you're so concerned, why is he still here? Why not take him someplace else?" Bella couldn't withhold the questions any longer. She wouldn't leave Jax in these conditions. Not for any reason.

"Desperation. Dalton's parents didn't want him at home any longer. I don't generally tell the entire story because the family is influential in their community. Having a son with mental issues embarrasses them. They think he's weak and cowardly because he doesn't snap out of it, but they pay the bills here. Right after Dalton was admitted, his mother said the care was too expensive and intimated he might not live long. They could afford to keep him here for years, so I was unnerved by the comments. His father is a hard, harsh man. Because I worried about Dalton not getting proper care, I interviewed for a job and got one. I don't object to anything because I want to stay near him, and I don't leave because I fear what might happen if I do. Now, he's gone anyhow." Her voice broke on the last phrase.

Sarah sounded sincere. Was she? Or was she a talented actress? Bella wasn't ready to admit her own role, but she had already been caught in the room, lock pick in hand. If the nurse wanted to cause her trouble, she need only report Bella. "Do you know who's behind patients being missing or found dead?" Would Sarah answer honestly, if she did?

"I'm not sure." The nurse wrung her hands. "Billings and the Lennings. Surely, at least one of them has information. Mrs. Lenning is increasingly vague and confused. She may know and forget, or she may not be aware of what's going on."

"I've heard you talk with the major and the doctor privately."

"About Dalton. He's the only reason I'm still here. I hate the place, but I feared leaving him here." Sarah gestured around the room. "I should've figured out something else for him. I will if he's safe."

"Right now, I want to find out what happened." But how? Bella wished a good idea would arise. Again, she wondered about relying on the other woman.

A moment passed before Sarah spoke. "I'll help you."

In the semi-darkness, Bella didn't have a clear view of Sarah's face, but her voice trembled. Since dilly dallying wasn't an option, Bella went with her intuition. Sarah acted and sounded as upset as Bella felt. "All right. Jax and I were planning to go to the little library, since we think there might be a passage outside there. We've both been in big houses with interior access to a storm cellar, and a cellar could be a hiding place."

"Jax?"

A resigned sigh escaped Bella, who explained the investigation before saying, "We're both temporary sheriff's deputies."

"You have a lot of courage to be his partner in such a perilous situation."

"I couldn't leave him on his own as a patient here."

"Then, you understand why—despite everything that's wrong with Poplar Pines—I wouldn't leave Dalton, either."

"Yes, I think I do." Bella's mind returned to the case. "Is there a storm cellar on the property?"

"Probably so, although I don't know where. There should be a place to go in case of a tornado. They're fairly common. You must remember the big outbreak last year on Palm Sunday."

"I do, although the storms didn't affect this immediate area," Bella replied. "Since this place was built as a residence, a lovely one, it makes sense to have a way out from inside. Have you been in the little library?"

"No. I've seen Marjorie go in there, but when she saw me, she shut the door."

"The same thing happened to me. She told me it used to be the schoolroom for the children of the house staff, back when the place was a home."

"I believe that's right. I've only gotten a couple of glimpses, but there are a lot of bookcases."

"I got a quick peek, and a door could be hidden behind one case. Whatever we do, we need to get going, but there's another concern. Just after midnight, I saw two people in the garden. They embraced before heading toward the river."

"It had to be Ian and Marjorie heading to his cabin."

Although Sarah's statement was firm, Bella still asked a question. "Are you sure it wasn't Anita? Marjorie said the girl has a crush on Ian."

A humorless laugh escaped the nurse. "He's a charmer, as you've probably noticed. Anita responds favorably to anyone who's kind to her, but it's Ian and Marjorie who are involved."

The information wasn't shocking, and it could be important. "What if we run into them while we're looking around?"

"We won't. When they have an encounter, she doesn't come back until shortly before dawn. Anita saw her twice, since she starts work very early. Evidently, Marjorie was later than usual. She told Anita to keep quiet, and she did, except for telling me. But I was already suspicious."

"Why?"

"Marjorie and Ian have talked about wanting to move to a big city. A couple of times, the two of them were off the same days. Supposedly, he gave her a ride to see friends. Maybe he did, but I believe they spent most of their time together. Once, I told her to be careful."

"What did she say?"

"She said young women have more freedom these days, and she planned to enjoy it."

The revelation matched much of Marjorie's demeanor. "Do you think Ian is serious about her?"

"I don't know. I have no specific reason, but I don't trust his type. Too flirtatious and full of himself."

"I agree." Since time was passing quickly, Bella returned to matters at hand. "I'm not sure how long ago Jax and Dalton were nabbed, so they may have been taken directly to the river."

"With the full moon, I doubt it. Both Falconer and Smith disappeared during waning moons and on cloudy nights."

"Aaron Corning has been gone for almost a week, hasn't he?"

"He has, but there have been clear nights ever since. He could still be here."

"I hope so. I wish I had a weapon."

Sarah reached into her jacket pocket and extracted a pistol. "I do, and I can use it. Actually, it belonged to Dalton, and he taught me to shoot before he left for France. I took it with me when I sailed."

Amusement and confidence were in her tone. Both buoyed Bella's spirit. Sarah was no weak-kneed young lady. "Let's go downstairs and see what we can find."

The women proceeded quietly and slowly. Not wanting to garner attention, Bella kept the flashlight off. When they reached the corridor by the kitchen, Sarah spoke again. "Maybe we should grab a couple of knives. If we find the men, they're apt to be bound."

"I'm sure they are." Bella only hoped their bonds were rope and not shackles. "Let's get those knives and go on."

After they retrieved two large blades, Sarah led the way to the closed library door. "It's locked, which is typical."

"I'll use the pick." Bella pulled it out, and once again, found it to be an excellent tool. "Let me go in first, but keep your gun handy." For a fleeting moment, she wondered about being too trusting. With few options, Bella moved forward and hoped for the best—not a bullet in her back. The room was dim, so she flipped on the flashlight and glanced around.

Suddenly, Sarah gasped. "There. On the floor. It looks like Dalton's overseas cap."

Bella watched as the nurse went to pick up the battered flat headgear.

"It's a talisman for him. A comfort. He always keeps it with him. I had to argue with the Lennings and Billings about it. They didn't want him wearing it, but he could keep it in a pocket." Her hands shook as she held it to her chest. "He and Jax had to be in here. Maybe Captain James, too."

"Probably so," Bella murmured. Despite the chill in the room, sweat beaded her forehead. Her mind churned. While the entire case was important, the whereabouts of Dalton, Jax, and the others meant far more. She swung the light around the room. "Look. One bookcase is ajar. A lever has to be hidden somewhere." Bella approached the shelves and ran her hand along the side. At first, she felt nothing. Finally, she encountered a slight projection where the middle case wasn't flush with the two on either side. Bella gripped the vertical edge and yanked. When it didn't budge, she put one hand on the adjacent shelf and tried again. Abruptly, the hidden access opened.

"Jack...Jax, Dalton, and James must've been taken this way." Sarah came to stand by Bella. "Are we going ahead? Or will you call for help?"

A shuddering breath left Bella. They couldn't wait, and she explained why. "The closest help is twenty minutes away. That's if I reached the sheriff in Bridgeling. He wouldn't come alone, so he'd have to call his deputies." With Richard and Nolen an hour off in another direction, Bella knew summoning assistance wouldn't work. "Besides, the telephone is at the front desk, which is too close to the bedroom suites of the Lennings and Billings. They're all suspects."

"I agree. I don't think we should wait, either."

When she turned toward Sarah, Bella saw determination in the other woman's expression. "It's just the two of us, then. Let's go." She slipped into the corridor, which was narrow but straight. The dirt walls on either side gave it an earthy odor, but no cobwebs impeded the women. Evidently, the route was being used regularly, something that heightened Bella's sense of urgency. Within a few moments, they reached the end and a locked door. Once again, Bella used the pick until the door swung open. "Just as we thought. It's a cellar." When no sounds reached her ears, Bella shone the flashlight into the blackness. She pointed the beam straight down. The few stairs were old but solid, and the women descended with caution. When she reached the bottom, Bella stopped. "Jax, are you here?" She kept her voice low and hushed. Several seconds ticked away before a response came.

"Bella?"

She strained to hear his rough whisper. "Yes. Are you okay?" He sounded terrible, which only increased her dread. Was he badly injured? What about Dalton and James and Corning?" She continued to swing the beam around.

A strange voice made the reply. "We're all bound hands and feet. Jack has to be in pain after the rough handling, but he hasn't admitted it. Dalton seems okay, except for being trauma-tized. Aaron is very weak."

"I'm all right." Another unfamiliar, somewhat wobbly, male spoke. Corning?

Relief and hope lifted Bella's spirits. It had to be, since Dalton never spoke. "We'll come in and get you loose." In the single light, two figures became visible. Bella rushed toward them with Sarah on her heels.

"Who's with you?" Jax asked as Bella cut his bonds while Sarah worked on Dalton.

"Sarah—Nurse Bailey—is here. It's a long story, but I was glad to have help," Bella replied.

"You could've had plenty of assistance if you'd called Rufus and Richard." Jax only sounded a little peeved.

"No time, I'm afraid." Bella swung the light around and saw two others. James was familiar, so the other man must be Corn-ing. Sarah was still on her knees by Dalton, so Bella hurriedly set Aaron loose. "Have you been down here since last week?" While Bella helped Corning, Jax assisted James.

Corning nodded. "I'm afraid so. Ever since Smith came up missing last month, Billings has gotten skittish, I guess. When they nabbed me, McNulty and Drier argued about whether to dump me in the river or wait until after the full moon. They definitely didn't want my body found."

A shiver rippled through Bella. She wanted more details about all the disappearances, but now was not the time. Getting away was imperative. "Sarah has a pistol, but that's our main weapon." Knives would only work at close-range.

For a moment, Jax bowed his head. When he lifted it, he squared his shoulders. "How far is it to the Chummy from here? Farther than from the house, I'm guessing."

"It's more like two hundred yards," Bella replied. "I hate to go back into the building, though. Remember, there's a path leading from the gazebo toward the river."

"There's another door," Jax said. "Over at the far end of the cellar. I assume there's another set of stairs, maybe leading up beneath the gazebo. Or someplace in the garden."

"That seems right," Aaron added. "The gardener has come and gone that way a few times."

The comment revealed another suspect. Maybe two. Could Marjorie be involved? Bella didn't want to think so.

"Our captors leave a lantern hanging by the steps. I believe they have matches there, too," James rubbed his wrists as he spoke. "I'll grab it."

"Good," Bella replied. More light would be useful in getting out, and getting out was their primary and immediate goal.

Sarah, who had helped Dalton to his feet, spoke. "The gazebo is in the middle of the garden. The passage we used had to take us almost that far."

Bella considered the nurse's observations. "You're right." Bella headed in that direction. Behind her, Jax groaned again.

When she glanced back, he was on his feet and following her. Slowly but surely. She kept going.

When they got to the far door, he pulled it open and stepped back to allow Bella to examine what lay beyond. Jax peered over her shoulder. "This has to go to the base of the gazebo. Once we get up there, it's going to be a long trek to the car for Aaron. Despite his protestations, he has to be weak. For Dalton, it'll be a challenge, too. James can help one of them, and I'll aid the other." Jax leaned against the door frame as he spoke.

"I think you should concentrate on staying upright yourself," Bella said with asperity.

"I'll be fine. The sedative is wearing off." Jax weaved slightly, but righted himself.

"Sedative? Couldn't you avoid taking it?" Bella asked.

"Unfortunately, we all got injections tonight, but we can go over details later. The sooner we get away from here, the better I'll feel." Jax went to Aaron. "You okay."

"Better than I was before the ladies got here."

"Same with me," James agreed. "Let's move out."

"Yes, sir, Captain." A low laugh escaped Aaron.

"Miss Bailey, may I have your weapon? Then, you can assist your fiancé." Jax addressed Sarah.

"Of course," she replied. "In fact, you can have the gun and the knife."

Bella also handed her knife over. Now, Jax, James, and Corning were armed.

Within moments, the group headed up the stairs. Bella held the flashlight while Sarah and Jax assisted Dalton. James, lantern in hand, and Corning brought up the rear. By the time they were all at ground level, she heard multiple gasps for breath. Up close, Dalton Miniger appeared to be in poor physical condition, and the other two weren't a lot better off. The trek to the Chummy was likely to take a bigger toll.

"Shine the light around, Bella. I need to look at the lattice-work." Jax sounded short of breath. "If this has been an escape route, at least one section is probably loose."

She did as he suggested. The gazebo floor was three feet above their heads, so the decorative panels—if taken out—would provide sufficient space for the group to exit the enclosure. "That one looks moveable." Bella kept the beam on it.

"It does." Jax crawled over and pushed it out. "Come this way, everyone."

They scrambled out. Following the path between tall shrubs took them farther from the parking area. Since it couldn't be helped, Bella tried not to worry. Both Dalton and Corning moved excruciatingly slowly, so Bella increased her estimate of how long it would take to get to the vehicle. As she did, a solution arose. "I'll get the automobile and pick the rest of you up."

"Good idea." Sarah, who had an arm around Dalton, was clearly winded.

James was dividing his help between Dalton and Aaron, while Jax took most of the latter's weight. "I agree." The captain was also breathless.

"I'll go with you." Jax panted between words.

Bella wanted to say she would make better time alone but resisted. They needed to keep moving, not debate options. "All right."

As they headed toward the Chummy, Jax's tension was a palpable force. Once again, Bella was reminded of how much was on his shoulders. His weary shoulders. To bolster him up, she tried for reassurance. "It won't be long before we're away from here, and I'm guessing you know enough to put the guilty parties away."

"We'll see, but I think so."

Jax wanted to tell Bella to stay behind while he got the Chummy, but truth be told, his shoulder and upper arm ached with every step while his left wrist throbbed incessantly. To say they had handled him roughly was an understatement. Although staying on his feet was a sore trial, Jax felt stronger with Bella by his side. When they reached the vehicle, he made no objection to her driving. Not that he ever did. She was the best driver he knew.

Within moments, they stopped for the others. Jax sat in the middle of the front seat by Bella, while Corning squeezed in beside him. The rest scooted into the back. Then, they were going down the driveway and on to the main road. Jax let his head rest against the top of the seat.

"How are you?" Bella's question was a mere whisper, but concern underscored it.

Although he was hurting and exhausted, Jax tried for a reassuring reply. "Doing okay."

"Which means you're in pain. Being without the sling can't help."

Certainty competed with distress in her tone. "It got discarded in the tussle."

"Is shrapnel coming out again?"

Denying the obvious was futile. "It happens from time-to-time."

"The doctors told you to keep the area clean when it does, which was impossible in that dirty cellar."

While her worry was reassuring, Jax intended to ignore it. He had too much to do before resting. "I wasn't there long, and I'll get it tended to after we round up the suspects. We don't have time now, even if we had supplies."

"What about your wrist? How is it feeling?" Bella asked.

Jax hesitated a moment. His throbbing wrist vied with his bicep and shoulder for the most piercing pain. "It'll be fine."

Her fingers slid down his arm to clasp his left hand. "I hope so, but if Richard and Rufus come back to make arrests tonight, you'll join in."

He wouldn't deny a statement of fact. "Head to Bridgeling. We'll get Rufus, so he can call Richard. As far as nabbing them tonight, maybe. Maybe not."

"We're making good time," Bella commented.

Actually, she was driving like she was in a race. Jax didn't complain. When he returned to his job as a constable, he'd be concerned with such infractions, but speed was advisable in these circumstances.

As she drove down the road to Bridgeling, Bella repeatedly glanced into the rearview mirror. No headlamps were visible, and after a time, she relaxed. "The sheriff's office won't be open, so where are we headed?"

"Ayling lives a block down from there," Jax replied. "After our meeting last Friday, he described the house and location to me, just in case we needed to hurriedly head this way. I guess he has a lawman's sixth sense, too. Anyhow, it's a white bungalow with several maple trees in front."

"With the gas streetlights, I should be able to find it." Bella was right, and a short time later, she pulled to a stop at the curb.

"Is this the place?" Sarah asked from the backseat.

"It is, but wait here while I go to the door. I don't want to alarm Ayling with a crowd in his front yard." While he spoke, Samuel James got out. Jax followed suit. He leaned into the vehicle. "Hang on. There must be a physician in town, so we'll get help in short order."

Neither Aaron nor Dalton had made a sound during the drive. Bella hoped that wasn't a bad sign. She watched as Jax went to the porch. An eternity passed before the door swung open. Another few moments ensued before Jax was back at the Chummy with Sheriff Ayling alongside.

"Jax says we've got two of you who may need tending. My wife's calling our town doctor, so he'll be here soon. In the meantime, we'll get everyone inside."

When the group entered the house, an older woman, clad in a dressing gown and nightcap, ushered them into the front parlor. Ayling introduced her as his wife before letting Jax present the others. "I'm happy to have all of you here. Doc is on his way, and I have coffee going," she said with a smile. "Rufus will get a fire started to take the chill off, and I'll be back with refreshments shortly. Is there anything else we can do to make you all comfortable?" Concern knit her brow as she focused on Aaron and Dalton.

The former replied, "No, ma'am." Dalton had no response.

In the light, Corning looked pale and drawn. His pajamas hung on his thin frame, and his bare feet were dirty. A shudder went through Bella when she thought of how long he had been in the damp, dark cellar. Her attention moved to Dalton, whose vacant stare remained. Sympathy for him and for Sarah swelled Bella's heart. The war had wrought terrible changes in many lives and although losing her brother had crushed Bella, she felt fortunate he wasn't suffering like Dalton. Nor was Jax, despite his wounds—old and new. "Let me help, Mrs. Ayling."

The older woman nodded. "Thank you."

Bella followed Mrs. Ayling. The aroma of fresh coffee hit her first as soon as they entered the kitchen. A cup would perk her up, which she needed. Now that the nervous energy had worn off, fatigue blanketed Bella.

"Rufus told me about your role in this case last week. You're a brave young woman to go undercover in that place." Mrs. Ayling clucked her tongue. "He's been concerned for a while, but got no answers out there. Looks like you and your beau have done the job quickly and well."

Heat flooded Bella's cheeks. Jax wasn't exactly her beau. Not yet, at least. She avoided the topic and focused on Poplar Pines. "We found out some important information tonight after Jax, Dalton Miniger, and Samuel James were taken. They were all in the storm cellar with Aaron Corning."

"Rufus said you and Miss Bailey rescued them. How in the world did you know where they were?" As she spoke, Mrs. Ayling put cookies on a platter and poured coffee from the pot into a flask. "Would you put the sugar bowl and cream on that big tray?" She gestured to the table.

"Of course." While she worked, Bella responded with her plan to search with Jax and revealed how she and Sarah had crossed paths in the patients' room.

"Oh, my. You must've been terribly upset to find them missing."

Upset barely scratched the surface of what she had experienced. Bella forced the memory away. "Nurse Bailey and I were both taken aback. Without her help, I couldn't have gotten them out."

"I'm glad you did. The goings-on out there have weighed on me, too. Now, let's get the refreshments to the parlor. Doc will be here any time."

When the two women re-entered the room, they found the men—all except Dalton Miniger—in deep discussion. After seeing that everyone had coffee and cookies, Bella took a seat next to Jax. "How are you feeling?"

A smile tugged at one corner of his mouth. "Probably better than I look."

Bella certainly hoped so, but she withheld the comment. "Has anything been decided about how to proceed?" She kept her voice low so only Jax would hear.

"I spoke with Richard. He'll get Nolen. Since they're coming from the opposite way, we'll meet at a filling station a mile from the sanatorium. Rufus called his deputies, and we'll pick them up on our way. James is well enough to go along, but the other men obviously can't." Jax took a long swallow of coffee.

"How many people are involved? From what Sarah said, Major Billings must be a key player." Bella kept her voice low, but James shifted toward her.

"I'd say so," the man put in, "but he sent his minions after us. He's the type who doesn't want to get his hands dirty."

"I agree with his overall involvement," Jax replied.

"He wasn't around when I got taken, either." Aaron Corning made the remark. "I'd complained a few times about treatment. The last time was only two days before I got nabbed. Billings made it clear I'd regret being a problem, and he told me about my wife's flapper activities. He said she loved to spend money on nights out and fancy clothes, and she'd be able to spend freely, if I was out of the way." His jaw tightened. "I can't say I was surprised, since Constance made it clear long ago that I was a burden."

Sympathy and anger collided inside Bella. What an awful woman. If she had paid to have Aaron eliminated, she needed to be brought to justice along with the others.

"Interesting information," Ayling observed, "and enough to question Billings. The others may decide to share details, once they get interrogated."

"We had time for discussion before Bella and Nurse Bailey rescued us." Jax smiled at Bella. "I, for one, will be forever grateful to them."

Bella's heart swelled at his sincere appreciation. "How long were you down there?"

"We were taken from the room shortly after eleven," Jax replied.

"How long did they plan to keep all of you?" Ayling asked.

Corning folded his arms over his chest. "When I got dumped, I heard them talking about waiting for the waning moon and a cloudy night. You worried them with your probing, Sheriff. They weren't willing to take chances with you and your deputies coming out from time-to-time. Otherwise, we'd all be in the river or woods."

"Then, I'm glad we went out there regularly, even though we didn't seem to make headway," Ayling said. "Your sister coming also put them on alert, I'm sure."

Corning's eyes went wide. "My sister. The last I knew Eleanor was ill."

"Her physician gave approval for her travel, and she came straight here to check on you," Jax said. He briefly explained Amos Derringer's role and why both had left.

Relief spread across Aaron's face. "I'm so grateful to them and to you." He looked from Jax to Bella. "Both of you."

"It was a team effort." Jax looked at James. "You were about to tell us your situation when Bella and Nurse Bailey came into the cellar."

James nodded. "First off, my name is really Seth Jensen. I served in France and saw some soldiers with shell-shock. One was a dear friend, Arthur Bland."

"Lieutenant Bland was one of our patients," Sarah put in. "His family took him home last month after only a few weeks."

"They were concerned about his condition. Arthur was no better and possibly worse after his stint at Poplar Pines." James ran one hand over his face. "The last time his folks visited, they met with Billings, who mentioned how much money they were spending on a hopeless case."

"How awful," Bella said.

The man nodded. "They certainly thought so, which is why they arranged to care for him at home. I went to visit shortly after he got back. His parents told me the story, and I looked into it." James briefly paused. "I'm a newsman by trade. When I explained the details to my editor, he agreed we needed to look into Poplar Pines. Turns out Arthur's sister was considering it for her husband. Anyhow, I had a friend have me admitted. He pretended to be my older brother. Dumped me off and didn't come back, so we could see what happened. I spent a week in the attic, complaining the entire time. When I got to a room, my first procedure—after the lecture from Billings—was an ice bath. Had a couple of those. Then, back to the attic for a while."

The observations sent a shiver through Bella. "You were there for a story?"

The reporter nodded. "An expose, which is why I used an assumed name. My editor did some research and learned about Falconer and Smith. Both of us wanted to dig into the place."

"Did you tell Miss Bounder about being a newsman?" Ayling asked. "She mentioned you to Aaron's sister but didn't have time to explain why."

"I didn't confide in her, but she recognized me from my picture. She brought it up one day because she was afraid someone else would identify me, too. Before the war, my photo ran with my feature stories. My editor and I only thought my name might be known. I look different than the old photograph, but Miss Bounder knew me."

Now, his dismissive attitude at the table the other evening made sense. "Do you think that's why you were targeted?" Bella asked.

"I'm not sure," Seth replied. "Drier and McNulty didn't reveal why they were taking us."

His revelations brought major questions to the forefront of Bella's mind, and she shifted toward Jax to ask. "Is it likely someone suspects you?"

"Not as far as I know," he said. "Why the three of us were nabbed remains a mystery. We should find out when we make arrests."

"Why take Dalton?" Sarah asked. "He wouldn't have reported on them."

Jax shrugged. "Perhaps, they didn't want to take chances, and it might've been a better story that all three of us took off."

"And drowned?" Bella asked.

"Maybe so, or died from exposure or hypothermia. It can get chilly at night now," Jax said.

"That's true." As Sarah spoke, she reached for Dalton's hand. "Temperatures in the forties and fifties can lead to death, especially when folks aren't dressed warmly."

"Which we definitely aren't," the newsman observed.

"What awful people." The cruelty left Bella reeling. Arrests needed to be made soon. Then, the remaining patients would be out of danger.

"I agree," Jax said.

"We'll get them. Before we head out, I'd like a few more details. You gave the main ones to Richard over the telephone?" Ayling posed the question to Jax.

"I did. We're sure Billings is highly involved, since he counsels relatives about costly care for hopeless cases. Dr. Lenning is probably involved, too. As far as the mother, it's impossible to know at this point." Jax took another sip of coffee.

Aaron Corning shifted forward in his chair. "Nurse Mayfair brought food to me after I was taken. Escorted by the gardener."

The observation supported Bella's wariness about the young nurse. Dismay momentarily held Bella mute. "Do you think she was forced to help?"

"Not really. She might be sweet on him," Aaron said. "At least, they acted lovey-dovey."

"Anita saw her sneak out at night to join him. The first time, Marjorie ran into her in the hallway and told her to keep quiet," Sarah said.

"I saw them, too. Just a couple of hours ago. They were headed toward McNulty's cabin." All eyes were on Bella as she spoke.

"You didn't have time to tell anyone, but what about Anita? She didn't report her to the Lennings or Mrs. Barley?" Jax asked.

"She was afraid to, and I agreed." Sarah laid her free hand on Dalton's arm. "Anita hasn't been allowed to go into town since Smith disappeared and the sheriff came out multiple times. I'm sure Billings was worried she'd tell all she knew and not come back. I'm surprised Marjorie helped in a criminal endeavor, though. I would've told on her myself if I had suspected. Maybe no one else would've been taken." Her teeth toyed with her lower lip, and she blinked hastily, as if to clear tears.

"Highly unlikely that would've made any difference," Ayling put in. "But it's important information in planning our arrests. If McNulty and Mayfair were together tonight, it must've been soon after you three were nabbed. And it indicates she's involved, too."

"I'd say so," Jax agreed. "What about Mrs. Barley? Is she taking part in any way?"

"I never saw her at all," Aaron replied. "Food was only brought down late at night, probably long after the cook went to bed, or well before dawn."

"I've known Mae Barley for years," Mrs. Ayling said. "I would be shocked if she engaged in such goings-on. If anything was wrong, she would've reported it to Rufus."

"She certainly tried to be helpful," her husband added. "Unfortunately, we weren't alone during the interviews, and she doesn't drive, so coming into town was impossible. She'll undoubtedly share her suspicions once we make arrests."

"Without more evidence, how will Billings be taken in?" Bella asked.

"We may have to rely on Drier and McNulty to turn on him and on the Lennings, if either or both are involved." Jax ran one hand over his face in a gesture of deep fatigue. "Nurse Mayfair might talk for a reduced charge."

A knock at the front door interrupted the conversation. The sheriff went to answer and returned with a tall, lean man in his forties. "This is our local doctor, Zeke Collins." He quickly introduced the others. As he did, his wife rose.

"I have the extra bedroom ready. Since it has two beds, I thought it was the best place," the older woman made the statements as she headed into the front hall.

"Very good," Collins said. He glanced around the group. "Who are my patients?"

While Aaron got up, Sarah helped her fiancé to his feet.

The doctor nodded. "Both of you can come along."

"I'm a nurse," Sarah said, "and I'd be happy to help."

The physician welcomed the assistance and let Mrs. Ayling usher the group out of the parlor. Once they were gone, Seth got up, too. "Sheriff, you said I could borrow some clothes. Perhaps, I could change now."

"Certainly. Come upstairs with me." Ayling led the way out of the room.

When the pair was gone, Bella put her coffee cup aside and focused on Jax. Not only was the sling missing, a bruise darkened the skin over his left cheekbone. His pajamas were torn and dirty, and his feet were bare. How had she missed these details at Poplar Pines or in the Chummy? In good light, he looked dreadful. "You should borrow warmer clothes, too."

"I will." A grin curved his lips. "My attire is pretty ragged, but yours is very interesting. I thought you weren't wearing knickers any more. That's what you said more than a year ago." His teasing tone took any sting from the observation.

Heat bloomed in her cheeks. "I said I wasn't wearing hand-me-downs any more. I bought these before my college girlfriends' reunion in June. Since they're more functional than a skirt, I brought them along. Just in case I needed to scout around."

"They're more stylish than Matt's castoffs," he observed.

Last year, he had teased her about wearing her brother's old knickers until her mother put a stop to it. Now, the appreciative gleam in his eyes had Bella glancing down at the navy knickers with their matching stockings. "I wasn't worrying about style." But she couldn't deny liking Jax's reaction. Perhaps, she should buy more of the trendy pants.

"In any case, the overall effect is lovely."

"And functional." Bella hesitated only a moment before voicing a new idea. "I can ride along, or even drive. Marjorie would feel more comfortable if I'm there. Perhaps, she'd be more cooperative, as well."

The levity left his expression. "We need to make the final arrangements with Richard and the others, but it'll be tricky, Bella. Drier and McNulty might come willingly. So, might Nurse Mayfair. On the other hand, the men may put up a fight, and she could, too."

"You think all the men might resist?" The idea deeply disturbed Bella. The group had already killed twice. Aaron Corning was safe, but Miss Bounder's fate remained a mystery. Perhaps, they'd murdered her along with Falconer and Smith.

"I don't know," Jax replied. "Warren Starling isn't involved at all, as far as anyone has seen or heard, but Dr. Lenning probably is, even if it's only to take a cut of the money. His mother is a wild card."

Fresh apprehension tore at Bella. "Sarah had a revolver. Mrs. Lenning and Marjorie might, too. That could mean six people to fight you. Four men and two women."

"We'll have more on our side, and we'll all be armed." Jax scratched his sprained wrist. "I sure didn't expect to be abducted myself."

The memory of finding his room empty and disheveled made Bella's insides knot all over again. "I was shocked when I got into your room and found no one."

"What made you get Sarah? That seems risky."

"I didn't get her. She likes to visit Dalton as often as possible, and that's what she was doing. I'm surprised you didn't see her before tonight."

"I haven't been in the room for long."

"That's true."

Bella revealed what the nurse had told her about Dalton's parents, and Sarah's anxiety about his safety. "She felt she couldn't complain about anything without taking a chance on being fired. Then, Dalton would've been very vulnerable."

"She's been in a tough spot."

"You've been around Dalton for a few days. Do you think there's any chance he'll ever be better?" Bella asked.

"Until tonight, I would've doubted it," Jax replied, "but he put up a solid defense against Drier and McNulty. That surprised me."

Bella scanned his face. "It looks like you put up a tough battle, too."

One hand went to his blackened eye. "Dalton was already fighting Drier. I couldn't do any less."

"And you probably did a lot more," Bella said in a wry tone. "If you're going back tonight, you need a new sling and more wrapping on your wrist."

"I don't want a sling, since I'll be driving."

"Driving?" Alarm flashed through Bella. "How will you drive? It was hard enough when you only had old wounds to your right arm. Now, those have been aggravated, and you have a sprained left wrist. Not to mention, you've got a black eye that's nearly swollen shut."

"Ayling is picking up his two deputies. James...that is, Seth Jensen, and I will go together. As you could see, he's limping. Probably sprained his ankle, although he won't admit it. He can't drive, so I will." Jax put the heel of his left hand on his forehead. Weariness rolled off him in waves, which only increased her anxiety.

"If you and the sheriff are going in separate vehicles, I'll drive you, and I'll stay out of the way when we get there. You have my word." His lashes swept down, whether in fatigue or in dismay, Bella didn't know. She waited for what was probably a minute, but seemed like ten.

"How we proceed remains to be seen. We still need to find out who killed Falconer and about Smith, but that won't be tonight. Today. Night will be over soon." He shook his head.

"You're exhausted," Bella said. He hadn't responded directly to her suggestion. Would he? Or would she need to press the point?

"You have to be tired yourself." Jax turned toward her.

Bella pursed her lips. "But I'm not injured. If I drive, you can catch a quick nap. At the very least, you can sit back and relax without stressing your arm and wrist." When he didn't immediately reply, she emphasized her argument. "You said you were mostly relying on me in this case. Did you mean it?"

When he lifted his right hand to cup her cheek, Jax winced. "All right. I'm worn out and hurting," he admitted. "Of course, you're my partner. Now and in five other cases. When I get back to being the Moreley town constable, I hope you'll be my partner going forward. And not necessarily only in solving crimes." His thumb gently brushed her lower lip. "And, as usual, you're right. I'd be better off not driving."

The sensations evoked by his touch and words nearly made Bella forget what they were about to do and why. Nearly, but not quite.

Whatever else she might have said was stopped by Sheriff Ayling's return. Seth was with him. Jax dropped his hand and sat back.

"We need to get going. I'll pick up my deputies and meet you two." He looked from the newsman to Jax. "We should've asked Richard and the Moreley deputy to come in two vehicles, since neither of you is really fit to drive. We may end up with several folks under arrest. I want to get them in my jail as soon as possible."

"They may come separately. In any case, Bella can drive my Chummy." Jax made the statement without hesitation. "She'll stay out of harm's way when we get to Poplar Pines."

Ayling glanced at Bella and nodded. "You're still deputized, so having you as a driver makes sense."

"Thank you," she replied.

The sheriff turned his attention to Jax. "Seth is changing into some clothes our son left here. You need something else, too. Go on upstairs. First door on the right. My wife laid things out. They should fit decently, and you won't be barefooted."

"Thanks," Jax replied. "I'll be right back. Richard will bring other clothes for me, too, since I'm not sure how long I'll be here." Jax headed into the front hall and up the staircase.

Bella slumped back and tried to release the fear and tension plaguing her. In a few hours, the worst would be behind them. Or so she hoped.

Chapter Twelve

After putting on the borrowed clothes and shoes, Jax headed back to the parlor with Seth. Bella and Ayling rose immediately.

"We need to get going in order to meet the others on time. They have farther to come, but we have two stops." The sheriff glanced at Bella. "Just follow me. Both of my deputies live in town. Then, we'll take the main road to a filling station about a mile from the sanatorium. That's the meeting place. Seth can ride with me for now."

Bella and Jax seated themselves in the Chummy and were soon on the road. "Why don't you rest for a while?" she asked.

"I couldn't sleep right now. Later on."

"Did you make a detailed plan with Richard? I feel like I missed some things while I was in the kitchen with Mrs. Ayling."

Of course, she would feel that way because she had. Jax had no compunction about sharing details with her. "Only a partial one. We'll flesh it out when we meet Richard and Nolen. You heard most of the discussion. Drier and McNulty are involved. Probably mainly as the strong arms to move patients."

"I'm not surprised about Drier, since he acts very tough. McNulty seemed more affable, even flirtatious."

"That's how he got Marjorie involved, I'm sure."

"Her participation shocked me, but so did seeing the two of them sneak off together. I never expected that, but I agree about him sweet-talking her into administering shots, taking food, and keeping quiet." Bella exhaled sharply. "I wonder what else she knows."

"Maybe not a lot," Jax replied, "although I hope she has some information. She's the most likely candidate to tell all for a deal on her own case." Frustration bubbled up in Jax. "There are a lot of questions remaining."

"Like why you and Dalton were taken."

"Yep. As for Seth, someone else must've recognized him."

A gasp left Bella. "Marjorie's parents live in the Columbus area, and she grew up there."

"Seth said the paper only used his photograph with his articles before the war, but Marjorie would've been rather young then."

"She's twenty-two now."

"Then, around fifteen or sixteen." He mulled the idea over. "She could've seen his picture and recognized him. Maybe not immediately, which would explain why he wasn't taken sooner."

"It certainly would," Bella replied. "If Marjorie is sweet on Ian, she might've carried the tale to help him and their plans to leave. She made excuses for staying at the sanatorium. Believable excuses like wanting to make more money to move to the city and having trouble finding a job there."

"If she's involved in the crimes, she's making more money here than as a nurse in a big town."

"It's worse that she might've been the one to point Seth out." A heartbeat passed before Bella went on. "Please be careful."

Jax let his head fall back against the top of the seat. "We will. We should get there before Marjorie takes the next meal to the cellar. Corning indicated she comes every day at the same times. One is just before dawn. We have enough time to set a detailed plan and still have cover of darkness. Rufus provided guns to Seth and me. He and his deputies are armed. Richard and Nolen will be, too. That's eight of us with guns. Like I said already, we outnumber them, and we have the element of surprise." Jax reached into his pocket. "I've got Sarah's pistol for you. After all, you're still a deputy and my partner." Although Jax preferred Bella stay out of danger, he realized smothering her wasn't a good way to press his suit—which he planned to do as soon as possible. And he would feel better if she could defend herself.

"Thank you." Her voice was a soft murmur that barely carried to him.

"I'm the one who needs to thank you," he replied with sincerity. "You took a big chance going undercover at Poplar Pines. When Drier and McNulty came into my room, my first fear—my primary fear—was for you. I was terrified they'd gotten on to both of us and nabbed you, too." Jax didn't keep the emotion from his voice. All the way to the cellar, he had fretted over Bella's fate. "When the three of us were tossed into the hole, I worried you'd be there, too. I was relieved beyond words when you weren't."

"Tossed in. Did they throw you down the stairs?"

"About halfway down, and there aren't all that many steps."

"Oh, Jax. No wonder you look so banged up. And your shoulder, arm, and wrist."

"I'll be fine," he assured her. "My point was being worried about you. Since you weren't abducted, we can safely assume no one knows we were undercover."

"Probably so. Sarah and I won't be missed until well after dawn. By the time breakfast is served, almost half of the employees may be under arrest."

"With luck, they will."

After Ayling picked up his deputies, the two vehicles headed to the filling station. Once there, Bella pulled the Chummy to a stop beside Richard's Winton Touring Car and hopped out. Nolen's new-to-him battered roadster sat next to the bigger automobile. The men were already talking when Jax joined her. They headed to where the rest of the group was and exchanged greetings.

"Arabella, I understand congratulations are in order." Richard stepped forward to shake her hand. "You and one nurse went to the rescue."

"They sure did," Seth said, "and I'm beyond grateful. Corning had it much worse. Of course, Jax and I got roughed up pretty bad. We all did to some extent."

"I want to find out why you were taken." Richard turned to Jax as he spoke. "But first, we need to go over our plans and execute them."

Bella listened while the men discussed how to proceed. Much of the information had been shared at the Ayling house. When they got to details on where all the suspects would be, she attended to each comment.

"Nurse Artem will be on duty and sleeping until five o'clock?" Ayling asked.

"That's her typical pattern. As far as I can see, she isn't involved at all," Bella said. Until recently, she thought of the older nurse as a far better suspect than Marjorie.

"I agree. She's a curmudgeon, but there's no evidence of her participation." Jax folded his arms over his lean waist. "There are two main issues to my way of thinking. One is exactly who is in charge. The other is who all the accomplices might be. Billings seems to have a big role, but Dr. Lenning may, too." He summed up his discussion with Bella and then, said, "We'll need to apprehend Marjorie, of course."

"After we talk with her and the others, the truth should come out," Richard said. "At least some of it should."

Jax braced one hip against the vehicle's bumper. "I wish we'd had a little more time to investigate. The mother is still a question mark."

Bella shared Sarah's assessment of the older woman, along with her own. "I'm not sure what to think about Mrs. Lenning," she added at the end.

"I understand her odd behavior, but Jax is right. We don't know for sure, so let's be cautious. In that same vein, we'll need to ensure those who aren't involved don't get used as hostages," Ayling put in.

"From what you've all said, it sounds like they hadn't figured out who you were." Richard made the observation to Jax and Bella. "Nurse Mayfair recognizing Seth is the more likely situation."

"I should've considered that, I suppose," the newsman said. "It's been a long time since my picture appeared with my byline. Neither my editor nor I gave it a thought."

"That's behind us, and you're safe. All of you, which is a relief. Plus, we've discovered a lot about their operation," Ayling said. "I just wish the suspects weren't spread throughout the property."

"I have an idea." Jax stepped away from the automobile. "Seth and I could get back into the cellar to wait for food to come. Drier and McNulty will be with Marjorie. Aaron only saw McNulty and Marjorie bring food, but he heard Drier holler down to them to hurry more than once. We discovered that when we were in the cellar together. Anyhow, we could arrest three that way."

Seth added. "They won't expect us to be armed, so you and I could grab the two who come downstairs right off."

"Several of us should be involved," Richard suggested.

"That's my exact thought." Jax's tone was optimistic. "A couple of you could be outside near the trapdoor under the gazebo. Drier probably stays on the back path, but he could be easily overpowered. The shrubs there are tall, so you could be well hidden until you jump him." He explained where and how they had escaped.

"I agree," Richard said, "but we're also arresting Lenning and Billings. While we don't have the same powerful evidence against them, we have reason. Do you want to go after them first? We've got some time before the food will be delivered to the cellar."

"Seth and I can head there. Two of you could be nearby, just in case they come early," Jax said. "Maybe the others can go after Billings and the Lennings."

Bella didn't like the idea of Jax and Seth being sitting ducks, but, try as she did, no better idea came to her. Maybe someone else had a better plan. But no one did. Instead, a chorus of agreement went around the group. Resignation filled her. They were close to arresting the suspects and solving the case. Then, the danger would end for everyone.

"The cellar is really dark, and we were all tied near the wall. Far enough apart that they won't realize there's only two instead of four until they're close enough for one of us to jump McNulty. The other can get Nurse Mayfair out of the fray."

"She might be armed herself," Bella pointed out, "so, be careful."

"Good point," Jax agreed.

"And those who are outside can get Drier," Ayling said. "A sound plan. After we get Lenning and Billings secured, I'll leave one deputy with them. I looked around already, when I was here in the past, and those suites are secluded. Even if those two put up a fuss, no one will hear."

"That's true." Bella chewed on her lip before continuing. "Their rooms are accessible from the foyer. I can show you the fastest way. I have a pistol, just in case. But I'll stay away from the action." She added the last to emphasize her willingness to cooperate.

"That would be helpful," Richard said.

"I agree," Ayling put in. "Now, we only need to decide who will be where, and get back on the road."

Bella noticed Jax didn't add his support, but she didn't let that bother her. Within moments, they were headed to Poplar Pines, so her focus was on what lay ahead.

They hadn't gone far when he spoke. "You didn't say anything about my plan."

Her gaze flickered to him and back to the road. "It's risky for you and Seth, but sound." She paused briefly. "You didn't mention how you felt about my idea."

"It's dicey for you, but you'll be cautious, and so will I."

The knot in her chest loosened. "I'll be glad when this is behind us, and we're back in Moreley."

"I will, too." He shifted to look at Bella. "If it wasn't for you, this wouldn't be happening. The four of us would still be tethered in the cellar. With the waning moon coming soon, we'd have been taken and dumped in some remote place, I'm sure. Maybe in a couple of days."

Bella shot him a sidelong glance, but only his profile—a dark silhouette—was discernable. "I was so relieved when we found all of you safe and relatively sound."

A chuckle escaped Jax. "*Relatively sound* is accurate, but I don't have any injuries that won't heal."

"That's good." Bella returned to the case. "I'd like to find out who else is involved, but, as Richard said, we may learn a lot from the ones who get arrested. Do you agree with him?" The possibility of the entire group staying mum was disturbing. Although McNulty, Drier, and Marjorie were clearly implicated, Billings and the Lennings had been careful not to get their hands dirty.

"I think so." His exhalation was audible. "With multiple suspects, someone usually cracks. After we discover who's in charge, we need to get details on relatives and their involvement."

"It makes me sick to think anyone would have a loved one killed because the care was costly."

"Some folks don't want the burden or the expense."

"So very sad." Once again, Bella's heart ached.

"That's for sure," Jax replied. "As far as finding out who paid and why, there should be some sort of record. We'll dig around and see. After the arrests."

Neither spoke for the rest of the brief trip. A new knot formed in Bella's stomach when the sheriff's vehicle turned into the sanatorium driveway. Richard followed, and she swung in behind them. Sweat dampened her palms as she came to a stop in a thick stand of spruce trees near the main road. They went on foot from there. Bella hoped her legs didn't shake too badly but anxiety was a palpable force. As they approached the building, Jax reached out.

"Be careful, Bella. You're a fine detective, but you haven't taken part in a raid. It can go wrong fast. If something seems amiss, hide yourself. We'll find you later."

The urge to protest rose and plummeted. Jax had taken part in raids, while she hadn't. "I won't take any foolish chances, and I hope you won't, either."

He gently squeezed her fingers before releasing her. "I won't. I have too much to look forward to." Then, he was escorting her to the circle of lawmen waiting just ahead.

"My deputies and I will split off," Ayling said. "Miss Stewart, we need you to show us the shortcut to the private suites. I only know the way from the foyer."

Bella didn't like being separated from Jax, but she saw no choice but to agree. "Of course."

"The rest of us can go through the little library to the passage and get in place that way," Richard added.

After a brief exchange by the back door, the group broke into two teams. Jax said nothing more to Bella, but she watched until he and the others—Seth, Richard, and Nolen—were out of sight.

"Lead the way, Deputy Stewart," Ayling said. "We're right behind you."

The sheriff and his two deputies drew their guns as Bella carefully crept down the hallway. The group slowly and quietly moved along. Their flashlights provided sufficient illumination, and they reached the far end within moments. She gestured down the corridor leading to the suites. "From what I've heard, Major Billings has the space nearest here. Mrs. Lenning's suite is farthest away." She kept her voice soft and low.

"Our best strategy may be to make some noise and draw him out," Ayling whispered. "Maybe Lenning will come, too."

Ayling turned to his deputies. "The two of you can post yourselves on either side of the door. Deputy Stewart, you get back in the other hallway. I'll be out of immediate sight, too, but the three of us can jump whoever comes in."

Bella agreed and went to where another corridor led to the front of the building. As she got settled, she pulled the pistol out of her pocket. Within a moment, the sound of the door banging open filled the air. She held her breath. Soon, footsteps came down the hallway.

"Who's in there?" A male voice shouted from near Billings' suite.

Another man spoke. Dr. Lenning? "Come out right now."

Sweat broke out across Bella's brow while she waited for what seemed like forever. What if the two men didn't come any farther? If the sheriff and his deputies stepped forward now, they couldn't get the drop on Billings and Lenning. The success of the plan—here and in the cellar—hinged on surprising and overcoming the suspects.

"We're both armed, so you'd be wise to show yourself," the first man said.

Again, a period of silence ensued. Then, the two voices were too soft to be understood. What were Lenning and Billings planning? Apprehension escalated inside Bella. They were at a standstill. What could she do to change that? Throw something at the far wall? Could a noise there get the pair moving forward? Something had to happen, since they couldn't stay out of sight and nab them. Because she only had the gun and lock pick, Bella tossed the latter with all the force she could muster. A whack sounded before a man swore. When footsteps hurried forward, Ayling's voice rang out.

"Stop where you are and put up your hands. You're under arrest."

The next few moments were a blur of activity and a whir of noise. Bella again turned on her flashlight to see one lawman snapping handcuffs on Lenning and the other doing the same with Billings.

"What is the meaning of this?" the doctor asked as he struggled to get free. He was no match for the lawman, but he stared at Bella. "What is she doing here?"

"Acting Deputy Sheriff Stewart is helping with your arrest." Although Ayling's expression was stern, amusement was in his voice.

"What?" Billings stated at her open-mouth and eyes wide.

Lenning looked at Bella with the same shock. "What is the meaning of this, Miss Halliday? Or Deputy whoever you are."

"I'm Arabella Stewart and, as the sheriff said, I'm a temporary deputy."

"Why are you here? All of you? There's no earthly reason for it," Lenning insisted.

"No, none," Billings agreed. "Get these cuffs off us." He jerked at the manacles.

"I'm afraid we can't do that, but we'll escort you to the kitchen where our colleagues and your accomplices should be soon." Ayling gestured toward the door. "We'll have the two of you go ahead of us."

Even in the dim light, their expressions went from surprise to dismay to resignation. No additional details were need to realize both men were involved in the deaths and disappearances. Their guilty reactions told the story.

"Accomplices. We have no accomplices," Lenning protested in a weak tone lacking conviction.

"We know different," the sheriff said. "By now, Drier and McNulty are probably cuffed, just like the two of you. Nurse Mayfair, as well."

Billings shook his head. "If the three of them are doing something illegal, we have nothing to do with any of it."

"We're sure that's not the case, but let's go," Sheriff Ayling said. "Our colleagues will be expecting us."

Bella hoped they were all waiting. No sound had emanated from the direction of the cellar, but it was a ways away. Not too far for gunshots to go unnoticed, though. She wouldn't relax until she knew the other men, most especially Jax, were safe.

"I have no idea what you might mean." Lenning's voice quavered, which sapped strength from his assertion. "What's going on here?"

"That's what we want to discover. Get going to the kitchen." The sheriff gestured with his revolver.

Billings and Lennings, their hands secured behind them, ambled along.

When Jax heard people coming down the corridor, he bowed his head in relief and gratitude. Billings and Lenning entered ahead of the Moreley lawmen. Finally, Bella came into view. He wasted no time studying the other men. All his attention was on her. A smile touched her lips when their gazes met, and he grinned in return. She was safe. They were all safe. The dangerous part was behind them. Closing the investigation was still ahead.

"I'd like to get everyone back to town. We can question them there," Ayling said.

The male suspects were silent, while Marjorie sniffled quietly.

Ayling glanced from Richard to Jax. "We need to split these folks up. Drier and Billings can ride with me and one of my deputies. How about you and your deputy taking McNulty and Lenning, Richard? The woman can go with Jax and Bella, if that works."

"Where are the cook and her assistant?" Richard asked.

"Anita has a room on the third floor. Mrs. Barley's room is down past the little library," Bella replied. "What about Mrs. Lenning? She didn't come when Sheriff Ayling made noise to draw those two out." Bella gestured toward Billing and the doctor.

Lenning's nostrils flared with a sharp intake of breath. "My mother won't wake up for a few hours. I gave her a sedative last night."

Bella was quick to ask, "Why?"

Lenning bowed his head, but Billings replied. "He always drugs her when she gets nosey. She's been asking too many questions lately. Otherwise, she might wander down here for cocoa and cookies sometime during the night and see something she shouldn't."

The pair had added to their woes with the last admission. Jax hoped they would be equally chatty about which relatives had been open to having their boys murdered.

"Very interesting," Richard said. "We should have someone here, someone reliable, check on her."

"Mrs. Barley is a heavy sleeper, but she'd watch out for Mrs. Lenning." Marjorie's voice was hushed and shaky. "Anita would, too."

"Be quiet, Marjie." The gardener made it an order. "Don't help them. They're trying to put us behind bars."

Bella saw moisture fill the young nurse's eyes, but Marjorie said nothing more.

"Before we move on, maybe you'd go with me to wake both, Deputy Stewart." Ayling addressed Bella with a grin.

"Of course," she agreed.

"What about Nurse Artem and the other orderly?" Richard asked. "We're pretty sure they aren't involved, but we need to check on them." His gaze went around the suspects. "Any of you want to say where they are? Cooperation is always a positive factor."

Bella focused on Marjorie. "Do you know if they're all right?"

"Keep your mouth shut, girl." Ian, his gaze flashing with fire, showed no trace of his previous charm.

The nurse focused on Bella. "Wanda is sleeping, as usual, I'm sure. Warren worked last night and all day today. That's the usual schedule when they want him of the way. He's probably asleep, too, and locked in his room, just in case he wakes up."

"My deputies can check on both of them and bring them down here," the sheriff said. "Meanwhile, the rest of you could get our suspects ready to leave. Richard, I'll leave that to you."

Jax helped get the prisoners settled outside, but his thoughts were on Bella. His mind didn't rest easy until, a short time later, she and Ayling emerged from the house.

After everyone—lawmen and lawbreakers—were in the vehicles, Jax turned to Bella. "You're the driver. I secured our prisoner in back and shackled her to the door handle, just to be on the safe side."

"Clever." Bella got behind the wheel while Jax took his place in the passenger seat.

He glanced over his shoulder. "I've got my gun in my hand, so I advise you to sit still and be quiet." When Marjorie didn't reply, Jax looked at Bella. "What was the cook's reaction to you and Rufus getting her up?" He kept his voice low, so it didn't carry to their prisoner.

Bella replied in a similar hushed tone. "Mrs. Barley truly is a sound sleeper. Once she finally came awake, she was happy to cooperate. She's suspected odd goings-on and wanted to tell Sheriff Ayling, but she hasn't been able to get to town for a while. When she noticed food missing and the larder disturbed months ago, she questioned Anita, who swore she had nothing to do with it. But both of them were scared enough to stay out of the kitchen late and early."

"Not a nice way to live. Did you speak with Anita?"

"She came down when we woke Mrs. Barley. Anita was going to start breakfast for the staff, but there won't be many this morning. She'll help with Mrs. Lenning and tell Warren Starling what happened. Nurse Artem, too." Bella paused briefly. "Mrs. Barley thinks he'll be relieved, since he'd also been warned about snooping."

"We don't have any evidence of his involvement, and Marjorie's words support him being innocent." Jax voiced another issue on his mind. "We'd already ruled Artem out. What about Mrs. Lenning? Her son drugging her and her confused mental state indicate she wasn't involved, although she had to know something."

With one forefinger, Bella tapped the steering wheel. "She's very groggy but able to understand about the arrests. The poor woman cried and cried. Mrs. Barley was comforting her when we left them. Being drugged by her son is really appalling."

"It sure is." Thinking about the next few hours, Jax slumped back in his seat. Rufus would head the interrogations, but he and Bella would need to share their findings. Putting it all together would be time-consuming but essential. "There's still a lot to do on this case."

"We can't do any of it right now, so why don't you relax the rest of the way? You've had a hard, long night," Bella observed, "and you aren't apt to get any proper sleep until much later today."

"All right," Jax replied, but he had no intention of dozing off. Although Marjorie was well-secured in the backseat, she merited monitoring.

Chapter Thirteen

Two hours later, Bella sat in the corner of Rufus Ayling's office, jotting down more notes. Lenning and Billings, who had been interviewed separately, had gone back to feigning innocence. After that, McNulty had been questioned. He provided no information at all. Stoic summed up his attitude.

Now, Drier, hands cuffed behind him, sat at the big table in the middle of the room. Richard, the sheriff, and Jax were on the opposite side. All three looked worn out, but Jax appeared much the worse for wear. He had allowed the town doctor to check him out, provide a new sling, re-wrap his wrist, clean his shoulder, and tend his black eye. He had refused pain medication and insisted no more shrapnel would poke through. Since he was wearing a dark jacket, no one except Jax would know if it did. Bella wished they could wrap things up and head home. If only one suspect would break down, the case could move toward a speedier conclusion. As things stood, they had no new information and scant evidence to hold Billings and Lenning.

Maybe Drier would be the one to crack. Or perhaps Marjorie would share more.

Ayling glanced over the paper in front of him before focusing on the orderly. "You and Major Billings came to work at Poplar Pines the same month, which was shortly after Captain Falconer was admitted. Since I don't believe in coincidences, I have to wonder why."

The statement hung in the air for long moments while Drier shifted restlessly but said nothing.

"Drier, you're the most vulnerable suspect. Jensen and I can testify you abducted us from our room and imprisoned us." Jax leveled a steady gaze at the man.

The orderly's chin went up as he stared at Jax. "You was only in that cellar a little while, and you fought hard when we went in your room. Besides, McNulty was with me."

Jax's fingers went to his puffy eye before moving to his ribcage. "You beat and kicked me as well. That's assault of a lawman."

Bella tried to repress a shudder. Jax must have more bruises hidden by his clothes.

Drier's jaw tightened. "I had no choice."

"You had a choice not to harm and kidnap patients," Richard said, his voice as sharp as a knife. "You had a choice not to kill them."

Drier was quick to respond. "I didn't kill nobody. I swear I didn't."

A tap at the door interrupted. "Yes," Ayling called out.

One of his deputies stepped inside with a paper in hand. "We just heard from Agent Derringer." The young man crossed the room, handed the missive to Ayling and left.

The sheriff scanned the document before handing it to Richard, who passed it on to Jax. Bella was dying to discover what it said. She didn't wait long to find out.

"Mr. Drier, since your work record at the sanatorium indicates you came here from Washington, I contacted a colleague there a few days ago. I called again this morning, and he went to the local police department himself to expedite the information." Ayling leaned back in his chair and folded his arms across his chest. "Would you like to tell us the truth, or should we go over your record?"

A stricken expression covered Drier's face. "Billings will say I'm lying. Him being a retired officer, he'll get believed. Not me."

"You don't need to worry about what he says," Richard put in. "The man's in trouble, although not as much as you, since he didn't abduct anyone. Or attack a deputy sheriff. You could do yourself some good by telling us how deeply Billings is involved in the disappearances and deaths. We've got some interesting information here, sent by a federal agent. If you provide more, I'll make sure it's taken into consideration in your case."

Derringer, who had a vested interest in solving the case and the connections to speed up the flow of information, had clearly done so. As promised, he had continued to be involved, even at a distance. Bella gripped her pencil tighter and waited to hear what was said next.

The orderly bowed his head. "I were under the major's command in France. When I were supposed to be sent to the front, he kept me back at headquarters. Course, I didn't want to go to the trenches again. Already had two friends and my little brother die. He said I could repay the favor later. I been paying ever since."

When Bella glanced up, Jax nodded at her. Maybe they were getting the big break that would unravel the entire operation. He looked as hopeful as she felt.

Jax turned his attention to the orderly. "In what way, and why would he let you stay at headquarters with him?"

Drier wriggled his shoulders and shifted in the chair. "I were on burial detail and got roped into taking a couple bodies for special interment. They was sons of higher ups." His gaze darted to the table top. "Had some cash on them, and Billings saw me stuff it into my pockets. They wasn't gonna use it, and their folks had plenty of dough."

The revelation made Bella sick at heart. Stealing from the dead was awful.

"Billings blackmailed you then?" Jax asked. "Why?"

"He needed a flunkie, so I done some things for him in France," Drier replied. "He were always greedy, and he had another guy helping him snag supplies meant for the front. Billings sold the stuff on the black market and made some good money. Least he did until Captain Falconer got assigned to our unit."

Bella's head shot up as she stared at the orderly, and Jax voiced the thought echoing in her mind. "Falconer reported him."

Drier nodded. "Threatened to report Billings, but didn't have no chance. The major made sure he got sent to the front before he could. The Meusse-Argonne offensive were underway, Captain Falconer were shot up. Lost most of his platoon before that. Not surprised he was in a bad way with his thinking."

The observation made Bella's heart constrict with sympathy. With the back of one hand, she brushed away tears. So many lost lives. So much devastation. And the suffering of some hadn't ended with the Armistice. After several moments of silence, Richard addressed Drier.

"What brought you and Billings to Poplar Pines?"

Again, Drier's head fell forward. "Like I said, the major kept me at his beck-and-call ever since the war. I were with the major at his last post. That's when I first came across Lenning. I found out then, they met on the ship over to France. The two of them talked about how to make money after their army days. Lenning had been a small-town doc, and he didn't want no more of that. Got paid mostly in eggs, other food, and such. His pa had died and left his ma a nice house. Lenning planned to talk her into selling and buying a big place out in the country. Not sure how he heard about Poplar Pines, but he thought it'd be perfect."

"He planned to make it a place for shell-shocked soldiers from the start?" Jax asked.

"Yep. Lenning and Billings both seen some of those poor boys—in France and back home. Lenning put out how he helped some during the war." His head came up, and he shook it. "He might've seen some in bad shape, but he treated injuries. Not no brain trouble, and he don't know more about it than other doctors. To top if off, he likes the bottle. Says it helps him forget what he saw overseas."

Although the assertion was true and troubling, Bella felt no sympathy for the physician. Or for his accomplices.

"So, Lenning got money from his mother to buy the sanatorium," Ayling put in.

"Yep, and we come here right off," Drier said.

"What brought Captain Falconer to the place?" Jax asked.

A shrug moved the orderly's broad shoulders. "He were also at the last army camp with Lenning and Billings. The captain were in terrible shape—shaking and confused—but he knowed

Billings right off. I ain't sure what happened, but I'm thinking Falconer threatened to tell on the major. The major don't like to take chances, so he talked to Falconer's wife about getting help for the captain. Not that Billings actually planned to do something good for him, and maybe the missus didn't care." A humorless guffaw escaped Drier. "She come to visit back then and were upset by her man's condition, so she brought him to Poplar Pines soon after it opened."

"Did Mrs. Falconer and Billings plan to kill Falconer from the start?" Richard posed the question.

"No idea," Drier said. "She visited a few times. Easy to see she was disgusted with Falconer. Billings always talked to her privately, so he probably convinced her after a bit. He and Lenning got paid off by Falconer's wife, so did McNulty and me. I got the least cuz I wouldn't take no part in dumping his body. McNulty got Marjorie to give Falconer a big dose of drugs. Knocked him out. Then, Billings and McNulty hauled him outside. It were a cold night, so Mother Nature did the rest."

As Bella listened, she found herself both appalled and convinced. Falconer's situation, like so many others, was heartbreaking. Drier's explanation seemed straightforward and honest, albeit horrifying.

"They found Falconer frozen to death the next morning," Jax said.

"That's right," Drier agreed.

Richard leaned forward. "What about Smith? What happened to him?"

Although Smith was most likely dead, Bella held her breath while waiting for Drier's reply.

"His kin was fed up when they brung him. Since Mrs. Falconer paid to get rid of her man, Billings and Lenning decided to see if others would do the same. They was careful in not doing it too soon, but Mr. and Mrs. Smith was more than ready to stop spending money on their boy. From the start, the pa was plenty mad about him going off to war. Then, him being crazy-like were the final straw. Don't know exactly what were told to them or how it were done cuz I was away. Had no part in him being carried off, but I knew and kept quiet."

"Did he actually drown?" Ayling posed the question.

"As far as I know, he did." Drier shrugged.

"And Aaron Corning? Why was he abducted?" Ayling asked.

"He weren't as bad off as the other two. He shared a room with Smith. Marjorie was supposed to dope him up, too, but she didn't give him enough, and he saw Smith get grabbed. He didn't say nothing for a while. Later, he asked some folks about how Smith coulda drowned. Billings caught wind of it. He'd already talked to the young missus about a way to get rid of her man. Only saw Corning's wife once. She was a looker. Sassy short hair and flashy clothes. Skirt at her knees." Drier turned to the sheriff. "You and your deputies coming and asking lots of questions made Billings and Lenning uneasy, so they wanted him hidden. Put him up in solitary for a short bit. They was gonna get rid of him when his sister called, so we took him to the cellar. The clear nights made them nervous, too. We gotta use flashlights and lanterns to go to the river or into the woods at night, and they're visible to others in the building or passersby, who are few but no need to take chances. Anyhow, they got rid of Falconer and Smith when it were cloudy with no moonlight."

"And Samuel James aka Seth Jensen?" Jax asked.

A snort left Drier. "Miss Marjorie said all along he looked familiar. Finally, it come to her just yesterday. You can bet the major and the doc didn't waste no time in getting him in the cellar. Having a reporter around made 'em all plenty jumpy."

"Why nab me and Miniger? Did someone get suspicious about one or both of us?" Jax glanced at Bella as he spoke.

"There were worries all along cuz Miss Sarah were Miniger's sweetheart. His folks dumped him, but she kept a close watch. Not sure if she figured things out or just fretted for him. We didn't have no idea you was a copper." Drier turned to Bella. "Or you, either."

"Then, we weren't suspected?" Bella asked.

Drier shook his head. "The two of you being with the reporter was a worry. You was seen chatting at dinner. Miniger ain't talking, but you could." He nodded toward Jax, "Billings and Lenning decided all of you needed to go. Marjorie give the three of you big doses. McNulty and I were surprised the three of you fought us, and you fought the hardest. Didn't think you could with the bad arms. I'm sorry I had to kick you, but the major woulda been mad if you'd somehow gotten away."

The excuse infuriated Bella, who could no longer hold her tongue. "You refused to carry Falconer outside, so you could've refused to assault Jax."

The orderly looked at her. "I paid dearly for not helping back then. Real dearly."

Bella didn't want to consider what Billings might have done to Drier, but the information might help convict the major. Before she pursued the topic, Ayling interceded.

"We can discuss that later. Right now, we need more information on the case at hand." Ayling drummed his fingers on the table. "You really didn't suspect Miss Stewart of being a deputy?"

"No," Drier replied. "Her being a copper is pretty unusual for a lady."

"It has been, but nowadays women are working with police departments and even with federal agencies," she replied.

"Takes a brave woman," the orderly commented.

"It certainly does." Jax replied to Drier, but kept his attention on Bella. "Miss Stewart...Deputy Stewart, that is, did a great job."

Warmth touched her cheeks at the praise, and she bowed her head so the others wouldn't see how strongly Jax's words affected her.

"She most surely did," Ayling agreed before returning to specifics. "What was the plan to get rid of all four?"

Drier's nostrils flared as he inhaled long and low. "Not sure. Billings and Lenning argued about what to do other them put them away. Few folks know about the cellar. It's a good hiding place, for sure. Nice and isolated. Maybe kill the bunch there. Or haul them out one at a time."

A shudder ran through Bella as the mental image arose. Drier was right about the secluded aspect of the pit. As she glanced around the group, she saw grim expressions on the lawmen's faces. Jax looked morose but, when he caught her gaze, he gave a slight nod. All she managed in return was a faint smile. Then, Bella posed a question that had plagued her since the start. "Why does Major Billings wear his uniform? He's retired."

Drier gave a harrumph. "He's always been power mad. Anyone lower in rank were worthless to him. Wearing his dress khaki with all the medals makes him feel like a big man."

Not the best reason, Bella thought, but probably an accurate one.

"Thank you, Mr. Drier. I believe that's all for now." Ayling crossed to the door and called his deputies, who escorted the prisoner out. He returned to his chair and sat down. "He was more forthcoming. I'm not sure confronting Billings and Lenning with the information will get them to talk. We need corroboration to pressure them."

"Marjorie might tell what she knows," Bella put in. "She's given us a little already."

"It could help if you do most of the interview with the girl," Jax said to Bella.

"A good idea," Richard put in. "Let's discuss our strategy before we get her."

The next few minutes were spent going over questions. After they finished, Ayling left to retrieve Marjorie. When they returned, the young woman's hands were cuffed in front of her instead of behind as Drier's had been. To Bella, the girl was less likely to resist. Evidently, Ayling agreed.

"We only want to ask a few questions," Bella said.

The young nurse, her face ashen, looked at Bella. "I don't know much."

"You won't help yourself by lying. We already know you gave sedatives to the men who were taken from their rooms." Bella spoke in a soft voice. "And you took food to the cellar."

"Three of us can testify to you giving us shots last night," Jax put in. "Miniger was knocked out immediately. James and I followed fast."

Marjorie's eyes widened. She briefly bowed her head. "Ian convinced me to help. At first, I didn't want to." Her voice was barely audible.

"But you did because you were sweethearts." Bella made the suggestion.

The nurse released a long sigh. "Yes. We planned to move away from here, get a place in the city, and marry. We were saving money, but it was so slow. Neither of us wanted to wait much longer, and Ian said he couldn't marry me while we both worked at the sanatorium."

The entire revelation left a foul taste in Bella's mouth. "So, you got involved in killing patients for money."

"I didn't kill anyone," Marjorie replied in an urgent, pleading tone.

"But you made it so others could. And you got paid." Bella didn't keep the edge from her voice.

Color formed splotches on Marjorie's cheeks. "I only drugged the men and took food to the cellar."

Key steps in the overall plan. "Why were certain patients targeted?" They needed substantiation, and Bella planned to get it.

Long moments passed while silence echoed in the room. Finally, Ayling spoke. "Miss Mayfair, you are in serious trouble. We have strong suspicions and some evidence about what occurred and why, but we need verification. We've gotten some. If you provide more information, you may help clear yourself of the most serious charges. Otherwise, being charged as an accomplice in multiple murders is a distinct possibility."

The color drained from the young nurse's face. "Ian sweet-talked me into meeting with Dr. Lenning about administering an extra dose of sedatives to some men in order to get them out of their rooms. At first, I thought they were being taken to isolation."

"And when you knew what happened to Falconer?" Bella asked.

Marjorie laid her manacled wrists on the table. "Ian said to keep quiet, so I didn't ask for details. I was scared to talk. He can be very sweet, but he can also be rough. I love him, though."

The young woman sounded pathetic. Bella didn't want to hear excuses, so she asked a pointed question. "You didn't get paid?"

Fresh color surged into Marjorie's face as she bowed her head. "I was well-paid, and so was Ian." She bit on her lower lip.

"How did you get the big doses of drugs to inject?" Marjorie's justifications infuriated Bella. Not only did patients receive little or no care, they were in danger of being killed for money. And with a nurse's help. She didn't believe for one minute Marjorie hadn't known what would happen to the patients involved.

"No one checks on how much medication is used or when. My biggest concern was getting upstairs after Nurse Artem dozed off. She's lazy but nosey," Marjorie said.

"You were willing to help kill men because McNulty convinced you." Jax let it stand as a statement and a query.

A half-shrug lifted one of the nurse's slender shoulders. "Captain Falconer was a mess. No treatment or drugs would've helped him. Dr. Lenning said as much."

Bella saw anger flash in Jax's eyes and felt it echo inside her. "So, it was okay to murder him," she said.

Marjorie's chin went up. "He froze to death."

"Because he was drugged and dumped outside in frigid temperatures." Jax kept his voice well-modulated but fury flashed in his eyes.

"I don't know about that," she mumbled.

"But your beau does." Bella watched her carefully for an emotional reaction. She was not disappointed.

Anger and anxiety crossed the nurse's face. "Ian wasn't the mastermind. Billings and Doc worked together on all that. Doc is the expert on whether or not patients can be helped. He decided all of them were useless and always would be." The words poured like water from a fountain.

"He isn't experienced in dealing with mental disorders," Bella said.

"In France, he saw plenty of soldiers who couldn't cope. He and the major saw some at their last posting, as well. Weaklings who couldn't deal with war. Captain Falconer was one of them. He even had delusions." Marjorie shook her head. "His poor wife would've been stuck paying for his care forever. No chance to remarry or have a family. She was suffering more than he was."

"You talked to her?" Jax asked.

"No, the major told me. Smith was much the same. Families shouldn't have to deal with fragile, broken men." Marjorie made the assertion with confidence.

"What about Corning? Why was he targeted?" Bella knew what they had been told already, but additional corroboration would be useful.

"He witnessed some things. Smith being taken, for one," Marjorie said. "He wasn't as confused, but he wasn't apt to get better, either. According to Major Billings, his wife wanted to go on with her life."

"And was willing to pay to do so." Bella made the comment. Drier hadn't mentioned that motive, but it seemed likely.

"I believe so. She never visited. When his sister did, Billings and Lenning decided to keep him around. They were already fretting because the sheriff and deputies kept coming, so they stuck Corning in the attic for a time. We all knew he was there, so no one mentioned him disappearing because he hadn't.

Then, the decision was made to get rid of him. But his sister arrived the same day, so he was put in the cellar."

"With the plan to kill him," Jax suggested.

Marjorie lifted her chin. "Like I said, I was only involved in sedating the men and taking food down to the cellar. That was done on doctor's orders, so I shouldn't be under arrest. I did what I was told." Despite the assertion, her tone was like that of a weak warbler.

"For money." Jax kept the contempt out of his voice.

Marjorie said nothing.

Bella watched with contempt and anger. The young woman was a nurse, someone who should put the well-being of patients first and foremost. Maybe love for McNulty had gotten her involved, but that was no excuse.

"You recognized and reported Seth Jensen," Richard put in. "That wasn't under orders, and it makes you look like you wanted to hide the goings-on."

A scowl formed on Marjorie's face. "I thought he might be released from the sanatorium because of being a reporter. I wasn't involved in getting him to the cellar."

"But you're the one who sedated him," Jax observed. "What about Dalton and me? Why grab us?"

When she didn't respond, the sheriff spoke. "You'd be wise to tell all you know."

Marjorie released a long breath. All the starch seemed to go out of her as she slumped forward. "Miniger's folks were tired of paying and disgusted with his weakness. Sarah told me as much. That's why she wanted to work at Poplar Pines. To take special care of him. She still hopes he'll get better, but his family is probably right. He'll always be a burden."

"Did his parents plan with Billings or Lenning to kill Miniger?" Jax asked.

Again, she didn't reply right away. When Marjorie did, she spoke in a resigned tone. "Not for sure but, from what I heard, they discussed the idea. I'm guessing they would've paid good money to solve the problem."

Problem. What kind of people considered a sick relative a problem? What kind of nurse did? Any solution should involve restoring the ill to health. Not eliminating them. Bella couldn't fathom the depth of callousness involved.

"Why was I taken along with Dalton?" Jax asked.

Bella knew he was seeking support for Drier's assertions, and she was ready to jot the information down.

"To eliminate a witness, I think. Billings and Lenning got very nervous after the sheriff came out several times. Especially after Miss Corning showed up." Marjorie clinked the cuffs as she spoke. "This was going to be the last time for Ian and me. We planned to quit soon because we've saved enough to get a start in the city."

A knot formed in Bella's stomach. The nurse and gardener planned to use their ill-gotten gains to finance their future. Appalling.

After Marjorie's interrogation wrapped up with confirmation of a few details, Ayling called on his deputies to put her back in a cell. Then, the group went over the latest information.

"It's worse than we initially figured." Jax slumped back in his chair.

"It is," Ayling agreed. "We still need to prove people paid Billings and Lenning to get rid of their sons or husbands."

"Any paperwork would be locked away. Maybe in Lenning's office or suite. Maybe in Billing's." Bella tapped her pencil on the edge of the table. "There are some dreadful paintings in the doctor's office. A safe could be behind one of them."

"Very possible," Jax agreed.

"I planned to go out with my deputies and talk to other staff," Ayling said. "And with Mrs. Lenning, if she's more alert. We need to make sure families are notified right away because the patients can't stay there with so few employees left. Some relatives live at a distance. I can leave one deputy at the place. If Sarah Bailey will help, that'd be two nurses, the cook, the cook's helper, and one orderly. Do you think they can manage for a couple of days, Deputy Stewart?"

Bella couldn't help but smile. When Jax grinned, too, pleasure spread through her. "I'm sure they could. Dalton, Seth, and Aaron won't be going back, which leaves seventeen men," she said.

"Neither will I," Jax added. "At least not as a patient."

"True," she replied.

"Both of you deserve to take it easy, but I'd like you to come with us to look for papers. If we're lucky, Billings or Lenning might tell us where to find them. I plan to ask," Ayling said.

Chapter Fourteen

Dr. Lenning was more voluble when the Sheriff spoke with him again. He not only revealed the hiding place, he confessed to going along with Major Billings' scheme because he owed the officer money.

When the physician was led out of the office, Jax grimaced. "A doctor willing to harm patients to pay off gambling debts. Lenning is truly despicable."

"I'm surprised he admitted his reason," Bella put in.

"Probably hoped he'd get some sympathy," Ayling said. "It won't work with me, and I hope the prosecutor will be as hard on him as on Billings. But I'm glad we know his motivation. A ghastly one."

The group agreed.

After arriving at Poplar Pines, finding the needed evidence didn't take long. As Bella had suggested, and as the doctor had admitted, a safe was behind one of Lenning's ugly paintings. In it were notes from relatives of Falconer and Smith, along with a check written by Aaron Corning's wife. A carefully worded letter from Dalton's father inquired about workable solutions for his son's ailments and how much such interventions would cost.

"Before you all go back to Moreley, I'd like to review a few things," Sheriff Ayling said. "First, I need to go over information my clerk gathered while we were out at the sanatorium. I promise not to keep you for long."

When the group reassembled in the sheriff's office, Jax thought back to the previous Friday. The case had wrapped up faster than he had figured, for which he was grateful. A few loose ends remained, but none required Bella and Jax to stay in Bridgeling.

"As I said earlier, I spoke with Amos this morning after we got back here," the sheriff told the group. "He'll contact Miss Corning, pick her up, and come for Aaron. He'll be staying with my wife and me until they arrive."

"What about Dalton Miniger?" Bella asked. "Will he and Sarah go back?"

Ayling tapped one paper he had retrieved from the front office. "Nurse Bailey agreed to help at Poplar Pines while patients are still there. Our doc examined Dalton, and he's more optimistic than others were. He's also said he'll run out from time-to-time and check on the patients."

"Miniger putting up a fight must be a good sign," Jax said.

Ayling nodded. "That's what our doctor told me." He lifted another sheet. "I heard from the constable in Miss Bounder's hometown. He finally located her. She was afraid of being tracked down because she knew so much. That's why she and her aunt went to visit relatives. They'll come home today, and I'll speak with her after that."

"That's great news," Bella said, and the others agreed.

"I'll also contact the police in the various towns and speak with local prosecutors about how to proceed regarding the families. As far as the suspects, we've got plenty to hold and charge them." He leaned back in his chair and glanced around the table. "We couldn't have solved this case if not for all of you."

"Arabella and Jax deserve the biggest thanks," Richard added.

A grin softened the sheriff's hard mouth. "I've been pleased to have you two as deputies."

"Thank you for letting me take part," Bella said. "Not every sheriff would."

The man shrugged. "Short-sighted of them."

"I suppose my tenure has ended now." She glanced at Jax. "Yours, too."

"Yep," he replied without hesitation. "I'll help in any way I can and testify in court when the cases come up, but I'm ready to head home, unless you need me here, Sheriff."

"You can leave any time. I understand wanting to be home," Rufus replied. "You're going back to your job as constable, Jax."

He nodded. "Not right away. I'll take some time off." Jax was seriously thinking about surgery on his arm, but he hadn't told Bella yet.

"Which you should do," Richard said. "Jenny and I are happy to stay as long as you need us."

Jax didn't want to talk about his pending decision in this forum, so he simply said, "I appreciate that."

"I'll keep all of you posted on the cases," Rufus said, "and on the future of Poplar Pines. It's a lovely place, so some other doctor—one who knows what he's doing and cares about patients—may buy it, eventually. It'll take time to sort things out."

"Won't any sale be complicated by Lenning's criminal prosecution?" Bella asked.

"I've got good news on that," the sheriff replied. "The property is in his mother's name. Evidently, their attorney insisted on it. She'll stay on for a time at least. Mrs. Barley, Anita, Starling, Nurse Artem, and Sarah Bailey will make a good team. That will give families a chance to find another place, or maybe leave their sons and husbands if a qualified physician is found. Mrs. Lenning may not be as mentally deficient as we thought. When I spoke with her lawyer, he was perplexed and said she was sharp as a tack when he last saw her a year ago."

"Do you think her condition was from being drugged?" Dismay underscored Jax's question.

"Quite likely," Rufus said.

"By her son, which is appalling." Richard shook his head. "The man ought to be sentenced for that, too."

"We'll charge him for that, if we can." The sheriff offered the assurance.

"What about the men there now?" Bella asked. "What will happen to them if their families don't want them?"

"I spoke with Mrs. Barley a while ago. Arrangements have already been made for several to go home. The rest should be fine with the current staff for now. Maybe longer if Mrs. Lenning gets back to normal. My deputies and I will go out and check from time-to-time, just to be sure," Ayling said. "Depending on what charges are leveled, there may be substantial fines, but she's in the clear on the criminal side."

"The poor woman." Jax shook his head. "She was used by her son and Billings."

"Will everyone involved be prosecuted for murder?" Bella asked.

"Billings and Lenning were the instigators, so they'll be tried for homicide. As will Ian McNulty. He finally admitted he and the major took an unconscious Falconer outside in freezing temperatures. They also put Smith in a shallow grave and laid out the slippers and robe to mislead people. I'll arrange a search for his body. Probably too late to determine the exact cause of death. Drier didn't participate in that effort, and no one else is willing to tell," Rufus replied.

Jax shifted restlessly in his chair. "Do you think Smith will ever be found?"

"I hope so, but I'm not optimistic. His aunt wants to give him a proper burial, so we'll make every effort," Rufus said. "Once charges are filed here, Seth will write a series of articles. I'll cooperate, and I imagine all of you will, too."

The others concurred.

"What about Marjorie and Arnold? No murder charges for them?" Bella asked.

"Probably not," Rufus replied. "Their cooperation will benefit them, but they'll undoubtedly serve some time."

"Deservedly so," Richard put in.

The sheriff glanced at his watch. "It's been a long, long day for all of you, and you've got an hour's drive ahead, so I don't want to hold you up."

Richard turned to Jax and Bella. "I've got my vehicle, and Nolen left already. Go ahead. I want to talk with Rufus longer."

The pair made their farewells and headed to Jax's Chummy. He opened the driver's door for Bella, and she slid on to the seat.

"Planning to sleep on the way home?" she asked with a smile.

"I'm not sure about that, but I'm too banged up to take the wheel." After he got in the passenger side, Jax glanced at her. "You look upset. Our part in the case is over, except for testifying. It's tough to think about the men who died and the families willing to pay to have them killed."

After pressing the starter button, she looked at him. "It's not that. When Drier was questioned, you said he beat you and kicked you. Your arm, wrist, and eye must be painful, but you've winced when moving around. Did he break your ribs?"

Jax reached to cup her cheek. "McNulty told him to kick me. Drier didn't put much effort into it, but I wanted to pressure him to talk, so I made a bigger deal out of it. I've got bruises, but no breaks. The doc here looked me over, and I'll heal well with time."

"Good, let's get home."

"Home. What a wonderful word." He let his hand fall away and sat back in the seat. "The only place I want to be from here on out is Moreley."

"Me, too," she agreed. "This investigation didn't drag out like I feared, but it was challenging."

A low laugh escaped him. "Challenging is a good word."

"Difficult is better." Bella steered the vehicle on to Main Street and headed out of town.

"You did great, Bella. No seasoned law officer would've done better."

Warmth spread through her. "Thank you." She cleared her throat of the emotion threatening to choke her. "I didn't follow the guidelines about only carrying messages."

"If you had, I might not be sitting here."

His statement was correct, and too true for comfort. "We're both safe now, and it's not likely we'll have another investigation like this one. Or any mysteries at all."

He snorted. "I've said that frequently, and I was always proven wrong."

"Moreley has had more than its fair share of problems. Since we'll both be there for the foreseeable future, I doubt if we'll need to sleuth around soon."

"Maybe not, but I may not be in town all the time."

Tension immediately gripped Bella. "What do you mean? I thought you left the Bureau. I thought you were taking your constable's job back."

Jax laid his left hand over her right one, where it rested on the gearshift knob. "You know, I've been thinking about having surgery on my bicep. It's the only thing that might help."

Bella glanced at him and back at the road. For months and months, she had hoped he would have the operation. "Are you really going through with it?"

"That's my plan. I'll need to see the surgeon in Toledo, of course. I'm not sure how soon he'll do it, but Richard will stay on until I'm ready to go back to work. I talked it over with him and Jenny last week."

"They told me."

A beat of silence passed. "Are you mad I didn't tell you first?"

"Not really. I figured you were working it out in your mind and talking with them would help." The feel of his hand on hers was enough reassurance to continue. "I've pestered you to have the operation because I could never understand why you gave up all hope of living out your dream of being a golf professional. I shouldn't have kept bothering you about it because it's entirely up to you." Since that had been a previous point of contention, she was careful in her wording.

"Not entirely. Your opinion means a lot to me. Everything, really. I'm still not sure I'll ever be able to play well enough to go back to being a pro, but I can't be sure until after I have surgery and some time passes."

Her heart beat faster as she considered the possibilities. "You'd consider that?"

"If I heal well enough, yes. But don't count on it or on me working at Ballantyne. I don't want you disappointed. Not in me. I've already let you down too much and too often."

"Oh, Jax. That's not so." She took a long breath. "You shouldn't have ever blamed yourself for my brother's death."

"Maybe not, but I should've done better in comforting you when we met at the field hospital right after Matt was killed. I'll always regret that."

The memory of him turning toward a young French nurse and away from her still stung. The woman hadn't had close ties to Jax, but he hadn't explained the situation until last year. Since then, she understood that the Frenchwoman had been involved with a friend of Jax and Matt. With understanding, she had forgotten the pain of that day. Pain from misunderstanding was the worst kind of suffering, and it lingered the longest. But now, it was gone. "That's all behind us. You won't be in Toledo for long, and I can visit there and when you recuperate at home."

He squeezed her hand. "Maybe you'll read to me. You never got a chance at the sanatorium."

The comment jogged her memory. "When we talked about me reading to you after your tonsillectomy, I asked if you didn't want Matt to know I chose *little girl* stories. You never said why you didn't want him finding out."

Jax released her hand and slumped back in his seat. "Matt was my best friend, and we were like brothers."

"I know, but what does that have to do with it?"

"I'm an only child, but siblings tease one another."

"True." Bella mulled over his point. "You and Matt sometimes teased each other, but I don't remember anything about me reading you stories."

"Not about stories. Or even about us spending time together when I was sick." Jax paused before going on. "He liked to say he'd be my best man when you and I got married."

Bella shot Jax a sidelong glance. "Even back when we were young?"

"Yep, and he never stopped. He always thought you and I belonged together. It was one of the last things we discussed."

Tears pricked Bella's eyes as she thought about her brother. How she wished Matt could be in her wedding. Then, she chuckled. A wedding couldn't happen unless a courtship did.

"What's amusing?"

"Nothing much. I was thinking about the future."

"Good. Last April, we agreed to step out when I left the Bureau, and I'm officially finished. For the foreseeable future, I won't have a job. We're both exhausted now, but what about a picnic on Sunday and a moving picture next week?"

Her heart lifted at the suggestions. "I'm free every Sunday and every evening."

Jax chuckled. "You aren't unless you want to be."

"Are you offering to fill my calendar with social engagements?" Her spirit took wings.

"I am," he replied, "and I'm hoping to close out the year with one very special engagement. If you're willing."

Bella's pulse raced with excitement. "I believe I am."

About the Author

D.S. Lang started making up stories to entertain herself as an only child, and she is still making them up. Now, she puts them in writing.

After earning Bachelor's and Master's degrees in education, D.S. worked as a golf shop manager, teacher (junior high, high school, and college), program manager, tutor, and mentor. She has a lifelong love of history and often gets sidetracked on research when she should be writing.

When she is away from the computer, D.S. enjoys reading, swimming, spending time with family and friends, and walking her dog Izzy.

Thank you for reading this book! If you have time, please rate or review it. Reviews help other readers find new authors.

For more information on this series and other books by D.S. Lang, please visit: https://www.dslangbooks.com You can also sign up for her monthly newsletter

Books in the Arabella Stewart Historical Mystery Series

To order any of the above books, and for more information,
please visit: https://www.dslangbooks.com